THE FIRE-DWELLERS

MARGARET
LAURENCE

The
Fire
Dwellers

ALFRED A. KNOPF   NEW YORK

This Is a Borzoi Book
Published by Alfred A. Knopf, Inc.

Lines from "I'll Be Seeing You" are reprinted
by permission of Williamson Music, Inc.
Copyright 1938 by Williamson Music, Inc.
Copyright renewed.
Lines from "There's a Gold Mine in the Sky"
are reprinted by permission of Bourne Co.
Copyright 1937 by Bourne Co., New York, N.Y.
Copyright renewed.
An excerpt from "Losers" by Carl Sandburg
from SMOKE AND STEEL *is reprinted*
by permission of Harcourt, Brace & World, Inc.
This book was published, in an abridged form, in the
March issue of The Ladies Home Journal.

If I pass the burial spot of Nero
I shall say to the wind, "Well, well"—
I who have fiddled in a world on fire,
I who have done so many stunts not worth doing.

CARL SANDBURG, *Losers*

THE FIRE-DWELLERS

ONE

>ᴧᴠᴧᴠᴧᴠᴧᴠᴧᴠᴧᴠᴧᴠᴧᴠ<

Ladybird, ladybird,
Fly away home;
Your house is on fire,
Your children are gone.

—— Crazy rhyme. Got it on the brain this morning. That's
from trying to teach Jen a few human words yesterday. Why
anybody would want to teach a kid a thing like that, I wouldn't
know. Half those nursery rhymes are gruesome, when you come
to think of it. Here is a candle to light you to bed, and here
comes a chopper to chop off your head. Just the thing to make
the sprouts sleep soundly, especially if followed by that prayer
about if I should die before I wake. Maybe it's okay, though.
Prepares them for what they can expect. Stacey, you sure are
joyful first thing in the morning. First thing, hell. It's a quarter to
nine, and here's me not dressed yet.

The full-length mirror is on the bedroom door. Stacey
sees images reflected there, distanced by the glass like humans
on TV, less real than real and yet more sharply focused because
isolated and limited by a frame. The double bed is unmade, and
on a chair rests a jumble of her clothes, carelessly shed stockings
like round nylon puddles, roll-on girdle in the shape of a tire

1

where she has rolled it off. On another chair, Mac's dirty shirt is neatly folded. Two books reside on the bedside table—*The Golden Bough* and *Investments and You*, Hers and His, both unread. On the dressing table, amid the nonmagic jars and lipsticks are scattered photographs of Katie, Ian, Duncan and Jen at various ages. Hung above the bed is a wedding picture, Stacey twenty-three, almost beautiful although not knowing it then, and Mac twenty-seven, hopeful confident lean, Agamemnon king of men or the equivalent, at least to her. Sitting on the bed, Stacey sees mirrored her own self in the present flesh, insufficiently concealed by a short mauve nylon nightgown with the ribbon now gone from the neckline and one shoulder frill yanked off by some kid or other.

—— God knows how old this damn nightie is. I've got to get some new ones. One, anyway. We're not all that broke any more. I'll get two, today, both fancy as hell. What difference will that make? None. Look at that Christly book—why do I keep it on the bedside table? I'll never get around to reading it. *Essential background,* the guy kept saying. He had probably read it a thousand times. If I wanted to take yet another evening course, why did I have to pick Mythology and Modern Man? Sounded classy, that's why. I went twice. Fees wasted.

Stacey looks at her underwear on the chair but makes no move toward it. Her eyes are drawn back to the mirror.

—— Everything would be all right if only I was better educated. I mean, if I were. Or if I were beautiful. Okay, that's asking too much. Let's say if I took off ten or so pounds. Listen, Stacey, at thirty-nine, after four kids, you can't expect to look like a sylph. Maybe not, but for hips like mine there's no excuse. I wish I lived in some country where broad-beamed women were fashionable. Everything will be all right when the kids are older. I'll be more free. Free for what? What in hell is the matter with you, anyway? Everything *is* all right. *Everything is all right.* Come on, fat slob, get up off your ass and get going. There's a sale on downtown, remember? Singing ad on local station—

Dollar Forty-nine Day plink plink. Funny thing, I never swear in front of my kids. This makes me feel I'm being a good example to them. Example of what? All the things I hate. Hate, but perpetuate.

Stacey gets dressed and takes Jen, two, over to Tess Fogler's, next door. Tess is still in her housecoat, but being tall and slender looks as though ready to receive the Peruvian ambassador. Tess's hair is honey-blond and even this early in the day is done in a flawless French roll. Stacey, who is shorter than she would like to be, is wearing her pale-blue last year's spring coat and, because her dark unruly hair needs doing, a small white veil-enfolded straw hat which she dislikes.

—— My God I look awful how does she always look so
Tess, it's terribly kind of you.

Heavens no, I'm always glad to

Well I certainly appreciate

Jen's no bother, are you honey?

Mumble mumble squawk

My, she's determined not to communicate, isn't she?

—— That's right, rub it in. If you had kids, you'd know it's not such a laugh.

I guess the other kids wait on her too much.

Come on, honey, want a cookie?

She's just had breakfast.

—— Don't feed the animals. I know your cookies. Shortbread. Last time she threw up when I got her home. God, I'm ungrateful.

Tess, thanks a million—I'm really grateful.

It's nothing. Now you run right along now.

—— What cat noises go on in her head? Maybe none. Maybe only me. Stacey, you rotten old bitch.

Tess, Katie will pick up Jen on the way back from school at lunchtime if I'm not back, okay?

Sure, okay.

Stacey walks to the corner of Bluejay Crescent and gets

3

the bus downtown. But she does not go to the sale. She gets off near the waterfront and starts walking. She is not cracking up. It is just that she has lived in this city, jewel of the Pacific Northwest, for going on twenty years, and she does not know anything about it. Inexplicably and suddenly, she feels it is time she learned. She knows she will not learn this way.

The pigeons are shitting all over the granite cenotaph, she is glad to see. Stacey stops and reads the inscription. *Their Names Shall Live Forevermore.* And on another side, *Does It Mean Nothing to You.* No question mark. Along the steps at the base, three old men sit in the feeble sunlight, coughing and spitting, clenching their arms across their skinny chests, murmuring something to one another, memories, perhaps, or curses against now.

— I guess they feel at home here. It was their war, my father's war. He spoke of it once, just once. Mother was out one evening, and Rachel was seven and asleep. He told me about a boy of eighteen—hand grenade went off near him and the blast caught the kid between the legs. My dad cried when he told it, because the kid didn't die. My dad was drunk, but then he wouldn't have spoken of it if he hadn't been. Mac never talks about his war, never has, not that he talks much about anything any more. Ian was ten this year and Duncan seven. Well, even if I'd had four girls, so what?

The streets are just beginning to waken. They keep late hours at night in this part of town. A few men in windbreakers and jeans are hanging around café doors. At Ben's Economy Mart, the windows are full of little penned cards—*Get a Load of This Bargain Only $10.95, How About This at $4.75? We're Cheating Ourselves at $9.95*—and other pieces of folk literature, propped against suitcases, kitbags, lumberjacks' boots, bush knives, thermos flasks and shiny double-bitted axes. In the lobby of the Princess Regal Hotel, some yawning yellow-toothed fishwife, fleshwife, sagging guttily in a print dress sad with poppies, is sweeping up last night—heel-squashed cigarette butts, Kleenex

4

blown into or bawled into, and ashes. Old men are sitting there, too, sitting in the red plastic-covered chairs, waiting for the beer parlor to open, so somebody can stand them a drink and they can accept haughtily, their scorn some kind of sop to their pride.
—— What is it like, really? How would I know? People live in those rooms above the stores, people who go to the cafés and bars at night, who prowl these streets that are their territory. Men down from the forests or off the fish boats. Faithless loggers clobbering their faithless women. Kids gaming with LSD—*look at me, Polly, I'm Batman—zoom* from sixth floor window into the warm red embrace of a cement death. Ancient mariners tottering around in search of lifeblood, a gallon of Calona Royal Red. Whores too old or sick-riddled to work any classier streets. Granite-eyed youngsters looking for a fix, trying to hold their desperation down. Is it like that? All I know is what I read in the papers. "Seventeen-Year-Old on Drug Charge." "Girl Kills Self, Lover." "Homeless Population Growing, Says Survey." "Car Smash Decapitates Indian Bride, Groom." "Man Sets Room Ablaze, Perishes." All sorts of cheery stuff. What do I know of it? I see the dead faces in a mocking procession, looking at me, looking again, shrugging, saying *There's stability for you.* Do I deserve this? Yes, and yet goddammit, *not* yes. Nearly twenty years here, and I don't know the place at all or feel at home. Maybe I wouldn't have, in any city. I never like to say so to anybody. I always think they might think it's obvious I'm from a small town.

Stacey Cameron, nearly nineteen, expert typist, having shaken the dust of Manawaka off herself at last. Stacey, five foot three, breasts like apples as it says in the Song of Solomon. Stacey in scarlet dressmaker suit, fussy lace blouse. Good-bye, beloved family. Good-bye to the town undertaker, her father, capable only of dressing the dead in between bouts with his own special embalming fluid. (Dad?

I'm sorry. But I had to go.) Good-bye to her long-suffering mother. (Now I'm not sure any longer what lay behind your whining eyes.) Good-bye to Stacey's sister, always so clever. (When I think you're still there, I can't bear it.) Good-bye, prairies. On the train, a New-foundland woman with six kids, going to join her husband in an army camp in Chilliwack. None of them had ever seen a train before. One of the kids vomited in the Ladies', and Stacey started to help her wipe it up. Then the porter came in and said he'd do it. He was brown and big and he looked at Stacey with amusement. It hadn't occurred to her that on a train you weren't expected to clean up as you were at home. The lady left with her bleak brat, and the porter said *Where you going?* Stacey told him Vancouver, and he asked if she had a place to stay. She said, chirpy as a sparrow now, out of pure need, I thought I'd look around. *Don't look around, sweetheart,* he said. *Go to the YWCA. That's what I tell all the prairie girls.* So she did that. Small-town girl.

Stacey's children will need to know this city. At present, the boys' domain is only the back yards, the white-flowering dogwood trees for climbing, the alleys where garbage tins teeter and lean castaway cats scrounge, the garages empty in daytime and littered with planks and tins of nails and stiffened paint-brushes—the places where children plot their secret revolutions.

—— Maybe the best thing would be to bring them up in the very veins of the city, toss them into it like into a lake and say swim or else. But I couldn't bring myself to do that. Mac would think I was off my rocker even to think of it, if I ever mentioned it to him, which of course I wouldn't.

Stacey walks more quickly and uneasily. Then she finds she is beside the harbor. The gulls are spinning high, freewheeling. Wings like white arcs of light crescenting above the waterfront. Voices mocking piratically at the city's edges. But the city is doing too much shrieking itself to hear the gulls.

—— If they're prophets in bird form, they might as well save their breath. They aren't prophets, though. They only look it, angelic presences and voices like gravel out of a grave. Birds in prophet form. They couldn't care less. They scavenge from the city, that's all, and from those black rusty freighters doing their imitations of monolithic ghosts, clanking and groaning out there. If this city were gone, the wings would skim unmourningly away, off to deride and suck up to some other city, if there were any. Even if there weren't, the gulls wouldn't be too upset. Change of diet, that's all. No more sea-sodden bread crusts and waterlogged orange peel.

> At the beach, once. Stacey watching a gull repeatedly dropping a closed clamshell from a great height. Finally the shell cracked on a rock, and the bird landed and calmly fed. Stacey had to admire such a simple knowledge of survival.

—— I don't want to look any more. Why did I come here? I want to go home. The kids will be back from school for lunch. What'll they think if I'm not there? Katie will make the sandwiches for the others. That's no excuse. Mustn't rely on her like that. She's only fourteen. It's not fair to her. Ian won't be worried, but Duncan will. *Where's Mum?* He always thinks I've been run over or something. Who made him that way? Where's the bus stop? Here. Come on, blasted bus—I've got to get home, right now. *Ladybird, ladybird, fly away home*—now, stop it, Stacey. Just cut it out. They are perfectly all right. Everything is all right. Tomorrow I will go on the banana diet. With luck, I should be able to lose seven pounds in seven days. Will Mac ever be surprised. Yeh, you do that, Stacey, doll. You just do that, eh?

7

Stacey sits very quietly on the bus, looking out the window in the belief that if she does not look at other people, they will not look at her. It is her matronly coat, hat and gloves which make her self-conscious. She feels more at home in slacks, but cannot wear them downtown in case it should embarrass her children to know she had done so.

—— Must've been off my head, wandering around the harbor so long. Didn't even get the nightgowns. Are the kids okay? Damn, I wish I didn't always have to be home at the right time. At the Day of Judgment, God will say *Stacey MacAindra, what have you done with your life?* And I'll say, *Well, let's see, Sir, I think I loved my kids.* And he'll say, *Are you certain about that?* And I'll say, *God, I'm not certain about anything any more.* So He'll say, *To hell with you, then. We're all positive thinkers up here.* Then again, maybe He wouldn't. Maybe He'd say, *Don't worry, Stacey, I'm not all that certain, either. Sometimes I wonder if I even exist.* And I'd say, *I know what you mean, Lord. I have the same trouble with myself.*

The bus crawls. The traffic is like two shoals of great metallic fish, frantic to get back to the spawning grounds, but not moving with the fine silence of fishes. Hooting and honking. Grinding of gears. Starting and stopping. And people yelling. The noise strikes at Stacey.

—— I'm getting so I can't stand uproar any more. I never used to be this way. Now one of the kids shrieks and I pounce, snarling. It's unnatural. I used to have very steady nerves. Sometimes I look through the living-room window at the snow mountains, far off, and I wish I could go there, just for a while, with no one else around and hardly any sounds at all, the wind muttering, maybe, and the snow in weird sculptures and caverns, quiet. I said some of this to Jake Fogler once and he said I had a death wish. So now I don't think I've got a right to think that about the mountains. How can you win? On the other hand, since when is Jake a psychiatrist?

8

The buildings at the heart of the city are brash, flashing with colors, solid and self-confident. Stacey is reassured by them, until she looks again and sees them charred, open to the impersonal winds, glass and steel broken like vulnerable live bones, shadows of people frog-splayed on the stone like in that other city.

— Lunatic. Mac says *Less danger now than ten years ago.* I guess he's right. I always say *I guess you're right.* More fool me, for agreeing so easily, but is it worth the upset not to? I ask myself. *Pre-mourning.* Such a brainy female she was—which evening course was that? Oh yeh, Aspects of Contemporary Thought. I asked her if she didn't worry. I'd worried for twenty years and couldn't seem to stop. And she said in that aloof crystalline voice, *Pre-mourning is a form of self-indulgence.* What should I do? Make a sign and hang it up in my kitchen?

A girl gets on the bus and sits beside Stacey. She has clear skin, unpimpled and unpowdered, and long straight blond hair which looks as though she has ironed it. Stacey smiles a little, being reminded of Katie. Then her smile is lost in self-awareness.

— What's she seeing? Housewife, mother of four, this slightly too short and too amply rumped woman with coat of yesteryear, hemlines all the wrong length as Katie is always telling me, lipstick wrong color, and crowning comic touch, the hat. *Man, how antediluvian can you get?* Is that what she's thinking? I don't know. But I still have this sense of some monstrous injustice. I want to explain. *Under this chapeau lurks a mermaid, a whore, a tigress.* She'd call a cop and I'd be put in a mental ward.

> Stacey Cameron, seventeen. Flamingo Dance Hall every Saturday night, jitterbugging. Knowing by instinct how to move, loving the boy's closeness, whoever he was, loving the male smell of him. Stacey spinning like light, like all the painted singing tops of all the spin-

ning world, whirling laughter across a polished floor. Five minutes ago. *Is* time? How?

Stacey gets off the bus at Bluejay Crescent. Then the sound she always dreads to hear. *Scree-ee!* Brakes. The white Buick shudders to a stop and the man climbs out. Very very slowly, as though he were moving underwater. He is terrified to look at the boy lying on the road. Stacey cannot see the boy's face. Only the blue jeans. He could be seven years old, or ten. He is not making a sound. No cry. Nothing.

Stacey does not go over to look, because she cannot. Instead, she begins running. Along the sidewalk, heels snagging on the cement, running crazily, until she reaches the big dark-green frame house with gabled roof and screened front porch.

Katie!

Yeh? What?

Where are the boys?

How should I know? They were here a minute ago. Where you been?

Stacey runs through the house and out the back door. Ian and Duncan are playing in the back yard. The two auburn heads are bent over the wheels of the bug Ian is making. They look up and see her.

Hi. Where *you* been, all this time?

Sorry. I—I missed the bus. I'll get your lunch right now.

Katie comes downstairs and looks curiously at Stacey, who is now sitting in the kitchen with her hands over her face.

Mum? You okay? Hey, what's the matter?

I'm okay. I thought for a second—there was this boy— an accident—white Buick—just at the corner. I didn't know—

Oh Mum. That's awful. Please, don't cry. Here—have a Kleenex.

Katie stands there, awkwardly, inexperienced at consoling, looking at Stacey from wide grey eyes. She is wearing a dress the startling color of unripe apples, and her long straight auburn hair looks as though she has ironed it, which she has. No

10

lipstick, but green eye make-up. For an instant Stacey catches hold of her hand and holds it.

—— It's supposed to be the other way around. What a rock of Gibraltar I turned out to be. Katie, you're so goddam beautiful. Sometimes I feel like a beat-up old bitch.

Katie, I feel about a hundred.

Well, you don't look so hot, either. Just at the moment, I mean. Want me to bring Jen downstairs? She's playing in her room. I fetched her from Foglers'.

Thanks, honey.

Normality is re-established, and Stacey takes off her coat and hat and starts making sandwiches.

> Stacey in hospital, holding Katherine Elizabeth, age twenty-four hours. Katie with eyes shut tightly, walnut-sized fists clenched, look of utter composure. *I did it. She's here. She's alive. Who'd believe I could have borne a kid this beautiful?* (Or any kind of kid, for that matter.)

—— You have to keep quiet about all that. Restraint. Some wise guy is always telling you how you're sapping the national strength. Overprotective. Or else, you don't really care about them—you're just compensating because you're guilty on account of the fact that in your core you're trying to possess them, like hypnosis. Or something. Article in magazine at hairdresser's. "Nine Ways the Modern Mum May Be Ruining Her Daughter." I should never read them, but I always do, and then I check in my mind to see how many ways I'm ruining Katie. But how can you tell? I can see the doll who wrote that one. Jazzy office stuffed with plastic plants and never a daughter in sight.

The boys come in. Stacey does not hug them. She restricts herself to putting a hand on their hair and mentioning the need for haircuts. Ian's hair is the exact color of Mac's, dark red, and Duncan's is a littler lighter, red-gold.

11

At quarter to one, Katie and the boys go back to school. Stacey watches them go. Ian walks ahead, as usual, slim and wiry, tall for ten, impatient, moving with a quick grace, perfectly in command of his muscles. Duncan rarely hurries, and is largely unaware of other people. Yet he will tell Stacey what he is thinking, sometimes. Ian guards himself at every turn.

—— What did I do to make him that way? It's the confusion that bothers me. Everything happens all at once, never one thing at a time, so how in hell do you know what effect anything is having on them? That other article, last week. "Are You Castrating Your Son?" God, Sir, how do I know? It's getting so I'm suspicious of my slightest word or act. Maybe I shouldn't have ruffled Ian's hair just now.

Stacey picks up Jen, who is robust enough but who seems fragile. Picking her up is like holding a kitten, when the first thing that is noticeable is not the softness of it but the fact that all its bones can be felt.

Come on, flower. Time for a sleep.

Babble babble

Come on, honey, *talk*. It's easy when you try.

—— Maybe she's got ESP, like those sickening kids in that SF movie, whose eyes glowed like lighthouses when they were communicating by mental telepathy with one another. She's probably chatting away silently this very moment with some mutated kid in Samarkand or Omsk. Oh God, it's not all that funny. What if there really is something wrong? Should I be doing something about it? What I should be doing right now is finding out who that boy is, and how badly hurt. I can't. It's all I can do to cope with what goes on inside these four walls. This fortress, which I'd like to believe strong.

After school, Ian and Duncan are in the back yard. The bug consists of wheels, planks, steering apparatus, nails, pieces of wire with some essential purpose. Ian works dartingly, knowing which hammer or screwdriver to use. Duncan has no mechanical know-how, but is trying hard to please Ian. Then wham.

Chaos. Yells. Imprecations, threats, denials. Poundingly, they are both in the kitchen.

Mum, tell Duncan to leave my bug alone!

You said I could help. You *said!*

I didn't say you could wreck it, dumb idiot.

I wasn't. I never.

You can't just nail on the wheels, you moron. How do you think they'll turn?

You think you're so

You keep your hands off it

I won't—it's not fair

You better, or I'll

Fighting, Ian holds himself back a little, using his brains to plan attack. Duncan fights with the flailing recklessness of the one who knows he cannot possibly win. The fury rises until at last Stacey is unable to bear their battle and their noise. Cain and his brother must have stared their hatred like this.

Cut it out! Both of you! You hear?

Slam. Only when she has done it does Stacey realize she has grabbed their shoulders and flung them both to the floor with as much force as she could muster. Ian does not cry. His pride sometimes permits him stomach cramps, but never tears. His bony face is bleached with anger. He rises and rushes outside, seizes the uncompleted vehicle and throws it down the outside cement steps which lead into the basement.

The hell with it then! I don't give a damn!

The wheels come off and tumble across the basement floor. The cracking sound is the nailed boards coming apart. Duncan, listening, looks blank with bewilderment.

He *can't.* He can't go and break it, Mum.

Duncan does not ever destroy the work he has done. He draws pictures of the shark-shaped rocket which will one day take him to Mars or Saturn, and of the scarlet forests he will walk there, under the glare of innumerable purple suns. He puts them away, and sometimes digs one out and looks at it with amusement as the product of an earlier self. But he never destroys them.

Ian looks at the shambles for an instant, his face desolated. Then he turns and runs to the garage, to the loft, full of tent poles and torn canvas chairs and sparrows' nests, where once Stacey found a scribbler half full of writing, headed "Captain Ian MacAindra His Direy of How We Beat Enimy." And she had wondered where he was bound for.

Stacey puts her arms around Duncan for a minute. Then he goes outside and glances up at the loft, as though wanting to go there but not daring. He stands on the lawn, looking as though he cannot figure out what to do.

—— If Mac knew, he would think I was unbalanced. He never hits the kids in anger. No, maybe not, but that icy calm of his is worse. Okay, so I'm trying to justify myself. Earlier, I was worried sick in case that kid was one of mine. Now, look. Why? What if I hit one of them too hard sometime, without meaning to? Am I a monster? They nourish me and yet they devour me, too. God, how can I make all this better as if it hadn't happened? No answer. No illumination from on high. As if I expected any. If I could only talk about it. But who wants to know, and anyway, could I say? I can't forget that piece in the paper. Young mother killed her two-month-old infant by smothering it. I wondered how that sort of thing could ever happen. But maybe it was only that the baby was crying and crying, and she didn't know what to do, and was maybe frantic about other things entirely, and suddenly she found she had stopped the noise. I cannot think this way. I must not.

Stacey pours herself a massive gin and tonic, and gets dinner. Mac is away on the road and will not be home until late tonight. The kids eat, do homework, look at TV. At eleven, even Katie is stashed away in bed and Stacey is off duty. She takes the current glass of gin and tonic up to the bedroom. She locks the door, temporarily, in case a kid wakens, strips and looks at herself in the full-length mirror.

Every time Stacey ran down the stairs from
the apartment above Cameron's Funeral Home,
which was home, she paused in flight like a
hummingbird or helicopter and sneaked a
glance into the mirror halfway down, circular and heavy, gilded in coy cherubs with
bunches of grapes draped over their private
parts. *Stacey, Stacey, vanity isn't becoming.*
The soft persistent mew from upstairs, the
voice that never tired of saying how others
ought to be and never were. And Stacey
would be off, to laugh and talk so loudly in
the jukebox-loud café that no one would
guess she cared about her ugliness.

—— She actually believed it was vanity, Mother did. *It's
not how you look, it's what you are that counts,* she used to say
—admirably, I guess, but brother, that was one of the finest lies
anyone ever spun me. Do I know that little about Katie now?
That old album—and when I saw a snapshot of myself, years ago,
I thought *My heavens, I was actually pretty—why didn't I know
it then?*

Stacey drinks the gin and tonic slowly, trying to make it
last. She brushes her hair and makes up her face and puts on
perfume. Then she looks in the mirror again. No change.

—— Oh Cleopatra. You old swayback. Four kids have altered
me. The stretch marks look like little silver worms in parallel
processions across my belly and thighs. My breasts aren't bad,
and at least my ankles aren't thick. Mac said once he liked the
color of my eyes, greenish-grey. But there used to be a slight
hollow on the side of my buttocks, a little concave place that
showed when I wore a tight skirt, and he liked that, too, and it
isn't there any more. Filled in with the slow accumulation of
flesh. Not flesh. Fat. F.A.T. I can make the hollow be there
again momentarily if I tense my muscles. But who is going to

go through life remembering to hold their thigh muscles in, just so they'll have an attractive ass?

Stacey slops on some more perfume. The gin is gone. She puts on her housecoat and tiptoes downstairs to refill the glass. She returns, sits on the bedroom chair, smoking, no longer looking in the mirror.

—— Why doesn't he get home? I want him. Right now, this minute. No, I don't. I want some other man, someone I've never been with. Only Mac for sixteen years. What are other men like? It's just as bad for him, maybe worse. He looks at the girls on the street, all the young secretaries stepping lightly, the slim fillies of all the summers, and his face grows inheld and bitter. I want to comfort him, but can't, any more than he can comfort me, for neither of us is supposed to feel this way. Except that I know he does. I wonder if he knows I do? Sometimes I think I'd like to hold an entire army between my legs. I think of all the men I'll never make love with, and I regret it as though it were the approach of my own death. I'm not monogamous by nature. And yet I am. I can't imagine myself as anyone else's woman, for keeps. What does Mac do when he's on the road? He doesn't sell vanilla essence every evening, that's for sure. God, I'm unfair. Are the small-town whores so glamorous? And anyway, it's only my conditioned reflex. I don't worry that much, whatever he does out there. It doesn't seem all that earth-shattering. It's jealousy, baby, admit it. He can and you can't. So okay. But apart from that angle, I'd like to be on the road. Not for anything but just to be going somewhere.

Mac on the road, soaring along as though the old Chev were a winged chariot, through the mountains and the turquoise air, into the valley where the rivers run with names like silkenly flowing water, Similkameen, Tulameen, Coquihalla, the names on maps, clear brown water over the shifting green stones, where the pine and tamarack and the thin spruce trees stand a little way off, blue-green and black-green needles dry in the dry gold air, where the tall barbed grasses are never touched or cut but

16

*remain eternally high with their pale seedheads like oats bent in
the light wind that blows always, where it is sun all the way in
the fields of purple fireweed where only the bees make their
furred music.*

Stacey knows it is not like that for him. He does door-to-
door. Nights, it is motels on the fringes of towns, gaudy dusty
shacks with names like Rainbow and Riverview and small neon
signs announcing *Eats* and *Vacancy,* where drowsy Alsatian dogs
sprawl on the gravel driveways and the proprietor's kids throw
stones at one another, and the cars rocket past—*ching! ching!
ching!*—like a roaring clock recording the minutes, and the rooms
are scantily clad in imitation furniture, the table covered with
burn scars and wet beer bottle circles, the floor buckling linoleum,
and a shower that dribbles lukewarm water unpredictably. Days,
and it is all doors, knocking and waiting, and flint-faced females
who imagine their unappetizing virtue to be in peril, so *slam.*

— He never talks of it. He won't. He refuses. Last week a
man knocked at my door, a young man with amber eyes pale
and circular behind magnifying glasses. He held out a pamphlet
in half-apologetic offering. *Safety in Time of War.* Ragged crimson letters like rising flames. I did a double take and saw the
smaller letters underneath. *God's War of the Last Day.* Oh, that
war. He was a Redeemer's Advocate. I nearly closed the door
quickly. But then I didn't. He was in the living room for an hour
and a half and I thought he'd never go. It can't be good, to have
a door slammed in your face.

Drabble's, as well as being purveyors of vanilla, lemon
and orange essence, peppermint and raspberry extract and
maple-type flavoring, also handle a wide selection of sprays—
Forest Petal House Freshener, Silk Brocade Hair Spray, Pink
Cross Athlete's Foot Spray, Angel-Breath Mouth Freshener,
Honey Blossom Garbage Tin Spray, and others. Mac has been
doing the circuit for Drabble's for seven years. He took it on immediately after he stopped selling encyclopedias.

— He was doing okay, in encyclopedias. He never lost his

17

job. He quit. He kicked himself for it afterwards. Listen, Mac, you did right. He's never mentioned it since, but I've never forgotten the night he told me what happened.

Mac, in a one-room flat above a store, near the docks. Going through the spiel. You, too, can travel to London, England, or Paris, France, or the frangipani-perfumed South Seas, through these spectacularly scenic pictures in *Once-Over World,* given free with every contract for a full set of encyclopedias, agreeable monthly or weekly terms. And the guy who was picking up the pen to sign was a pensioner, old retired logger, who wanted to see the picture of Piccadilly, London, where he'd once gone on leave in 1917 from the trenches. Mac suddenly grabbed the contract and tore it up, telling the old guy he needed encyclopedias like he needed a hole in the head, and there was a public library only a few blocks away. The old guy was furious, cheated. So much for gesture. But Mac went back to the office and quit, anyway.

—— At that precise moment, didn't I have to go and get pregnant? I shouldn't have. It was my fault. We were both a little stoned the night it happened. I thought I'd put the damn equipment in, but next morning there it was on the floor beside the bed. After I was certain, Mac didn't say a word. He went to work for Drabble's, which was the first job that came along. Was it then he started to go underground, living in his own caves? If I mentioned the possibility of trying something else, looking around for another job, he'd only say *I'm not complaining, am I?* I couldn't very well say *Yes,* but it seemed he was, in some way. I kept saying I was sorry, which must have got pretty boring for him. I *was* sorry, and yet I wasn't, too. I feel the exact same now. How can I regret Duncan, who isn't like any other person on this earth? When Duncan was born, Mac came to see me, and didn't ask about the baby at all, simply said *You okay?* I guess it was terrible for him. It *was* terrible. But it was his kid, too. It wasn't immaculate conception. Well, he took on the responsibilities, Stacey. What more do you want? After a while business picked up in the spray and flavor trade, and Jen was born, planned.

> Stacey in yet another hospital. Mac, handing her two dozen yellow chrysanthemums. *Hey, a girl, eh? You did well.* Stacey taking the flowers, smiling at him, suddenly knowing how late it was, unable to care at all what he said or thought about the new child. They're beautiful, Mac, the flowers. *Glad you like them.* Yes, they're lovely—thanks a million. *That's all right.* Everything was all right. Certainly. Of course. She held Jen in her arms and thought of Duncan.

Well past midnight, Mac gets home. Stacey wakens and hears his key in the door. He climbs the stairs slowly, his footsteps sounding to her like those of his father, like Matthew's footsteps on the front steps on Sundays, seventy-four years old.

— Mac, for Christ's sake, you're forty-three.

But when he switches on the light in the bedroom, and stands in the doorway, Stacey cannot see that he has changed all that much in sixteen years. He is still as lean as ever, and although his auburn hair has darkened, he has lost none of it. He is still handsome to her. The main change is in the webbed lines around his eyes and on his forehead.

— Worrying about how to support us? If I could only go away and leave him alone, take the sword off his neck. Would he want me to? No good saying he chose me and the kids. He didn't know what he was getting himself into, just as I didn't. Mac—let me explain. Let me tell you how it's been with me. Can't we ever say anything to one another to make up for the lies, the trivialities, the tiredness we never knew about until it had taken up permanent residence inside our arteries?

Hi. You're late, Mac.

My God. Is that my fault? I had to finish up before I started home.

I didn't mean it that way.

Well, that's how it sounded to me.

I'm sorry. I only meant you're late and isn't that too bad. For *you*, for heaven's sake, I meant.

Okay, okay, it doesn't matter.

Doesn't matter! That you misunderstand every single word I utter.

Oh Stacey, for God's sake. I'm tired. Quit exaggerating.

Okay, so I'm exaggerating. It would just be nice if you knew what I meant.

—— Why am I doing it like this? If I knew what you meant, as well. Oh Mac. Talk. Please.

I'm sorry. I'm obtuse—okay? But I'm bloody tired and I don't feel like starting one of these

I'm sorry. I didn't mean *that*

All right, all right. Let's forget it, eh? Let's just forget it. I've had about enough for one day.

—— And he has. He has. Let's forget it, then. When we're both dead, we'll forget it.

Mac undresses and climbs into bed beside her.

Christ, am I ever beat.

You better get to sleep right away, then.

I've got to.

It's okay, I know.

Well, I'm sorry

You don't have to be sorry

Yeh, but you've been alone all week

It's okay—I'm used to it

Look, are you sure you don't mind?

I don't mind. It's not that. Look, it's okay. Everything is all right—okay?

Yeh, I guess so. God, the traffic was terrible tonight, coming back in. Kids okay?

Yes, everything's fine here. How was it this time?

Oh—could've been worse.

Tell me about it.

Nothing to tell. Same as usual.

What's usual?

Oh, I don't know. Same old crap. Look, are you sure you're okay?

Yes, I'm okay.

Good night, then.

Good night.

> Stacey Cameron, twelve, visiting for a week with a remote cousin who lived on a farm fifty miles from Manawaka, hating every minute of it, knotted with strangeness and loneliness, scared of cows and coyote-like dogs, sickened by unfamiliar food, potatoes and apple pie at breakfast, thinking of home where she didn't want to be, either, the tomb silences between Niall Cameron and his wife. Stacey, writing her letter home. *How are you? I am fine.*

Beside her, Mac moans a little in his sleep, turns over and is quiet. Stacey is not able to sleep.

—— Damn him, snoring away so unconcernedly. I feel like giving him a sharp kick, so he'll wake up and at least we'll both be suffering. All right, God, don't tell me, let me guess. I'm a mean old bitch. I know it. But I ask you, Sir, is it fair that Mac should be systematically restoring his physical and mental energy through sleep while I lie here like a bloody board? What's that you say? You are suggesting that if I am expecting justice I am a bird-brain? You have a point there, Lord. I will have to mull that one over.

One of them cries. The games vanish. Stacey sits up in bed. Mac half wakens.

—— Which one? Duncan.

What in hell is the matter now, Stacey?

Duncan. I think he's having a bad dream.

Leave him. You're going to ruin that kid, Stacey. Boy of his age shouldn't have his mother tearing in to see what's the matter every time he wakes up.

The crying increases, thin, attenuated, frightened.

I can't just leave him, Mac.

Go ahead, then. What a man he's going to grow up to be.

Stacey stumbles out of bed and down the long hall, through the darkness, no light needed, every hillock of carpet known to her bare feet. It has been this way always with the boys. Ian used to have nightmares, and now Duncan does.

—— It's the one thought Mac can't bear, the insufficient masculinity of one of his sons. He wonders what will happen when they leave home, what unnatural flowering. He tortures himself (or so I think) with the idea, and then he turns on them and does his sergeant-major act, the toughening process, or so he believes. Sometimes I see it his way, and I think *How can I ever make up for what I've done to them? How can I ever answer or atone for it?* And yet I keep going to them when they waken and cry out. It's as though I'm compelled. What I cannot bear is the thought that one of them is trapped in his nightmare, alone in there. Then I think that lots worse things could happen to them than to be queer, and that when they're away and on their own, in some ways it wouldn't matter to me at all who they held as long as there was someone and they could bring themselves to cry out. If Katie grew up bent, would I feel the same? The question could never arise with Katie. Oh? There you are, doll—confusion again.

Duncan is partly awake, rubbing his eyes and trying to come back to the world.

Mum?

It's okay, honey. I think you just had a bad dream.

There was all these spikes coming up through my bed

It's okay—you're awake now.

It was a dream, wasn't it, Mum?

Yeh. Just a dream. Can you go back to sleep now?

Guess so

Duncan rolls over and is asleep once more.

—— Has the trap released him? It was of my making, wasn't it? What I did this afternoon to stop the noise.

Stacey kisses his forehead, touching his sweat-damp hair. Then she turns to go. There is a stirring from the other bed, across the room.

Mum?

Ian? You awake? Did Duncan waken you? That's too bad.

It doesn't matter. Good night.

Ian reaches out a hand. For him, this is extraordinary. Stacey holds his hand briefly, trying to interpret, then folds his blankets in around him.

Good night, honey. Sleep well.

Good night, Mum.

—— Has he forgiven me? Or does he only need my reassurance, at any price?

When she gets back to the bedroom, Mac is sitting up, smoking.

If you want a pansy for a son, Stacey, you're going the right way about it.

I don't think so.

I know so.

Didn't your mother ever get up in the night when you had a bad dream?

I didn't have any bad dreams that I can think of.

I don't believe it. You've forgotten.

I'm not in the habit of forgetting. Duncan would damn soon get over having bad dreams if he once realized you weren't going to trot in to him every time.

He doesn't do it on purpose. He was scared.

I'll bet. He quieted down soon enough once you traipsed in there.

23

Mac—don't be angry

I'm not angry

You are

Stacey, I am not angry. I am merely trying to point out that you are babying that boy and it isn't doing him any good. Can't you understand even that?

—— Even that. Among all the other incomprehensions? No, I can't understand even that. But if he's right, where does that leave me? Kid-ruiner. Also, his unadmitted fury. But the kids find mine the same. *Mum, don't be mad.* I'm not mad, I tell them. Spoken with deathly intent.

I don't mean to baby him. I'll try not to. Honestly, Mac, I will.

Well, really you should, honey. For his own good.

I will. Honestly.

—— I will. I will anything. I will turn myself inside out. I will dance on the head of a pin. I will yodel from the top of the nearest dogwood tree. I will promise anything, for peace. Then I'll curse myself for it, and I'll curse you, too. Oh Mac.

Honestly, Stacey, it's only because I

Yes, I know.

She gets back into bed. Then Mac is not too tired, just when she is. He draws her between his legs, and she touches him sirenly so he will not know. When he is inside her, he puts his hands on her neck, as he sometimes does unpredictably. He presses down deeply on her collarbone.

Mac please

That can hurt you   not that much   that's not much. Say it doesn't hurt.

It hurts.

It can't. Not even this much. Say it doesn't hurt.

It doesn't hurt.

He comes, then, and goes to sleep. The edges of the day are blurring in Stacey's head now.

—— God, Sir, do I know why? Okay, I've aged this man. I've

foisted my kids upon him. I yak away at him and he gets fed up, and he finds his exit where I can't follow and don't understand. There are too many people involved in this situation, Lord, you know that? You don't know. Well, Stacey, for heaven's sake get some sleep. Tomorrow everything will look better. Or at least different. Optimist.

The hillside is burning. Who dropped a lighted cigarette? Did she? Evergreen catches fire with terrible ease. In case of forest fire, all the men around have to go and fight it. That is the law of the land. Everyone has to obey the law of the land. But only the men are forced to go. The children have no business to be there. Don't they know they aren't supposed to be there? Only one way to get to them. A black fallen tree across the pit. A suspension bridge across the jagged rock canyon. Tree bridge. The ravine is so deep no one has ever dared look down. She will be all right, if only she does not look down. Come on, Stacey, only a little way. The hands. She is holding the hands of one. Which? She will not be allowed to return. Only this one can she take with her, away from the crackling smoke, back to the green world. She must not look to see which one. She must never look, never again, to see which one. She must never know who was left behind. She has to know. No. Not to be borne. Not to be born would be not to have to die. But that would be useless. Philosophy, my dear, is useless under certain circumstances. Their voices? Oh yes—no mistaking them. She would know their voices anywhere. She has to count the voices. But she must not. They know she can hear their voices. They do not know why she cannot come to them. Can she explain, while there is still a moment of time? No time

BR R R RING

—— Where's the damn alarm clock? Oh here. Shut up, you. That's better. Bloody morning once again.

TWO

>Λ(ᴏ)Λ(ᴏ)Λ(ᴏ)Λ(ᴏ)Λ(

The MacAindra residence on Bluejay Crescent is not classy, but it is not rundown either. Mac and Stacey have lived for twelve years within this large square structure with its high-gabled grey shingled roof, its evergreen-painted cedar-shake-covered walls and its only slightly sagging screened veranda. Stacey is attached to it, partly because she fears new houses and partly because her own veins and skin cells seem connected with this one.

— Mac hates it more every year because it's so dowdy and reflects on him, or so he thinks. Or so I think he thinks. One of these days he'll manage a switch, and we'll move to a pricey new split-level on the west side, furnished with that kind of sleek teak which will make me feel inferior to my own coffee table.

Jen is scrabbling around on the veranda floor. The afternoon has the feverish damp warmth of early summer, and Stacey is swinging in the brown-and-white-striped hammock, with tassled edges, which Mac refers to as The Anachronism. She is studying the front door, which is a lilac color.

26

—— What a fool I was. "Want To Be a Little Off-Beat?" Here's ten ways, the article said. A lilac door was one. So off I tripped to the nearest hardware store to assert my unique individuality with the same tin of paint as two million other dimwits. Conned into idiocy. My mind is full of trivialities. At lunch Ian said *Duncan's piece of cake is miles bigger than mine—it's not fair,* and I roared that they should quit bothering me with trivialities. So when they're at school, do I settle down with the plays of Sophocles? I do not. I think about the color of my front door. That's being unfair to myself. I took that course, Ancient Greek Drama, last winter. Yeh, I took it all right.

> Young academic generously giving up his Thursday evenings in the cause of adult education. *Mrs. MacAindra, I don't think you've got quite the right slant on Clytemnestra.* Why not? The king sacrificed their youngest daughter for success in war—what's the queen supposed to do, shout for joy? *That's not quite the point we're discussing, is it? She murdered her husband, Mrs. MacAindra.* (Oh God, don't you think I know that? The poor bitch.) Yeh well I guess you must know, Dr. Thorne. Sorry. *Oh, that's fine—I always try to encourage people to express themselves.*

—— Young twerp. Let somebody try killing one of his daughters. But still, he had his Ph.D. What do I have? Grade Eleven. My own fault. I couldn't wait to be on my own and out of Manawaka. Those damn freight trains—I can still hear them, the way they used to wail away far off at night on the prairies, through all the suffocating nights of summer when the air smelled hotly of lilacs, and in winter when the silence was so cold-brittle you thought any sound would crack it like a sheet of thin ice, and all the trains ever said was *Get on your way, somewhere, just so something will happen, get up and get out of this town.* So I did. Business course in Winnipeg, then saving every nickel to come out here. And look at me. Self-educated, but zanily. No wonder I bore Mac. Do I bore him? How do I know? The slightest effort at speech seems too much for him lately, too debilitating. What's he want? I'm not a complete dope. He wouldn't be any better off with someone like Tess Fogler, gorgeous though she may be. Would he? She had a sign made for their house—*Three Five Seven* in scrolled numerals and a bluejay perched on a crescent moon. *Get it, Stacey? Bluejay Crescent. Cute, eh?* And I said, *Gee that's really cute, Tess.* These lies will be the death of me sooner than later, if they haven't already been. What goes on inside isn't ever the same as what goes on outside. It's a disease I've picked up somewhere.

Everything drifts. Everything is slowly swirling, philosophies tangled with the grocery lists, unreal-real anxieties like rose thorns waiting to tear the uncertain flesh, nonentities of thoughts floating like plankton, green and orange particles, seaweed—lots of that, dark purple and waving, sharks with fins like cutlasses, herself held underwater by her hair, snared around auburn-rusted anchor chains

Hey! You asleep?

Mac's voice. Stacey leaps out of the hammock, disheveled in pink Bermuda shorts, and looks around for Jen. What negligence. Asleep on duty. Jen is playing quietly with her blue plastic tea set on the floor. Relief.

What on earth are you doing home at this time of day, Mac?

Mac does not reply at once. He stands there, looking pleased, the lines around his eyes easing a little. Then he points to a new teal-blue Buick parked in front of the house.

I've got a new job.

— A new job. He's got a new job. And suddenly I've got a weird feeling. As though I'd been forgiven after all.

Oh   honey that's wonderful. That's terrific. What doing?

No more door-to-door. Getting orders from drugstores, mainly.

What *is* it?

Richalife. I guess you've heard of *them*.

— I've heard all right. Full-page ads in newspapers. *Richalife—Not Just Vitamins—A New Concept—A New Way of Life.* With testimonials. *Both Spirit and Flesh Altered. Richness Is a Quality of Living.* Singing ads on local stations, blond angelic trilling. Rallies. Gimmicks falling like the golden shower of stars from fireworks. Oh Jesus lover of my soul.

Gosh, Mac, that's—why, that's wonderful.

Whatsamatter? You don't like it?

Sure I like it. Of course. I said so, didn't I? It's marvelous.

Well, I certainly *hope* you think so. Considering it's the best opportunity I've had in

I like it. I think it's great. I'm really delighted, Mac. Tell me.

It's go-ahead, that's all. None of this business of refusing to spend a dime to make a quarter of a million. National firm—headquarters in the east, but they really give the branches their head and let them decide how to handle the local campaign. Thor Thorlakson—he's the provincial manager—well, he's a young guy, but exceptional. Really exceptional. If you get a young guy who's good, he's in touch—you know. Thor's got everything going for him. He's quite a guy. You'll have to meet him soon.

I'd love to.

— Yeh, I can hardly wait. Dr. Spender, here I come for forty billion tranquilizers.

He wants to meet all the wives. He likes to find out what a guy's home atmosphere is like.

— Oh he does, does he? I'll turn up in long black tights, a green wig, and a feather boa, mouthing obscenities.

29

Why is that any of his business, Mac? I mean

All those things affect the way a man does his job. Surely you can see that.

Oh sure. I guess so. The Buick's lovely, Mac.

Yeh, and when I think Drabble's didn't even supply a car. I'm not going to sell the old Chev, Stacey. You need a car.

Me? Oh Mac—honestly?

Sure. You pleased?

Am I!

Stacey kisses him and he holds her unexpectedly closely for an instant. She feels his tremor—not sex, something else.

—— Mac, what is it? Are you nervous about taking on a new job? You're only forty-three, for heaven's sake. Or what is it? Why don't you say?

Mac—you're happy about it, aren't you?

I'm bloody delighted. Why ask? Can't you see?

Yeh, sure. The—product—it's okay, you think?

What do you mean? Of course it's okay. Listen, I'll bring the Chev home tonight, eh?

Gosh, Mac, thanks a million. It'll be a lifesaver it'll be absolutely terrific shopping taking the kids to the beach all the hundreds of

That's okay. I'm glad you're pleased.

Then Stacey realizes why he looks different and why she has been puzzling about it at the edges of her mind. He has a crew cut. His dark auburn hair is like a soft brush. Crew cut, fashion of his college days. He sees her looking and he reaches up a hand and touches his head.

Think it looks all right?

I *wondered* why you looked different. It looks great. Really great.

—— How many times has he protected me from the sight of myself? *Sure, Stacey, you look really good in that dress,* he said when I bought the green and gold last month. It was only later I knew it was Katie's dress, although wrong size for her. Mac,

30

you're only forty-three. Last time I thought that, I meant how relatively young. Now I mean how relatively not-young.

The evening they go to see Thorlakson, both Mac and Stacey are edgy. Stacey in their bedroom tussles with her hair, while Mac repeatedly clears his throat.

Hem hem hem hem

— Stop it, for heaven's sake, Mac, can't you? It's getting worse, and that awful cough at the end of the throat-clearing— *Whoop! Whoop!* The rosy-fingered dawn in this house sounds like it's playing bongo drums. But he keeps on smoking nonstop and gets mad as blazes if I say anything. It worries me, but it revolts me, too, to hear him hoicking up phlegm from his inner recesses. It disgusts him that I pluck out handfuls of my eyebrows with my fingers without knowing it. No one ought to have repulsive mannerisms. We all ought to be physically perfect. I need a state of unblemishment more as the years go by, but I have it less.

Do I look all right, Mac?

Stacey is wearing her black sheath dress, supposedly slenderizing. She tugs at the waist, trying to straighten the wrinkles in the material, but her hips are against her. Mac is looking at his watch and does not glance in her direction.

Fine fine fine you look fine. Aren't you ready *yet?*

Right this minute. C'mon then. *Katie!* No later than ten for you, and don't forget to pot Jen before you go to bed, eh? Ian—Duncan—you're to go to bed when Katie tells you, you hear? And no fighting.

A chorus of *Yeh, yeh, okay* comes from various corners of the house.

For Christ's sake, Stacey, they're all *right*. Can't you just leave them?

Sorry sorry sorry

— He's right. I fuss. Mother-hen type. All a load of nonsense. All unnecessary. Another nervous tic. How can I break habits I've acquired so gradually I'm not even aware of them until I see they drive Mac out of his mind?

> Timber Lake, sixteen years ago, had hardly any cottages. Jungles of blackberry bushes and salmonberry. Spruce trees darkly still in the sun, and the water so unsullied that you could see the grey-gold minnows flickering. You know something, Mac? *What?* I like everything about you. *That's good, honey. I like everything about you, too.*

—— Why should I think it unbalanced to want to mourn? Why shouldn't I wail like the widows of Ashur if I feel like it? I have cause. Come, come, Stacey. Act your age. That's precisely what I'm doing, God, if you really want to know. Too much mental baggage. Too damn much, at this point. More more more than I want. Things keep spilling out of the suitcases, taking me by surprise, bewildering me as I stand on the platform.

Whatever else you do, Stacey, for God's sake don't get into an argument, will you?

I won't I won't do you have to tell me?

I'm only thinking of the time you told Crimpton you were going to join the Redeemer's Advocates—that's all I'm thinking of.

Well, I *was* considering it, Mac. Serenity, I thought. I was going to give it a whirl. But I couldn't. Maybe it was the thought of your dad that stopped me even from going to a meeting. You know, having been a United Church minister and that. I thought he'd have a fit.

He wouldn't have been the only one. C'mon, we're here.

Thor's apartment is in one of the high-risers near the bay. There is a mirror in the elevator, and Stacey spends the up-flight in patting distractedly at her hair. Down a thickly carpeted hall, and then at the gentle bell buzz the door opens and a massive figure fills the doorway.

32

Hello there. Great to see you, Mac. And this

Thor turns to Stacey, gazes down at her, sizes her up, frowns a trace, then gives her an oblique and uninterpretable smile. Mac steps in.

Thor, I'd like you to meet my wife, Stacey.

Now Thor's smile broadens and widens, grows relaxed, genuine, sincere.

Well, hi there, Stacey. I've really been looking forward to meeting you.

Mutter mutter me too

Well, come on in.

Thor Thorlakson is not actually taller than Mac, but he carries himself carefully straight as though he practices every morning in front of a full-length mirror. His suit is a costly blue-grey, giving the impression of a luminous uniform, a doorman in heaven or perhaps a mace bearer behind the celestial throne. His features have clearly been sculptured by an expert, and his hair is silver. Above the out-jutting jaw and the young face, the silver hair forestedly flourishes, a lion's share of it which he tosses imperially back as they walk along a slippery hall.

—— How do you like that? How has he achieved that crowning glory? No peroxide in the kitchen sink for him, you can be quite sure. No damn crew cut, either. He looks vaguely familiar. I think I must've seen him in a magazine or newspaper. It would be funny if he'd ever been a male model. He looks as though he just stepped out of *The Venusian Warlock,* that SF movie I rushed off and saw once when everything got too much. I thought warlock was something like deadlock, but no, and when I saw the movie I thought brother things have come to a fine pass if I can learn from a piece of garbage like this. Thor's the wizard.

Thor motions Stacey to a royal blue canvas-looking chair shaped like an upside-down tent. She sinks down nervously. On the floor, a black-and-white fur rug looks as though it had been made from the skins of stillborn monkeys, softly eerie. The coffee table top is grey-veined marble. Voluminous white drapes are

33

like the heavy fine linens of ancient Rome. On the walls, two abstract paintings in selected shades of orange, black and white. On a sideboard, a sharply orange vessel like a misshapen triangle in thin glass. The place is both ascetic and voluptuous.

I've gone off booze ha-ha. Never was a heavy drinker but used to enjoy a martini before dinner. That was in the B.R. days—before Richalife. Same with caffeine and nicotine—you could say the shackles have been lifted. Yes, you could definitely put it that way—the shackles have been lifted. Once upon a time I could barely face the morning without three cups of coffee and as many cigarettes. Then I started reaching for a Richalife instead. I think we've all got to remember that we're not just selling vitamin pills—we're selling ourselves. I mean ha-ha that sounded a little ambiguous but what I was meaning to say was we stand as living examples. What program you got the family on, Mac?

Well, I haven't quite had time to get it worked out for all of them yet, but I plan to start them the beginning of the week.

—— You do, eh? Over my dead body.

Mac, you never said

Then Stacey's jaw clamps shut as her brain receives the signal from Mac's red-flare-sending eyes. His voice goes on without a pause.

I'm on 35–ADDB myself, Thor.

—— Another unknown. What has he been doing? Slogging down pills secretly in the bathroom? Now he won't look at me.

Oh yes—let's see now—35–ADDB—that's age thirty-five to forty, height medium to tall, temperament fair to medium calm, slight tendency to anxiety. Right?

Right. Can you remember them all, Thor?

Most of them. I couldn't have, at one time, of course, but I find now my memory potential was hardly being tapped at all, before. Alertness-wise, the change has been really gratifying. I always had a good memory, mind you, but not what you would call really excellent. Now I think I can honestly and truthfully say it's reached the excellent mark. Have you noticed much change in yourself, Mac?

I sleep better I think

—— He *sleeps* better? Better than what? Mac, who's never lain awake one single night in his life that I know of? Has he suffered insomnia in country motels I never knew? Counting cockroaches marching in procession across the floor or patterned petunias parading across the wallpaper?

That's splendid. Takes a little time for the changes in depth, you know. Even Richalife can't reach the deep cells of the mind instantly. I'm on 25–Triple A myself, that's twenty-five to thirty, height tall, temperament outgoing, slight tendency to variable depression. I remember when I began, just over a year ago now, it took—oh, I should say about three or four weeks, approximately, before the depth changes were really well established. These very slight depression feelings I used to get—they were alleviated almost right straight off, definitely alleviated, but it must have been more or less a month or so before they totally disappeared. Cut down any on smoking?

Mac, who has been reaching into his pocket for a cigarette, withdraws his hand.

Some

Well, I feel confident there'll be a marked drop. Let me know how you're getting on caffeine-wise, too, won't you?

Oh certainly of course

Stacey leans forward as far as the chair shape permits.

How do you decide who's to have which uh course of tablets?

Mac fixes her with a stone idol's eye.

I explained to you, honey. *You* remember. It's done by the Richalife Quiz.

—— Did he explain? He did a certain amount of yakking last night, and I was thinking all the time of how it could be that Duncan keeps getting such awful marks in arithmetic. I'm always wanting him to talk, and when he does, I'm absent. Sad defection of duty. Goddam, though, I'm not convinced that he *did* explain.

Oh sure. Yeh. I recall it now. It just slipped my mind for a second, there.

Thor smiles again and rises to his feet. Standing beside a grey-veined marble fireplace he looks almost as striking as he presumably intends.

Time your program was designed for you, Stacey. I'll bet you make lists so you won't forget things—come on, now, don't you?

Stacey nods dumbly. Thor's voice continues slow and dreamily, intimate.

Think of the moment when you can throw away your lists. That'll be a red-letter day. Not to mention energy. Are you satisfied with your present level of energy?

Well

Mothers very often aren't, I do know that. Kids can take a lot out of you, can't they? I know. I'll bet some days you feel just pretty beat and exhausted, don't you? It's certainly not a very pleasant feeling. I don't know from personal experience— never having been a mother ha-ha—but I surely can sympathize.

—— Come on, little fish, there it is. Boy, if Mac ever came home one evening and said *Honey, I'll bet you're beat,* I'd fall into his arms. Well, nuts. I'm not rising to this. No dice.

Thor looks at Stacey, and she looks into his blue eyes, blue as the copper sulphate that used to be put in the near-shore water of Diamond Lake to clear it of the snails that caused itch. Still blue eyes without any gleam or flicker of themselves in them, no fathoming of them possible. Then he glances towards the hallway.

Well, it's been just great talking to you two. I don't mean to hustle you good people off, but Mickey Jameson's bringing his wife in to meet me in another few minutes, and I've got Stewart Essex coming in after that with his fiancée. I think it's always more personal if you talk to people by themselves. Of course I enjoy parties as well. We're going to have to see about an office party soon. Small celebration. Because I just have this feeling that we're going places together. I think the Head Office is really going to sit up and take notice of the fact that in this province we're *moving* and we're not moving slow. Am I right?

Sure—you sure are.

Good-bye   good-bye

So glad to have met you

Thanks so much

A pleasure

Blabber blabber

Click.

The Buick zooms lightly over the bridge, and Stacey, looking back, can see the lights of the city, rearing neons in lightning strokes of color, jagged scarlet, blue like the crested heart of a flame. She puts down the car window on her side, and can smell the sea, salt warmth and decaying seaweed, like the presence of some rank stinking turbulent primeval creature which has not yet realized the fact of its own passing.

What was that bit about the quiz, Mac?

Just answering some questions. There's nothing to it.

What sort of questions?

Oh—about your personality, and what worries you, stuff like that.

I won't.

Don't be ridiculous, Stacey. Of course you will.

We'll see about that.

Oh God, Stacey, why do you always have to make everything so difficult?

I don't mean to

Well you *do*

I'm sorry. I *mean* it. I'm sorry. What about the kids?

I can answer for them. That's allowed.

Mac

What now for God's sake
What do you think, I mean, in yourself?
What do you mean what do I think in myself?
Just what do you *think?*
What do you *mean,* what do I think? Like what?
Well, I mean
Just what *do* you mean, Stacey?
I guess the product's pretty good, eh?
I told you.
What about—I mean, what do you think of Thor?
I think he's a guy with drive.
I think he's bat-winged Mephistopheles.
You must be out of your mind.
Are you leveling with me, Mac?
For heaven's sake. What is there to level *about?*
Why don't you say what you mean, just once? Why not?
Look, I *know*
You do, eh? You really think you do?

Stacey looks at him, at his face in the half-light of the
car, his face bitter and real.

> Cameron's Funeral Home in the prairie town,
> and Stacey, seventeen, coming in late from a
> dance, stepping behind the Caragana hedge
> to avoid encountering her mother, who had
> come downstairs and outside in her dressing
> gown and was trying to open the mortuary
> door, which was locked. *Niall—you come up-*
> *stairs and quit drinking. I know what you're*
> *doing in there. I know you.* And the low
> gentle terrifying voice in reply—*You do? You*
> *really think you do?*

No. I don't know, Mac. Okay, I don't know. Isn't it
strange? I thought it couldn't happen to me.
What're you talking about? What couldn't happen?
The silences

Oh God. What gimmick are we in for now?

Nothing. Look—nothing. It's okay. Everything's okay. I'll do the quiz.

—— I've just remembered. The pill parade Mac's on is for age thirty-five to forty. Exactly how young did he tell Thor he was? Well, whatever the game happens to be, it's a form of solitaire for Mac. He's decided on that.

Stacey, look—you know I don't want to be unreasonable, but

Yeh, I know. It's okay. I wish I knew more.

About what?

I don't know.

Six o'clock, the dinner ready, the kids groaning about their emptiness, and no sign of Mac. Stacey pours herself a large gin and tonic and raises her glass.

—— Here's to the god of thunder. He's right. If I spent my life pouring myself full of vitamins and tomato juice instead of gin, coffee and smoke, maybe I would be a better person. I would be slim, calm, good-tempered, efficient, sexy and wise.

Also beautiful. Beautiful and intelligent.

What did you say, Mum?

Katie has snaked in around the kitchen door.

Nothing. Just talking to myself, I guess.

When's dinner? Marnie and I are going to the show.

Who said? The local, you mean? What's on?

Just this experimental film.

Which one?

Oh, you know. *Psychedelic Sidewalk.*

You can't. It's an A.

Katie drapes herself slenderly across a kitchen chair. She is wearing a turquoise dress with canary-colored plastic earrings.

So what else is new?

I'm just telling you, you won't be allowed in, that's all.

39

Jingle-jangle. Coinage. Ever heard of it, mini-mind? You can get in anywhere if you've got the price of admission.

Well, that's pretty cynical, I must say. Anyway, what makes you think I'll let you go?

You said I could go tonight. You *did* say.

I didn't say you could go to that one.

—— What difference does it make? Why are we going on like this? Do I really believe it's going to alter her out of all recognition? No. I feel it's my duty to appear to be doing my duty, that's all. A farce.

Katie flies up from the chair like a rust-feathered pheasant from cover.

You said I could go and I'm going. I just simply am. That's all.

—— Such rudeness. I never spoke to my mother that way, at her age.

> Stacey Cameron, fourteen, dark hair set rigidly in rolls on top of the head, transference from movie star queens to a million clumsy-fingered small-town girls. Stacey with tomato-colored mouth, regarded by mother more in sorrow than anger. *You are certainly not going to a public dance hall, dear. You wouldn't want to be the sort of girl people wouldn't respect, would you?* It's a dance, Mother, for heaven's sake, not an orgy. Mother sniffling into lace-edged hanky. *I never thought a daughter of mine would speak to me like that. Your father's going to have to deal—*(But he was down among the dead men, bottles and flesh, and didn't hear when she called.)

—— I stand in relation to my life both as child and as parent, never quite finished with the old battles, never able to arbitrate properly the new, able to look both ways, but whichever way I look, God, it looks pretty confusing to me.

Katie   listen, I'm sorry   try to be reasonable

Why don't *you* try being reasonable for a change? You give with one hand and take away with the other, that's your standard pattern. It's not only inconsistent—it's—it's immoral.

—— Lord assist me not to laugh. If the worst thing on my conscience were refusing to let her see *Psychedelic Sidewalk,* I would be a happy happy lady. Yet from where she stands I look unreasonable, inconsistent and immoral. And I'm not certain I'm not.

Katie gives Stacey a look filled with something deeply her own. Scorn? Pity? Then her turquoise shoulders slope a little and her long loose hair falls across her face. She turns and walks upstairs. Stacey can hear her sliding the bolt across her bedroom door. Stacey reaches for the gin and tonic and drinks it as though she has just stumbled in from the Sahara.

—— Katie? Listen. Just let me explain. I can explain everything. Sure, Explainer of the Year, that's me. How can I explain anything? How can I tell you what you should be doing? I don't know what I should be doing. But I think if I don't tell you, it'll look bad. If I could level with you, would we be further ahead? Do you really want to know what I'm like? I can't believe it.

Stacey rounds up Jen and feeds her. The boys are playing in the back yard, and the fighting is at present suppressed and undeclared. Stacey peers into saucepans, turns the stove elements lower, and pours another gin and tonic.

—— Where in hell is he? Knocking himself out for Thorlakson. He's working too hard. Yeh, but doing well, you have to admit. Sure, doing splendid. On his way to a heart attack. If he'd finished university, everything would be all right. He'd have a profession. How come he could only stick to it for two years after the war? It was more fun to go out drinking with Buckle. I can't imagine Mac ever being like that. Damn you, Buckle Fennick, you ruined my husband's life. What nonsense. Things don't happen that way. It was Mac himself who had to quit university.

Because his dad was a minister? Because Matthew was upright
to the point of unbearability? If only Mac were a doctor, say, or
a lawyer. Yeh, that would solve everything. Last month in this
city two lawyers and one doctor killed themselves. The lawyers
used the exhaust pipes on their cars, the doctor simply swallowed
the appropriate pills. Come on, Stacey, let me freshen your drink.
That's what Tess says. Yes, she does. She is a very dainty type.
Freshen, indeed. Let me give you another slug of this drug—
she doesn't say that. She is also wont to say, in such places as the
City Hall or the Hudson's Bay Company, that she wonders where
the Little Girls' Room is, making the john sound like a council
hall for countless nymphets. I shouldn't talk. Katie is always saying how outdated my slang is. Gosh. Gee. Twerp. Heavenly days.

Clump-clump-clump. A man's footsteps, but not Mac's.
Stacey thrusts her glass into the deep concealing blue bowl of
the Mixmaster on the kitchen cabinet, and goes to the door.

—— Mac's father?

But it is not Mac's father. It is Buckle Fennick. He stands
there on the front porch, grinning. For Buckle, to swagger does
not mean to walk boastfully, or not necessarily. Buckle can swagger while standing still. He wears a sleazily shiny sports shirt,
cerise and silver, and jeans.

—— Man of his age, I ask you. His jeans are always too tight
and they bulge where his sex is, and it embarrasses me and in-
furiates me that it does, yet I always look, as he damn well knows
and laughs at, one of the many unspoken small malices between
us in our years of competition for Mac. No—that's unfair to all
of us. I didn't mean it. Oh?

Buckle is only slightly taller than Stacey, but he is stocky
with muscular hair-flecked arms. He has a face like an Iroquois,
angular, and faintly slanted dark eyes. His hair is night-black and
straight. He never loses the tan on his face and arms, not even
in the winter, and on the occasions when he goes to the beach
with Mac and Stacey and the kids, it surprises Stacey to see how
pale his legs are under the black hairs.

—— Okay, so he's sexy. It's an optical illusion. How many men do I see? You could count them on one hand, and most of those like Jake Fogler, about three feet tall with heavy-rimmed glasses and semi-collapsed chests, talking earnestly about media or some damn thing. Buckle's just around here half the time, that's all. Mac's dear old buddy from during the war. I detest him. I try to be nice to him for Mac's sake, but sometimes I don't try hard enough and make some private remark to Mac, very restrained, like *Why does that slob always drop in at dinnertime?* and then Mac is furious. He doesn't know that Buckle scares me. It's ridiculous. It's untrue. That article—"I'm Almost Ready for an Affair," which turned out to mean she wasn't at all, ending in an old-fashioned sunburst of joy, Epithalamium Twenty Years After, virtuous while conveying the impression that dozens of virile men would be eager to oblige if she weren't. She was probably like me—the only guys she knew were her husband's friends.

Hi, gorgeous.

—— Buckle, when are you going to stop talking like that? Where do you get your lines? Old B-grade movies? Oh God, I should criticize. Here's me, dressed in none-too-clean slacks and a blouse which Katie discarded when indelible red ink got spilled on it, so I look like I'm bleeding severely from a chest wound. Thrice hell.

Oh hi, Buckle. Come on in. I'm just getting dinner. Mac's not home yet, but he should be here any minute.

—— My good-wife-and-mother voice. I can't seem to talk to Buckle in any other way. I always sound so prim. Sometimes I wonder what kind of person he imagines I must be.

I just got back from a haul north, so I'm off for a coupla days. Thought I'd drop in and see how the guy's getting on with the new job.

Mac's getting on fine.

You don't sound too pleased.

Sorry—I'm tired. End-of-day bit. Want to stay for dinner?

Twist my arm.

43

—— Will I, hell. Your arm needs less twisting than anybody's
I know, you cheap bastard. Don't you ever have a meal at home?

Sure, do stay. There's plenty. Let me get you a drink.
Gin and tonic?

Don't mind if I do.

—— Buckle, can't you vary the response from time to time?
I once said this—*Don't mind if I do*—and Mac told me later it
was vulgar. I didn't tell him it had been a take-off. I was too overcome with shame at my spiritual acidity.

Jen is playing with her plastic tea set on the kitchen
floor. Buckle picks her up and swings her around above his
head. Stacey, preparing one drink, having adroitly lifted her own
out of the Mixmaster bowl, gazes in the hope that Jen will
scream bloody murder. But no. Jen chortles for more.

Hey, how's my girl friend, eh? How's the champion pisser
of the neighborhood?

—— Just once. Only, for heaven's sake, *once* did Jen wet
on him when she was a very young baby. He still thinks this
is the wittiest remark going. Take your hands off my kid, you ape.

Here's your drink, Buckle.

He sets Jen down and picks up the glass.

Here's looking at you.

How was the trip, Buckle?

Buckle is a trucker. He drives a diesel dinosaur, a steel
monster, innumerable great tires, heavy as a mountain, roaringly
full of crazy power. Buckle loves it. It is his portable fortress,
his moveable furnace. It is his lover and himself all in one. He
mainly goes north, up the Cariboo Highway and the Alaska Highway, up to the Peace River Country where the forests grasp
the ancient moss-covered rocks, to the last little towns raw in
the mud of new clearings.

Same old shit. Bananas this time. Had to unload along
the way, but the last of them had to get to Fort St. John before
they rotted black. So what happens?

What?

44

Ten miles out of Williams Lake the steering goes. She's supposed to be serviced before each haul. Those buggers of mechanics at Ace don't know a spanner from their own cocks. Lucky it was me driving. Slightest thing happens, Harvey's nerves go on the blink. I'd slowed to light a cigarette, and that was lucky, too. My luck's still in—I make good and sure of that. If ever I go, it's not gonna be that way, some dumb thing like the steering going. *Doing!* I brake. Hard, but not too hard, see? She shudders and skids and finally comes to a standstill. Oncoming car nearly swerves right off the road. Terrified tourist climbs out and screams *What d'you think you're doing? Listen, bud,* I tell him, very calm, *it's a lucky thing for you my reaction time's pretty good and this crate decided to go for the verge and not for you, or you'd be strummin' your motherfuckin' harp this very second, and don't you forget it, eh?* Harvey's sleeping in the back all the time. I swear that guy's made out of plasticine. Six and a half hours we're held up.

What about the bananas?

They got there okay. I never lost a load of anything yet. Harvey keeps peeking away at them, like he's a hen with unhatched eggs or something. I tell him, *Relax, I'll take the night shift and we can make time.*

I bet that pleased him no end.

He's no good any more. Too slow. He's getting on, and he gets jittery. I'm trying to work a change. I'd like to go by myself, if they'll let me.

You never get jittery, I suppose.

Look, Stacey, I've told you. Nothing can happen to me while my luck's in. See?

No.

No what?

I don't see.

Well, like I know every inch of that goddam highway, and I know my vehicle, see? I know how she responds, and what she'll do and won't do. She'll do what I want because I *know.*

Anyway, it's always Russian roulette to some extent. That's not bad. That's just the way it is. You know that before you start out.

— He's never consistent. He contradicts himself all the time, and there are things he only hints at, or else mentions as though you were bound to know all about them—as though they were commonplace. His luck—something apart from him and yet within his control, like the steering wheel, although with the possibility of abrupt change. His head must be full of unnamed gods meshing like a whole set of complicated gears. He's as superstitious as a caveman, but he always denies having any superstitions.

Anyway, Stacey, I don't aim to get taken by some bonehead mechanic's mistake, not if I can help it—I mean, not even something I did, or another driver.

What do you mean—another driver?

When I say another driver, I mean another *driver*, see? Not some jerk of a farmer or tourist. I don't include Mac in that. He drives a car, sure, but he's as near to a driver as you could get.

— Maybe Buckle has a recurring nightmare about being smashed by a Volkswagen. Fate worse than death. Well, so what? All he wants is a jury of his peers.

How do you keep your luck? Praying?

You kidding? None of that crap for me. Reilly keeps a St. Christopher medal strung up there in front so he can see it all the time. Lots of guys do. Everything from kewpie dolls to saints. I know a guy keeps his wife's picture up there, framed with doodads and plastic flowers. All a lot of bullshit. I'm not superstitious.

Yeh, so you've said.

— His shrines are invisible. I wonder what they look like, and what fetishes and offerings lurk on those altars? Yeh, doll, that evening course Man and His Gods. Great authority, you. What do you know of it? Don't be silly. Don't think of it. It always seems unbelievable that I met Mac through Buckle, in a way.

46

Stacey Cameron walking out of the brown-wainscotted office at five, wondering if she wouldn't be better off working for T. Eaton's or almost anyone rather than Janus Importers. *Stacey, well for the Lord's sake, is it really you?* Julie, a girl from Manawaka. Gosh, Julie, what you been doing? *I should only tell you, kiddo. Everything from fruitpicker to hairdresser. Married now. Yep. True. Mrs. Fennick, that's me. Real swell guy, a little on the nutty side but what a dancer. What about you?* Oh, I been working for these importers, but my boss makes horoscopes for people—I think it's some kind of a racket—think I oughta quit? Stacey went home for supper with Julie, to talk it over, and one of Buckle's friends was there. Clifford MacAindra. Six months later she thought how fortunate, to have her whole life settled once and for all, so ideally, at twenty-three.

Whatsamatter, Stacey?

Oh—nothing. Want another drink?

Twist my arm.

—— Julie left him four years later, when their boy was two. The last couple of years we saw very little of them. When she left, she never said why, not to me, anyway. She just lit out. Buckle blamed it all on her, how she complained about his long-distance driving and that, and wanted him to change, and he wasn't having any of that crap, et cetera. Only a long time later I began to hear in his talk just how often he claimed somebody was trying to force him somewhere he didn't want to be. I never knew how it was, for her.

How's your mother, Buckle?

Buckle's face takes on further concealment. He has lived with his mother in an apartment over a store on Grenoble Street ever since Julie left him. He has never asked Mac and Stacey there, so they have never seen the old lady.

Oh great. Always great, she is. She's only got one tune.
What tune is that?
Be careful on them dangerous roads, she keeps telling me. She couldn't care less about me, you understand. She just wonders what'd become of her if I went. I don't blame her.

—— Maybe he can't stand anyone to go to his place because she probably calls him Arbuckle, which is his name and which he hates even more than Mac hates his name, Clifford.

Click. Slam. Mac at last. Stacey now realizes that she has not gone upstairs to fix her hair or put on a decent dress.

Hi, Stacey.
Hi. Everything okay?
Mm. Everything's fine. You?
Fine. Buckle's here.
That's good.

—— The automatic kiss bit. Does he actually not see me when he kisses me like that, or is it really the opposite—out of the corner of his day-beleaguered eyes he sees his life's partner, slacks and scruffy blouse, sagging in all directions and doing damn-all about it, and he shuts off the sight like you shut off the street noises because if you didn't, one day you might run amok and that wouldn't do?

Mac picks up Jen.
Hi, princess.
Jen laughs straight from her belly, the deep delighted laughter of a child loved.

—— He's crazy about her. If ever I suggest maybe I should take her to the doctor and see about why she doesn't talk, he nearly has a fit. *Don't be ridiculous,* he says. It's because he can't bear to think anything might be wrong with her. Not with Jen.

Katie refuses to come down for dinner, and Mac inquires what the hell could possibly upset the kid like that. Stacey refuses to answer. Buckle goes into his steering story again. He is

48

interrupted by Ian and Duncan, who argue over the relative
size of each other's dessert, both claiming that the other has the
larger portion, until Stacey suggests that they trade, which both
refuse to do.

— Spoiled brats. What have I done to them? Fighting over
a square inch of frozen artificial cream. Not dying of hunger. Not
even aware of the possibility. Squabbling over nil. Who made
them so? What will happen when the horsemen of the Apoca-
lypse ride through this town? Oh Stacey, enough.

Mac finally cannot bear the uproar.

Shut up, for God's sake, can't you? Stacey, can't you
keep these kids quiet for one minute? Here, you two—neither of
you will get any ice cream, if that's the way you're going to carry
on. Just you leave the table right now. You don't know how damn
lucky you are. When I was a kid, ice cream was a treat.

— I was thinking the exact same. Yet when it's spoken, it
doesn't sound convincing. It sounds corny.

Mac—leave them. Please. They'll simmer down. C'mon,
kids.

— My placating voice. Running interference again, never
knowing if rightly or wrongly, or whose side I'm on or why I
should be on anybody's side. Am I undermining Mac? "Are You
Emasculating Your Husband?" I swear those articles are written
by male anarchists, delighting in the tapeworms of doubt which
they sound out to squirm through my guts. How do I know if I'm
emasculating him or not? Every time I disagree with him I feel
I'm knocking him down. So I agree with him profusely and then
it's me who'd doing the disappearing act. Now he's on the point
of real anger. Action, quick.

Ian! Duncan! You heard what your dad said. Eat your
ice cream right now and then leave the table and no more hors-
ing around, eh?

This is not what Mac has said, but maybe he will let it
pass. Stacey's voice sounds to her own ears like some harpy of
the mountains, the cold shrill of the north wind. And yet, after

49

dinner, Ian approaches Mac with no apparent qualms and it works.

Hey, Dad, you wanna see something?

What?

My bug. I got it finished today.

Yeh? How'd it turn out?

Not bad. You should see the steering—it's really neat, how I got it rigged up. C'mon—it's in the back yard.

Okay. Want to come, Buckle? Big deal, here.

Sure, okay. I'll come along. You know what you're gonna be, Ian? A long-distance driver like me. You got the feel for a vehicle, eh?

Naw, I'm gonna be an inventor.

Great, boy. You can support me in my old age. The hell with driving, like your uncle Buckle and I do. You invent a new-type rocket, see?

—— It's good when it's like that. Why can't it be all the time? Ian needs it so much. He doesn't give a damn for my approval. He knows he's got it anyway. It's Mac's he needs. And yet they turn around and knife each other with words, both suspicious. I should be able to prevent it, but I don't know how.

The gin has completely worn off now. Stacey clears the table and perceives that Duncan is standing by himself near the kitchen door. She puts an arm around him, asking him to help with the dishes because he is so talented in this way, and he consents to the deception for the sake of belonging somewhere. Stacey takes a bowl of stew and one of ice cream upstairs and leaves them outside Katie's door where Katie's dignity may permit her to claim them in due course. Then Stacey bathes Jen, puts her to bed, calls the boys, gets them stowed away after a one-hour exchange of repartee, and finally changes her own clothes, from slacks to bronze linen sheath with ersatz gold pendant.

—— Pour on the Chanel Number Five. Drench yourself in it, woman. Go on. Mac and Buckle will spring to their feet. *Gad!*

they will exclaim. *Who is this apparition of delight? Who is this refugee queen from The Perfumed Garden?* In a pig's eye, they will.

Mac and Buckle are not in the dining room or the kitchen or the living room. They are down in the basement, in the darkened TV room. Buckle is lighting two cigarettes, holding them both in his mouth at once. He hands one to Mac, who takes it without a word.

— I'd like to knock that damn cigarette to the floor and stamp on it hard. Yeh, that would be splendid. Mac would have me certified.

Stacey says nothing. She sits down and lights a cigarette for herself, crossing her legs so that her ankles, still slender, show. Or would have done if the room had been lighted and anyone had been looking.

— The Ever-Open Eye. Western serial. Sing yippee for the days of the mad frontier. Boys were sure men in those days all right and men were sure giants. How could they miss? Not with them dandy six shooters. *Tak! Tak! Splat!* Instant power. Who needs women?

The program ends, and then the News. This time the bodies that fall stay fallen. *Flicker-flicker-flicker.* From one dimension to another. Stacey does not know whether Ian and Duncan, when they look, know the difference.

— Everything is happening on TV. Everything is equally unreal. Except that it isn't. Do the kids know? How to tell them? I can't. Maybe they know more about it than I do. Or maybe they know nothing. I can't know.

It's depressing.

Don't look then, honey. Want a beer, Buckle?

Don't mind if I do. They oughta drop an H-bomb on them bastards.

You'd like that, wouldn't you?

What d'you mean, Stacey? It would settle them. It would settle a lot of things.

Yeh, so would slitting your own throat.

Stacey, would you kindly go and get a couple of beers for Buckle and me, if it's not asking too much?

I was only

I cannot stand these pointless arguments over nothing. Nothing!

There isn't any use in talking. It doesn't change anything.

— True. And he really can't stand it when I argue with Buckle. God, Mac's terrible need for quiet, and my denial of it. I'm sorry. I'll get the beer.

— Anyway, I probably exaggerate. Do I? *Doom everywhere* is the message I get. A person ought not to be affected, maybe. I've got an accumulation of years, and a fat lot of good it does me. I wish I could chuck it all away.

The Eye, shining, newly acquired, five or so years back. *Interviewer:* Now, tell me, Mrs. Frenfield, what effect has this new—uh—shelter in your basement had upon your peace of mind? *Mrs. Frenfield* (smiling anxiously, never thought she'd ever be on TV): Well, I used to have these very disturbed dreams, see, like I mean nightmares they were, actually. Now we got the shelter, I definitely got more peace of mind, like. I mean, it stands to reason. *Interviewer:* Yes, I see. Well, now, in an—um— emergency, what would you do if one of your neighbors who didn't have a shelter tried to— *Mrs. Frenfield:* Boy, let them try, that's all I can say, just let them try. My husband's got an old army rifle, and he— *Interviewer:* Well, thanks very much, Mrs. Frenfield. It's been been very interesting talking to you, and—uh —sweet dreams, eh?

— Around that time I used to figure out how we would get away if need be. We would all pile into the old Chev and rocket on up to the great north woods. Ignoring traffic jams, that is. I used to visualize us taking some little-known road which we would cleverly discover on the spur of the moment. Armed with radish seeds, we would conquer the muskeg, the rock and the green-black silences of the timberlands. We would hack out our village, grub up slugs for the soup pot, spear deer, and teach the kids all we remembered of Shakespeare. Only one or two snags. Neither Mac nor I could have mustered more than about two lines of Shakespeare, and neither of us would last more than twenty-four hours in the great north woods. Also, who would the kids marry? Incest was out. So I gave up on that one. It wasn't such a hot sedative.

Here's your beer.

Oh, thanks, honey. Listen, Buckle, I'm sorry, but I'm going to have to go up and do some work. Got to finish a report on sales. Seeing Thor tomorrow. You'd hardly believe it, but that guy keeps all the sales figures for each area in his head. Not just city, either—all over the province. See you around, boy, eh?

Sure. So long.

Buckle and Stacey remain looking at the screen. Buckle, who normally drinks a bottle of beer in four gulps, now sits holding it without drinking.

Guess Mac thinks this Thorlakson guy is okay, eh, Stacey?

Yeh. I guess so.

Sounds like quite a guy.

Yeh.

I noticed his picture in the paper few days ago. You see it? In connection with some kinda rally he's putting on. Pretty well-educated guy, would you say, Stacey?

—— I never before in my life felt sorry for Buckle Fennick and I don't want to now. It disorients me.

I don't know. Yeh, I guess Thor is pretty well educated. Funny name—Thor. Sounds made up.

53

Icelandic, I guess. Used to be lots of Icelanders in the prairies, around Gimli.

—— I wonder if I ever say Thor in Winnipeg or somewhere? Imagine Buckle feeling like that. I think I'm badly off with Grade Eleven. I bet he's got about Grade Five.

After Buckle has gone, and even Katie is now reluctantly in bed, Mac emerges from the study, which is his retreat, the place where he can shut himself away, amid his business files and racing car magazines and *Playboy,* away from the yammering of his wife and young.

Thought you'd gone to bed, Stacey.

Sorry. I didn't know you wanted the house to yourself.

—— Oh hell. Again. Grabbed for a rapier even before I found out whether a duel was intended.

Christ, I can't say anything right, can I?

—— He does feel like that. Of course. How is it we can both feel that way, simultaneously?

Mac, I'm sorry. I didn't mean

Skip it. I only wanted you to fill in this quiz. I should've asked you before, only Buckle was here.

Stacey reaches for the paper.

BLOCK CAPITALS PLEASE.

Name   *Address*

Year of Birth   *Month*   *Day*

Weight   *Height*

Any Illness in Childhood

Any Illness Since Age Eighteen (*Specify Year and Severity*)

Deficiencies I Feel in Myself

My Best Qualities Are

Qualities I Would Like to Have

54

My Energy Is: (a) consistently high

(b) variable

(c) low

Anxieties: (1)

(2)

(3)

Guilt Feelings: (1)

(2)

(3)

My Relationships With My Family Are: (a) richly rewarding

(b) satisfactory

(c) less than

satisfactory

My Goals Are (Specify Briefly):

(1)

(2)

(3)

—— Two more pages in the same vein. I have the feeling I've seen this form before. "Is Your Marriage Happy? Answer These Ten Questions." "How Do You Rate As Mother/Mother-In-Law/Auntie/Fairy Godmother?"

What's the trouble, for heaven's sake?

I don't want to fill it in, Mac.

Look, Stacey, it's late and I don't feel like standing around arguing.

Okay okay okay. Lies are permitted, I take it?

All right. If you're going to get all worked up about it, let's forget the whole thing. It was only a thought. Pardon me for ever suggesting it.

Do we have to do it?

We have been asked to do it. I thought I had made that fairly plain.

I'll do it, Mac. Please. Honestly.

Yeh, like you did with that form for Ian, I suppose.

> Ian MacAindra, seven, Grade Two. *You got to fill in this form for me, Mum.* Civil Defense. Name of child. Name and address of parents. Home telephone. Name, address and phone of person who could be contacted in National Emergency if parents not available. To the final question, Stacey had written: *Name:* God. *Address:* Heaven. Ian, stark-faced with fury, had stormed to Mac. *Look what she's written! I'm not taking that to school!* Why embarrass Ian, Mac said, quite rightly. So she wrote instead: Matthew Mac-Aindra (grandfather), Apartment 21, 704 Ballantyne Road.

That was three years ago, Mac. Can't you forget it?

Well, if you're all teed up for a wisecrack, you don't need to bother.

I get the message. You can even dictate the answers if you want. Here gimme the bloody thing   gimme it

Stacey

What?

If I were like Buckle, on my own, without anyone really around me, do you think I'd give a damn?

Stacey stares at him.

—— It's real. His acceptance of the responsibilities he took on long ago when he never suspected what they might mean. He doesn't intend it to be a gun at my head. Or if he does, in some crevice of his mind, he doesn't know. Just as my acting up isn't consciously intended to hurt him. My motives aren't any better or any clearer. Impasse.

56

Mac   I know   or I don't know. If we could talk about
It's late.
You're right. It sure as hell is.
What now? Sardonic implications again?
Let's go to bed, Mac. Let's just go to bed.
Yeh. Okay.

THREE

꙳ꙮꙬꙮꙬꙮꙬꙮꙬꙮꙬ

Stacey, my dear. How are you this lovely morning?

Matthew never knocks. He always walks straight in. This has irked Stacey for many years, although she is not convinced that she has a right to be irked by it.

— After all, he's Mac's dad and we're all the family he's got. It's mean of me, but I can't help it. I mentioned it to Mac once, and he said *He's got a right to walk in.* So that settled that.

Oh—hello. I'm just fine. How're you? Yes, what a lovely day.

— Burble-burble. I always talk to Matthew this way. I dread an uneasy lull or anything fringing on what I'm thinking about. I'm always afraid he'll guess. And yet I long to tell him I don't see life his way—gentle Jesus meek and mild and God's in his heaven all's right with the world. But I can't. Mac would be furious. Anyway, why do it? So I should be relieved of habitual fib-telling? It wouldn't be worth the commotion. Or is this just my excuse for being a goddam coward? God knows why I chat to you, God—it's not that I believe in you. Or I do and I don't, like echoes in my head. It's somebody to talk to. Is that all? I don't know. How would I like to be only an echo in somebody's head? Sorry, God. But then you're not dependent upon me, or let's hope not.

Where's Clifford?

Stacey turns her glance away so that Mac's father will not see her icicle eyes. Matthew is the only person who ever calls Mac by the name of Clifford, never apparently having realized that Mac discarded it deliberately.

Out washing the car.

Oh yes. His Sunday ritual. I forgot. For a moment I thought he might have gone to church.

— What in hell do you mean? You know perfectly well that Mac never goes to church. He was made to go, as a kid, to listen to you. Let up on him, can't you? He placates you in every possible way except that one.

Well no. He's washing the car, like I said. Ian and Duncan are at Sunday school.

Not Katherine?

Katie had a headache.

— This reason has been used too often lately. I'll have to find another.

Stacey moves into the kitchen and Matthew follows her. This is his custom. The instant she moves into the dining room, even momentarily, he will follow her there. Irritation flares in her like a struck match, but goes out as quickly. She looks at him, not knowing what could be done about him at no personal inconvenience to herself. Matthew does not have enough people to talk to these days, and practically nothing ever happens to him. He still attends the church where he once used to preach, but the people he knew there are getting fewer. The young minister is painstakingly cordial, but cannot think of anything Matthew could usefully do, and Matthew himself is afraid of getting in the way.

59

Matthew is a tall man, almost as tall as Mac, and he is careful to carry himself straight, a fact which only emphasizes his gauntness and assailability. His hair must once have been the MacAindra auburn, but now it is yellowish-white. The skin of his face stretches tightly over his big bones so that it appears exaggeratedly pale, almost transparent, lightly purple-etched with veins. He keeps himself scrupulously clean and neat, and his dark suits are never in need of dry cleaning. But he still wears shirts with detachable collars, and today he has put on a light-green collar with a blue shirt.

— If only none of the kids point it out. I'll clobber them if they do.

We had a guest preacher this morning.

That's nice. Was he good?

I think he promises extremely well. His theme was Christian humility, and although he might have chosen some of his texts more tellingly, he spoke quite well. He's young David Brownlee—I knew his father years ago. Dead now.

How've you been, yourself, this week?

Stacey can never address Matthew by any name. In sixteen years she has been unable to discover what to call her father-in-law. She cannot bring herself to call him Dad, for this still to her means Niall Cameron, long dead. Mr. MacAindra is out of the question, and only in her mind can she refer to him as Matthew. If the children are present, she calls him Granddad. If not, she cannot call him anything.

Oh, all right. My digestion's never very reliable, but it's no worse than usual. I eat very simply, as you know, but I fear I shall never get the hang of cooking. The apartment is very close these warm days.

Mac's mother died eighteen years ago and remains a mystery to Stacey, who knows about her only through Matthew's remarks, which tend to semi-canonize her, and the occasional remark from Mac—*She always went by what he said; she wanted me to learn to play the piano, but I wasn't very good at it.* Since her death, Matthew has lived alone. As long as he was preaching, he had a housekeeper. When he retired and moved into the small apartment, he began making his own meals. Mac's sister is married and now lives half a continent away.

— I know we ought to have him here. Don't tell me, God. I know. But when I think of it, I think—*mental hospital, here I come.* Following me around from room to room, desperate to make talking sounds, someone else who'd have to be told everything is all right.

I'll be taking the kids to the beach on Saturdays now that the weather's getting warmer. Why don't you come along?

— Madwoman.

Thanks, but I don't think I would be much of an addition, Stacey. The children think I fuss.

No, they don't. You must come.

We'll see.

His voice is quite gentle, and Stacey feels deservedly rebuked. Then Mac comes in from the back yard.

Hello, Dad.

Hello, Clifford. How are you liking the new job?

Fine. Just fine.

Well, that's wonderful. I always did feel that Drabble's wasn't really worthy of your abilities.

Yeh well

It's too bad you couldn't get something on the administration side with the new firm, though, Clifford. I've always thought that would be a better type of work for you, and it must be hard on Stacey to be on her own so much here when you're away. Perhaps in time you'll

Well, administration's not actually so much my line, Dad. I'm a salesman from way back.

It's too bad you never finished university, Clifford.

Yeh, well—that's water under the bridge. Lunch nearly ready, Stacey?

Just about. Only waiting for the boys to get home.

Mac lights a cigarette, draws on it and immediately begins coughing, at first politely—*hem hem hem*—then in deep chest-wracking spasms.

You shouldn't smoke so much, Clifford.

Yeh—*hack! hack!*—well, I've cut down.

You ought to give it up entirely. It's what I've always said. Even before these discoveries about how dangerous it is, I was always certain it was harmful. I always said so, if you remember.

Yeh. I recall your having mentioned it.

— That's the closest Mac ever allows himself to get to irony, with Matthew.

Katie sweeps in. Pastel-orange lipstick. Green-pearl nail polish. Eyeshadow like all the greenish-blue sea fern that ever flourished full fathom five. Burnt-orange earrings. Ocean-green dress. Long clean straight auburn hair.

— Katie, baby, how can you be so gorgeous? I love you for it, but it makes me feel about a thousand.

When's lunch? I'm starving. Hi, Granddad. How's tricks?

Mac frowns and Matthew tries not to look offended.

— Matthew thinks it's flippancy. But she's only trying to please, using slang which isn't hers and which belongs to some vague past. She's easy on him, but he doesn't see that. Everybody should stop from time to time and explain what they mean. But none of us in this house do.

Ian steams in, followed some dawdling moments later by Duncan. Ian has learned how to evade Matthew's Sabbath quiz. He begins talking about cars to Mac. Duncan, slower on the uptake, squirms at what he appears to feel inevitable. Matthew turns attention on him.

62

Well, Duncan, nice to see you. What did you learn at Sunday school?

Duncan, trapped, looks into the middle distance.

God loves birds.

Pardon?

Birds. Like sparrows and that.

You mean—"God sees the little sparrow fall"? Did you sing that hymn?

Yeh.

That's a fine hymn, especially when you really think about its meaning. It used to be your dad's favorite hymn, when he was your age. Did you know that?

Gee.

What else did you learn?

I got my paper. It's right here somewhere.

Duncan reaches into his pocket, then withdraws his hand hastily, as though he has remembered something just in time.

Guess I lost it, Granddad.

Stacey quickly picks up Jen and heads for the dining room.

Everybody to the table. C'mon.

Later, Stacey finds the Sunday-school paper where Duncan has crumpled it small and put it into his wastepaper basket upstairs. There is a rainbow-tinted picture of a sweetly innocuous and vacant-faced St. Francis surrounded by feathered companions. Around the edges, where there was a little blank paper, Duncan has put cramped and secretive pencil drawings—the various stages in the launching of a spaceship, its journey past moons and constellations, its arrival on a planet beyond our stars, where twining trees twist octopus-like and the stickmen are met by starfishmen.

—— Not the Stations of the Cross. Not any more. Whose fault? Mine? Or is it maybe better this way? I haven't done well by them. I've failed them by failing to believe, myself. I pretend to it, but they are not deceived. Yet I am the one who wakens them on Sunday mornings and shoves them off churchwards. One more strand in the tapestry of phoniness. I want to tell them. What? That I mourn by disbelief? I don't tell them, though. I go along with the game. It's easier that way.

> *Ye holy angels bright*
> *Who wait at God's right hand*
> *Or through the realms of light*
> *Fly at your Lord's command,*
> *Assist our song,*
> *Or else the theme too high doth seem*
> *For mortal tongue.*

My God, Stacey, what's happened to you, warbling hymns all of a sudden?

Nothing. It just came into my head. Used to sing it when I was a kid.

You should tell Dad that. He'd be pleased to think you even remembered. Hey—what's up, honey? You're not crying, are you?

No. Eyelash in my eye.

—— So why complain about Mac being guarded?

Morning, and the sky is like the light water-color blue from a paintbox. Warm-cool, the air smells of grass and last night's rain. On Bluejay Crescent the laburnum branches bend a little with the yellow wind-swaying burden of blossoms, and the leaves of the big chestnuts are green outspread tree-hands. Kids under school age are out already, whizzing up and down the sidewalks with wagons and tricycles. In the distance, the mountains form the city's walls and boundaries, some of them snow mountains even now, as though this place belonged to two worlds, two simultaneous seasons.

C'mon, flower. We're going shopping.

Jen replies unintelligibly, then begins to sing, not loudly, but recognizably the tune of a song Duncan once brought home from school.

Hey, that's marvelous. That's lovely. What about trying the words?

— I can see it all now. Jennifer MacAindra, The World's One and Only Nontalking Opera Star. Very funny, Stacey. In the meantime, have you taken her to Dr. Spender, just to check? You have not. He's so busy and I hate to pester him unless it's a real crisis. Mac thinks I'm nuts to worry, and probably I am. The truth is I'm scared to take her.

Stacey puts Jen in the Chev and they drive to the supermarket.

— Nobody could help feeling some lift on a day like this. I don't get out enough. My boundaries are four walls. Whose fault? Okay, mine. By the time the day ends, I'm too beat to seek rich cultural experiences, whatever that may mean. That babe in Varying Views of Urban Life. That's what she said. *What we must seek is rich cultural experiences.* I thought she probably meant she didn't get laid often enough. But I sat there nodding and smiling and agreeing with her. I swear I'll never take another of those damn evening courses. What's left of me? Where have I gone? I've brought it on myself, without realizing it. How to stop telling lies? How to get out? This is madness. I'm not trapped. I've got everything I always wanted.

Hang on, doll, and don't lean out the window, eh?

Down on the streets near the beaches where Stacey often takes the children, there are rows of high old shaky timber houses, no proper fire escapes. Dwelt in by whom? Sandaled artists courting immortality and trying to scrape by in this life? Extravagant-voiced poets preaching themselves? Semi-prophets with shoulder-length hair, baubled in strings of colored seeds or glass, pseudo gemmery, maybe not pseudo for their purposes?

65

Languid long-legged girls who speak a new tongue and make love when they feel like it, with whoever, and no regrets or recriminations?

—— It changes too rapidly for me to keep track. What do I know of it? Only what I read in the papers. What do they think about? Impossible for me to know? What do they think about me? "Love-In Held in Park." Newspaper couple of years ago. "We Aim to Love, Not Hassle, Says Leader." "Love who?" reporter asked. "Everybody" was the brave if reckless reply. Why did I have the persistent nasty suspicion that that generality and generosity would most likely stop just short of me? I wanted to explain myself. I still do. Wait, you! Let me tell you. I'm not what I may appear to be. Or if I am, it's happened imperceptibly, like eating what the kids leave on their plates and discovering ten years later the solid roll of lard now oddly living there under your own skin. I didn't used to be. Once I was different.

> Stacey, traveling light, unfearful in the sun, swimming outward as though the sea were shallow and known, drinking without indignity, making spendthrift love in the days when flesh and love were indestructible.

Here we are, flower. Let's hope it's not too crowded.

—— What'll it be like, when Jen is at school? I'll have to be careful, then, or I'll find myself speaking aloud one day when I'm alone among the Zoomy Puffs and the Choco-Corn Bleeps, and the young mums (damn them—they get younger every year, it seems to me) pushing carts full of groceries and babies will smile in embarrassment and pretend not to notice.

The long aisles of the temple. Side chapels with the silver-flash of chrome where the dead fish lie among the icy strawberries. The mounds of offerings, yellow planets of grapefruit, jungles of lettuce, tentacles of green onions, Arctic effluvia flavored raspberry and orange, a thousand bear-faced mouselegended space-crafted plastic-gifted strangely transformed sproutings of oat and wheat fields. Music hymning from invisible choirs.

I'll be seeing you
In all the old familiar places—

Diamond Lake, fifty miles north of Mana-waka. At night the spruce trees held them-selves intensely still, dark and immutable as old Indian gods, holding up the star-heavy sky. The path of the moon lighted the black lake. The fishes danced and the night birds dipped and pirouetted in obeisance towards the fallen light, the shreds of heaven. And Stacey Cameron, under the green-purple neon starlight of the Wapakata Dancehall, danced with the airman from Montreal. He held her close, his sex pressed against hers. Then miles along the beach, the sand still day-warm un-der their bare feet, until they reached the leaf-blanketed hillside. Feeling the tacit agree-ment of the forest for their unspoken plans. Stacey afraid, but wanting too much to let go. Unexpectedly rising to him, not having known before that it was to be like this, everything focused in the crux where they met and joined. They both cried out, and then they half slept and wakened tender and it was nearly morning there on the curled yellow-green moss of the spruce-screened slope with the lapping of the lake in their heads.

—— Whatever happened to him? How did he get on? Dead over Germany? The local paper only ever printed the lists of provincial casualties. Running a shoe store in Montreal? A bar in Antigonish? A ranch in the Cariboo? The unanswered questions.

Stacey suddenly realizes what is happening. Last week it was pop music, and the week before that. New manager now, maybe, someone who knows what age the women are who do most of the spending here.

—— Conned again. Conned into memory. Now I'm not even certain that this music hasn't been going on for weeks or months. How long have I been remembering without knowing it? Al, was it really more than twenty years ago? Al Duschesne, half French, half English, claiming he was doubly outcast. Belonging once for half a night in me. I remember everything about you. The way the hair was gold on your belly and forearms in the almost-morning. Your sex. Everything. I wish I could see you. No, I don't. I wouldn't want you to see me, not now, not in my present shape. Of course, you'll have changed, too. But not as much. Women may live longer but they age faster. God has a sick sense of humor, if you ask me.

Jen, sitting at the front of the grocery cart and dangling her short legs, begins to sing, a wordless humming but tuneful. Her narrow fine-boned face seeks Stacey's, and her eyes are watchful, hesitant with hope. Stacey smiles quickly.

Hey, you're improving, flower. That's great.

—— Stacey, how dare you complain about even one single solitary thing? Listen, God, I didn't mean it. Just don't let anything terrible happen to any of them, will you? I've had everything I always wanted. I married a guy I loved, and I had my kids. I *know* everything is all right. I wasn't meaning to complain. I never will again. I promise.

> Duncan and Ian last summer at the beach, wrestling and wisecracking, brown skinny legs and arms, the shaggy flames of their hair, their skin smelling of sand and saltwater. Sea-

68

children, as though they should have been
crowned with fronds of kelp and ridden
dolphins.

—— Please. Let them be okay, all their lives, all four of
them. Let me die before they do. Only not before they grow up,
or what would happen to them?

When Mac comes in that evening, he hands Stacey five small
boxes and five rolled-up scrolls. Gingerly, she unfolds one of
the scrolls. It tells her that Duncan Cameron MacAindra is seven
years old and has been enrolled in the Richa Younglife Program.
He is ABBD (Junior), and he promises to record on the following chart the zoom ratings of his energy up-go and his memory
snap-up. Stacey opens one of the boxes. Each pill occupies its
own nest. There are seven colors—pink, purple, peacock blue,
tangerine, canary, green and crimson. Stacey touches them
lightly.

Pretty. They'd make a nice necklace.

The kids better take them at breakfast, so they won't
forget. A color for every day, see, so it's quite simple. Only don't
get the boxes mixed up. Each one's got a different combination,
depending on which program the particular person is on.

Mac?

What?

When you worked for Drabble's, we didn't go around
spraying them with Angel-Breath Mouth Freshener.

Thor goes through the charts personally every month,
for all members of staff and their families.

He's got a nerve.

You can't mount a real campaign unless you've got a
hard core of support. If somebody can't even be bothered to
give them to his own family, well

Okay. Okay okay okay. Give 'em here. Let's round everybody up.

69

You are making things damn difficult, Stacey. I hope you're enjoying it.

I don't mean to. Honestly. Honestly, Mac. Mac?

What?

I'm sorry.

Yeh, so you say. Look, I don't want you to be *sorry*. Only quit bugging me, eh? Haven't you seen the Richalife displays in the drugstore down the street?

Yes.

Well, it's like that all over. Big displays. It's catching on. I suppose you don't want the kids to go to university?

Oh Mac. Of course I do. You know that.

Well, then. Get off my neck. I'm earning more than I ever have.

You're working too hard.

Stacey, I am not working any harder than I have to. Now, please.

Okay, honey. Really.

By seven in the evening, Mac is closeted in his study, as he has been every evening this week. Stacey knocks and enters. Mac is sitting at his desk. In front of him are many colored brochures, a map of the province, sales charts, and several Xeroxed memo pages—*Let's Talk Richness, A Quality of Living,* and *Getting Across the Message Audio-Visually.* Mac looks up, frowning.

Whatsamatter?

Nothing's the matter. I have to go over to Tess's tonight. I promised. What does he mean, A Quality of Living?

Stacey, I'm busy. Can't you see?

Okay, I'm just going. What did Thor say about my quiz?

He said he never heard of anybody feeling guilty because they couldn't bake bread. I told you you shouldn't have put that.

You laughed at the time. Don't deny it. What did he

expect me to do? Put down what I feel guilty about or something?

Ha bloody ha.

You never showed me what you put down.

It wasn't spectacular. Listen, Stacey, I'm busy.

Doing what? Yoga?

Everybody has to present their idea for totally new types of sales campaigns.

That's not fair. What's he trying to do?

How should I know? I guess he doesn't want any dead wood.

Mac—why did you say that?

A joke.

Yeh. Ha bloody ha. Mac?

Mm?

Are you afraid?

Me? What of? You must be kidding.

You're only forty-three. You're a damn good salesman. There have never been any complaints about you, that I know of. You've been working like a dog since you joined Richalife. You don't need to be afraid.

Stacey, for Christ's sake. I am not afraid. I am busy at the moment trying to work out ideas. Now will you please leave me alone?

You're really not—well let's say nervous—about Thor? He scares me. Something about him. I don't know.

Stacey, everything is okay. How many times do I have to say it? Can't you please for heaven's sake quit yakking about my work?

I'm sorry. But you won't talk. You won't ever say.

There is nothing to say.

Oh well in that case

Look, what do you *want* me to say?

I don't *want* you to say anything

Then why do you keep on

71

I'm sorry   it's just that

Well, everything is all right, see?

Yeh. Well, okay. I feel very strange sometimes.

What do you mean, strange?

Like as though everything is receding

Receding?

As though I'm out of touch with everything. Everybody, I mean. And vice-versa. If you see what I mean.

Maybe you need to see the doctor. Do you feel sick?

At heart

What?

Nothing. I don't know what I'm talking about. I'm sorry. It was—I don't know. Do you want some more coffee before I go?

No thanks. Are you okay, Stacey?

Sure. I'm fine. You're sure *you* are?

Yes, yes. Quite sure. Have fun at Tess's.

Thanks. I won't be late.

I may turn in early.

Okay. Well good-bye.

Good-bye.

Stacey goes upstairs to dress. No use in trying to compete with Tess, who would look splendid even if she were wearing an old potato sack tied with bindertwine. Stacey puts on her blue-silk suit. This is the first time she has worn it this spring, and the zipper on the skirt will hardly do up.

—— Hell. I can't have put on that much. Oh heavens—look at me. Feast your eyes on those hips. Tomorrow—I swear it—the banana diet. I will buy half a ton of bananas and eat nothing else. I'll stick to it. So help me, I will. What did Mac mean, nothing to talk about? He probably isn't worried in the slightest. I'm making him nervous. "Are You Increasing Your Husband's Tensions?" More than likely. Why should I think he's worried? It's only me that's worried—only I who am worried. Compared with mothers of fifteen kids who are swallowing only air in India or somewhere, have I got troubles? No. God, to tell you the truth, it's getting so I feel guilty about worrying. I know I have no right to it, but it keeps creeping up on me. I'm surrounded by voices all the time but none of them seem to be saying anything, including mine. This gives me the feeling that we may all be one-dimensional.

Very far away, in a galaxy countless light-years from this planet, a scorpion-tailed flower-faced film buff sits watching a nothing-shaped undulating screen. He decides he's seen enough. He switches off the pictures which humans always believed were themselves, and the imaginary planet known as Earth vanishes.

—— You're losing your mind, Stacey girl. Well, I may be, but I'm sure as hell not losing these hips.

Stacey is the first to arrive at the Foglers'. Tess is wearing an oatmeal-colored dress, straight and unadorned, with an Italian leather belt, costly in appearance, draped around almost non-existent hips.

—— How's she got such good taste in clothes and such awful taste in furnishings? Those drapes—demented turquoise trees and crimson-jacketed hunting gents on puffing black horses, and the entire scene shot through with simulated gold threads at regular intervals. Cut it out, Stacey. I'm getting worse. I used to be nicer. If I live to be ninety, I'll be positively venomous. My grandchildren will flee from me in terror.

Am I early, Tess? Gosh, I love your dress.

Not a bit. It's only Bertha and you coming. Glad you like it—I just got it this week. I think it's kind of fun, myself. Listen, I must show you what I got at Twiller's sale today.

—— Don't tell me. Let me guess. Ten cuckoo clocks, forty-seven TV tables with puce-and-orange ballerinas prinking on them, two hundred packets of bath salts done up to look like dinosaurs and labeled *Hers* and *His*, five thousand hankies embroidered with pink tuberous-rooted begonias, and a partridge in a plastic pear tree.

73

Yeh, I'd love to see.

Tess brings out two salt and pepper sets shaped like harlequins and colored lavishly. The salt or pepper comes out of the hats.

Oh, they're sweet, Tess.

I thought they were kind of cute, myself. We don't really need them, I guess, but I can put them away for Christmas or shower gifts. Jake isn't crazy about them, but then, he's kind of hard to suit, I guess, in a way.

Jake Fogler is a radio actor who is fond of talking about the breakdown of verbal communications and the problems of semantics in mass media. Stacey cannot imagine either of them needing any salt or pepper shakers whatsoever. Tess lives on pineapple and cottage cheese salads, and Jake, if Tess is to be believed, exists mainly on brandy and raw eggs. He has a talented voice, but he does not stand a look-in with TV. Sometimes he retires to the spare bedroom and broods, and then Tess goes over to Stacey's and says in her high light voice, *Jake's ulcer is acting up.*

The doorbell chimes softly in four notes, and Tess opens the door to Bertha Garvey, whose voice rasps anxiously.

I'm not late, am I?

Why no. Only Stacey's here. The Polyglam lady hasn't even got here yet. I hope she hasn't got the date wrong.

Bertha comes into the living room. Pressing sixty, corseted to the point of shallow breathing, grey hair with slightly too true-blue rinse and done in a profusion of springy curls, hands big and capable—telling what her lifework has been—eyes always a little worried behind up-curled green-framed glasses.

I would've been here sooner, Tess, but you know what Julian's like. Any time I'm going out—and goodness knows that's not often—he thinks of all kinds of things to delay me. Tonight nothing would do but I should get his navy suit laid out ready for him to take to the dry cleaners in the morning. Mercy, I could do it with no trouble at all before breakfast, I told him. But that wouldn't do. Oh no. Had to have it all ready in a shopping bag right that minute. I guess it's not his fault, really. He's getting on. And it's hard for him to be retired—he's never got used to it. You girls just wait. You'll see. Although I'm not saying it'll hit your hubbies that same way.

Julian Garvey is twelve years older than Bertha. He used to be an accountant. Now he putters around the house or does a little gardening, which he dislikes. He is small and dignified, meticulous-mannered with everyone else, but crabby with Bertha.

Bertha Garvey, one New Year's Eve, brought up a Baptist, only taking a drink on high days and holidays, as she said, and being quickly affected. Strapping efficient Bertha in Stacey's kitchen, shedding absurd cartoon tears (until Stacey looked again and saw them) into her Bloody Mary. *Hardly anyone knows, but I was born and raised in a lumber camp.* Stacey saying in amazement, good heavens, what's so awful about that? *Well it was the schooling I missed. My mother wanted me to go and live with my aunt and go to high school but Dad wouldn't hear of it. He was a high-rigger, my dad was, and when he got too heavy for it, he still went on, and then one day he lopped the top off a Douglas fir and lopped himself off with it.* Bertha had sworn not to marry a lumberman, so she had married Julian when he was a pay clerk in camp. *Julian was my fate, Stacey, but he can't forget I never went beyond grade school.*

The doorbell croons, and Tess patters excitedly into the front hall.

Oh—she's here, girls!

The plastic lady is petite and emaciated, high frothed-up

hair metallic blond, high thin teetery heels supporting bird-bone ankles, face gay-gay-gay with its haggardness fairly well masked by tan make-up and the scarlet gash of a lipstick smile. Her sleeveless silver dress shimmers like the scanty robe of some new oracle, and on the right breast it bears the iridescent ice-blue letters *Polyglam*.

Hello, Mrs. Fogler. Hello, girls. My, it's a real pleasure to meet you. Now, if I can just find a table.

Quick as a slickly sleight-of-handing magician, she hauls boxes in from her car and sets up shop in the Foglers' dining room. The company gathers. Stacey chain-smokes. Bertha knots her hands together, cat's cradles of broad fingers, and smiles hopefully. Tess sits wide-eyed like a child about to behold marvels. The marvels are there, arranged in heaps and rows on the table, plastic vessels gleaming softly, pearl-pink, mauve, green like the pale underthighs of a mermaid, blue as pastel as angel veins.

Picnic plates. Beakers. Sandwich cases. Pie containers. Cookie jars. Breadboxes. Buckets and dishpans. Dogs' feeding bowls. Infants' cereal bowls. Mixing bowls giant human and elfin. Ice-cube trays. Vats suitable for making wine or drowning enemies. Beach pails. Juice holders. Jugs all sizes from cream to martini. Tumblers and eggcups, plant pots and kid pots. To name only a few. The Polyglam lady takes her stance in front of the display.

Now, girls, just to get acquainted, we're going to play a little game. I think you'll all really enjoy it. All my clients say it's the nicest fun thing ever. It's a simple little word game—not *too* simple, mind you—that wouldn't do for you bright girls, eh? I'm going to give you each this full-colored Polyglam booklet, and on the first page you'll see the words *Polyglam Superware*. See? That's it. Now, see those blank spaces? I'm going to give you each a pencil, and I want you to see how many words you can make using only the letters in *Polyglam Superware*. We've got ten minutes. Ready? *Go!*

76

— My mind has gone blank. There's old Bertha scribbling away as though her entire future is at stake. Tess looks like Katie did once at about ten, when she had measles and wrote her exams at home—chewing her pencil, trying terribly hard.

Stacey after several minutes writes down *Mug*. She looks at the word for awhile, contemplating its inner truth. Then she writes *Pee*. She crosses this out and writes *Woe* instead. By this time the ten minutes are up.

Now let's just count them up, shall we, girls? Ho-ho Mrs. uh MacAindra, you haven't got very many, have you? Not to worry. It's only a game, isn't it? Mrs. Garvey, ten for you—that's fine. Mrs. Fogler, let's see now—*Glam, Spam, Lam, Pew, Sew, Are*—oh this is very good. Very good. Mrs. Fogler's got twelve words, girls! Isn't that nice? Now, Mrs. Fogler, it gives me real pleasure to present you with a little prize—this set of six Polyglam Juicicles. Yes, you can make your very own juice popsicles any flavor you wish. The kiddies can't get enough of them.

— Pure tact. She might have found out whether Tess had kids or not. I still wonder if it's by accident or design that she and Jake never have. Tess has never said.

Look—look at this, Bertha. Aren't they the cutest?

Real nice, Tess. Real handy. Really handy, that is to say.

Now if you'll just take your pencils again, girls, I'm going to let you in on a recipe which our Polyglam kitchens have just dreamed up—and is it ever a dream! It's the yummiest dessert you've ever tasted. We call it Tropical Paradise. I made it only yesterday for my own youngsters, and every single one of them polished their plates and asked for more. I'm positive your toddlers and teens will all be saying—*Mm—this is sure a tummy treat, Mum.* Okay? Ready? One cup maraschino cherries, chopped very fine. One cup melted marshmallows. One cup diced pineapple. Two cups whipped cream. A teaspoon of

Stacey writes *Safe in the Arms of Jesus*. Then she writes *Lost in the Arms of Morpheus*, followed by *Yummy Yummy Says*

My Tummy. After that, she has time for one quick game of X's and O's.

—— Without realizing it, that woman may actually be suffering severely from myopia. I'm only thinking of Bertha's toddlers.

Everybody got it all down? You, Mrs. MacAindra?

Yes, thanks.

Good. Now, then, I'd just like to point out a few features of this lovely Polyglam Superware—features you may not have noticed. For instance, would you ever guess just how durable Polyglam is? Oh sure, we all know it won't break, but the average person may not realize just *how* strong this unique material is.

Three lake-water blue dishpans, upturned, become the Polyglam lady's platform. She jumps up and down, tap dances, stomps with stiletto heels, leaps from one to another.

—— My God, what if she falls? I can see her skimming down, slamming her pointed chin on the grey Chinese carpet, unable to rise out of sheer mortification. Am I *willing* this to happen? Stop it, Stacey, for heaven's sake—you may not realize your own tremendous mental powers. Yeh, a likely thought.

The Polyglam lady does not slip. She does a ballet-like zigzag in the air and comes down in a proficient landing on two dishpans, legs outspread but not vulgarly so.

Now, I don't want any of you girls to feel you have to, but if you'd like to look at the various pieces of Polyglam

These sandwich cases are just perfectly

What adorable eggcups

It's this cookie jar that I think is so

—— If I get out of here for less than ten bucks it will be a bloody miracle. Two weeks ago it was copper-bottomed stoveware at Bertha's, and I bought a Dutch oven, which I needed slightly less than I need a Dutch uncle. I'm weak-minded, that's my trouble. Anything to look agreeable. Don't rock the boat. Why can't I? Why am I unable to? Help me. Who? How strange if Bertha and Tess were thinking the exact same thing. We could unite. This could start an underground movement. The Bluejay

Crescent Irregulars. I can see it all now. We're too damn complacent. No—we're not complacent one bit. We're just scared. Of what? Making a scene? Finding out we're alone after all—better not to test it out? How do I know what Tess and Bertha think? Am I going to risk offending Tess by asking? I have to live next door to her. She frequently minds Jen for me. Oh Katie, you're dead right about me, baby. I'm corrupt. Or was it immoral you said? Jesus, if I'm going to be immoral, I should scout around for some slightly jazzier way of being it.

Two and a half decades back, to the Dragon Lady of Terry and the Pirates. Wearing Stacey's face and a slinky black velvet ensemble that clings to her gifted breasts and friendly thighs. What was it you wanted to know, McNab? She is addressing the customs officer. Did you say smuggled opium? But McNab (about thirty, muscles like wire rope) can only stand and drool, overcome by his impossible desire. (Switch here from Saturday colored funnies page to elsewhere.) This way, McNab—nothing is impossible. Will it be the bed or the deck?

— I am either suffering from delayed adolescence or premature menopausal symptoms, most likely both.

When the purchases have been made, Tess serves coffee, two kinds of sandwiches, shortbread and layer cake with three-inch mocha icing.

— Shut up, God. I feel too lousy not to eat. Bananas tomorrow.

The Polyglam lady makes the first move to go.

It's been such a pleasure meeting you ladies, and thanks a million, Mrs. Fogler, and now I really must

Thank *you* for coming. We certainly all had a wonderful

I must be getting along now, too, Tess. Thanks loads

Lovely evening thanks   thanks

Thanks a million

Well, good night

G'night—watch the step, Bertha

Well, thanks again

A pleasure   thanks for coming

Well, good night

G'night, then, see you real soon

Yeh   sure thing   well good night

Good night

On the doorstep, as Bertha and Stacey are finally sidling out, Jake Fogler appears. His enormous glasses and slightly worn face give him the look of an aging owl-like boy caught in some moment of nefariousness.

—   How long has he been standing here waiting for us to go?

Hello, Jake.

Evening, all. Tess has foisted all the gimcrackery on you, I see. Christ, Bertha, you can hardly stagger under the weight of all that crap.

Oh *Jake*—don't talk like that to Bertha. Don't be an old

Sorry, dear. Do I spoil all your fun? Coming back in for a drink, Stacey?

Thanks, no. Got to get home. 'Night, Tess.

Good night, Stacey.

Tess's small puzzled voice is at complete variance with her impressively packaged exterior. She waves uncertainly, then follows Jake into the house.

Stacey, entering home, takes off her shoes in the hall, goes to the kitchen and pours a gargantuan gin and tonic. Mac is in bed and none of the upstairs lights are on. Stacey flicks on a small lamp in the living room and curls up on the chesterfield, the Polyglam booklet in one hand. Along with the Superware, families are shown on each page. Kids beam peacefully and undisturbedly. Mothers with young untired faces glow contentedly. Fathers with young untired faces smile proudly and successfully. Grandmothers with young untired faces gaze graciously and untroubledly.

—   Shit.

The booklet skids and lies still under the coffee table.

Stacey turns off the lamp and stands near the window, drinking and looking at the lights of the city out there. They flash and shift like the prairie northern lights in the winter sky, here captured and bound.

The thin panthers are stalking the streets of the city, their claws unretracted after the cages of time and time again. The Roman legions are marching—listen to the hate-thudding of their boot leather. Strange things are happening, and the skeletal horsemen ride, ride, ride with all the winds of the world at their backs. There is nowhere to go this time

—— Today I saw a girl walking up the street towards me, a plain girl unfashionably dressed, and from a distance I thought it was myself coming back to meet me with a wiser chance. But it wasn't.

No other facet to the city-face? There must be. There has to be.

Out there in unknown houses are people who live without lies, and who touch each other. One day she will discover them, pierce through to them. Then everything will be all right, and she will live in the light of the morning.

FOUR

)⋋⌒⋁⌒⋁⌒⋁⌒⋁⌒⋁⌒⋁⌒⋁⌒(

Come on, you kids. Aren't you ever coming for breakfast?

THIS IS THE EIGHT-O'CLOCK NEWS BOMBING RAIDS LAST NIGHT DE-
STROYED FOUR VILLAGES IN

> Mum! Where's my social studies scribbler?
> I don't know, Ian. Have you looked for it?
> It's gone. I gotta take it to school this morning
> Well, *look*. Katie, have you seen Ian's social studies
> scribbler?
> No, and I'm not looking for it, either. If he wasn't so
> Stacey, the party starts at eight tonight. Be ready, eh?
> Sure, yes yes of course. Duncan, eat your cereal.
> I hate this kind. Why do you always buy it?
> You say that about every kind I buy. C'mon.

WORD FROM OUR SPONSOR IF YOU HAVEN'T SEEN TOOLEY'S NEW
SHOWROOM YOU'RE IN FOR A REAL COOL SURPRISE

Chatter buzz wail

Okay, Jen, I'll be up in a sec. Are you finished? Don't try to get off by yourself—I'm coming.

You going to get your hair done, Stacey?

Yes, of course, whaddya think?

I only asked, for heaven's sake. No need to

I'm sorry, Mac. Yes, I'm getting it done this morning. Want an egg?

Please.

Mum, it's not *here*, and Mr. Gaines will be mad as fury. I got to find

Okay, Ian, one minute and I'll look. Where have you looked?

Everywhere.

ROAD DEATHS UP TEN PER CENT MAKING THIS MONTH THE WORST IN

I got to take fifty cents, Mum.

Duncan! What for?

Cripples or something

What?

It tells about it right here, in this piece of paper they gave us

Why didn't you show me this last night?

I forgot

So long, Stacey. So long, kids.

'Bye, Dad.

Oh   good-bye, honey. Wait—you didn't have your egg. It's just done now

Can't. Said I'd be in by eight thirty. You eat it.

I hate eggs.

Miss Walsh said earn it if we can but I dunno how to earn fifty cents

WHEN QUESTIONED THE BOY SAID HE HAD SEEN THE GIRL TAKING THE PILLS BUT HE HAD NOT KNOWN THEY WERE

Scream

Okay, Jen—I'm coming right now

Mother, what have you done with my orange earrings?

I never touched them, Katie, and anyway you can't wear them to

Who says I can't?

Mum, I've looked in the desk and everywhere and my social studies scribbler just isn't

YANCY'S FANCIES ARE THE BEST TASTE TREAT OF THE GOLDEN WEST

Maybe you could advance me fifty cents on my allowance and I could

Mr. Gaines will have hysterics I mean it boy you don't know him

They were on my dresser yesterday with my green earrings and now they're both

BRR-RING

Katie, answer the phone, will you?

I can't I'm in the bathroom doing my hair

Well, take Jen off, then, while you're there

Man, who was your servant last year?

Oh shut up and do as you're told

BRR-RING

Hello?

Oh, hello. Stacey?

Yeh. Hello, Tess.

Got time for coffee this morning?

Well, I have to get my hair done. Maybe a quick one.

Leave Jen with me, why don't you?

Oh, gosh, Tess, I can't ever pay you back. No, she'll be okay with me.

I don't mind having her a single speck, Stacey. Really and truly

Well, that's certainly nice of you we'll see look I gotta run now see you eh?

Sure, okay. G'bye.

G'bye. Come on, you kids! Ian, for the Lord's sake whatsamatter with your eyes? Your scribbler's under the cushion on the chesterfield. Here, Duncan, and please the next time let me know when you come home from school instead of springing things on me like this. You can earn it by clipping the edges on the lawn. Katie! You find your earrings?

Yeh. They were on the floor behind my dresser.

Well, next time don't be so

AND NOW THE PINK BALLOONS SINGING WELL WELL WELL WELL

Okay, you guys, everybody out of here. Got everything?

You missed your calling, Mother. You should've been in the army. You would've made a great sergeant-major.

Nuts to you. So long, Katie. 'Bye, kids.

'Bye.

Slam.

Okay, flower. Here's your cereal.

—— Quick, coffee, or I faint.

EIGHT-THIRTY NEWS BOMBERS LAST NIGHT CLAIMED A DECISIVE VICTORY FOUR VILLAGES TOTALLY DESTROYED AND A NUMBER OF OTHERS SET ABLAZE

Stacey stirs her coffee and lights a cigarette. Then she switches off the radio.

—— I can't listen. It's too much too much too much. What can you do, anyhow? Nothing. Just agonize. Useless. All useless. Me included. Listen, God, I know it's a worthwhile job to bring up four kids. You don't need to propagandize me; I'm converted. But how is it I can feel as well that I'm spending my life in one unbroken series of trivialities? The kids don't belong to me. They belong to themselves. It would be nice to have something of my own, that's all. I can't go anywhere as myself. Only as Mac's wife or the kids' mother. And yet I'm getting now so that I actually prefer to have either Mac or one of the kids along. Even to the hairdresser, I'd rather take Jen. It's easier to face the world with one of them along. Then I know who I'm supposed to be.

> *What's your name, little girl?* Stacey Cameron. *That's a funny name—Stacey.* It is not! It is not! It's my name and don't you say anything about it, see? *Stacey, don't be rude—this is Reverend McPhail, our new minister. Say you're sorry.* I will not. *Go to your room, then.* (In the bedroom, an oval mirror, and she put her face very close to it, so she could see deeply into her own eyes—Anastasia, princess of all the Russias; Anastasia, queen of the Hebrides, soon to inherit the ancestral castle in the craggy isles.)

Come on, opera star. Let's go and see Aunt Tess. We better put a few presentable clothes on first. Gosh, I wish I had a skin like yours, flower. Not a blemish. All the other kids have got a certain amount of freckles, but you're like milk. Too pale, maybe. Yeh, you could stand with a little more color. C'mon, this is where you're supposed to say nuts to you, Mum, I'm absolutely gorgeous the way I am. Okay—you've convinced me.

> Newspaper photograph. Some new kind of napalm just invented, a substance which, when it alights burning onto skin, cannot be removed. It adheres. The woman was holding a child about eighteen months old and she was trying to pluck something away from the scorch-spreading area on the child's face.

Come on, Jen, let's get dressed and get out of here.

Tess is waiting for them with the coffee cups out.
> Gee, that's a cute outfit, Stacey.

Like it? I got it for her last summer.

No, I meant your dress.

What, mine? Oh—well, thanks, Tess. I can hardly squeeze into it.

You haven't put on any weight, surely?

That's what you think. I'm on a diet this week.

Oh? What kind?

Well, I tried the banana diet, but I get so fed up with bananas that I'm not fit to live with. This one's high protein, no carbohydrates.

How do you find it?

It's hell. It's the bread I miss. I've got no willpower, that's my trouble.

Oh Stacey, you? I always think you've got terrific willpower.

Who, me?

I mean to say, all those kids and running the house and all.

That's not willpower. That's just elbow grease.

Well, my heavens, I know I couldn't do it. I tire so quickly. Sometimes it's like I can hardly lift a finger without getting all played out. I saw the doctor again about my blood pressure.

Oh? What did he say?

The usual. Take it easy. Keep up the pills. Salt-free diet. I didn't tell Jake I went.

Why not?

I don't know, Stacey. He doesn't like people not feeling well.

It's not your fault.

I know, but then again—well, I don't know. You know what men are like.

No, but I sure wish I did.

I wish I had your way of laughing at everything, Stacey.

I don't really

Sure you do. It's a real gift. My dad used to say, *Tess, when*

87

God gave out the sense of humor, he missed you. I've never forgotten that. I guess it's true. Of course, I mean, I like laughing. But I can never remember jokes and that. Did I show you the goldfish?

No. You got goldfish?

Yeh. Jake bought them for me. For company, he said. See, here they are. I like the little wee castle at the bottom of the bowl, there, don't you? And all those pink and blue pebbles. Kind of sweet, I thought. See, there's the big goldfish hiding behind that fern or whatever it is. Where's the smaller one got to? Don't tell me —no, there it is. There were three when Jake brought them home.

Did the other one die?

Well, not exactly. The big one ate it.

What?

Apparently it's a quite common thing among goldfish. Some just do. I saw it happen. It was kind of peculiar. The big goldfish bit it on the back of the neck, sort of, and it had this convulsion, like, and then the big one took it to the bottom of the bowl and just ate it. I saw the whole thing happen. It didn't even take very long.

That's gruesome.

Yes. It looked really peculiar, like I said. I am keeping my eye on this other one now. To see what happens

Can't you take it out? Or do something

Well, it's their natural way isn't it after all

What'll you do if it *does*

Jake said he would bring home another one tonight just in case

Expensive fish food

Oh, they don't cost very much

—— Dog eat dog and fish eat fish. Don't tell me any more because I don't want to know.

Thanks for the coffee, Tess. My appointment's for ten. I must get going

You'll leave Jen?

Well, I don't think I should

Sure. Leave her, Stacey.

Okay, if you're sure it's no

Oh, positive. She's as good as gold. You're as good as a little goldfish, aren't you, sweetie? No trouble

— Jen? You okay, flower? I want to take you along with me, but I don't know how to say it politely.

The hair dryer purrs whirringly like a metallic tiger. Stacey turns the magazine page. The article is entitled "Pruning Down with Prunes—New Concept in Dieting." She sighs, closes the magazine and looks around. The dryer prevents any other sound from reaching her, so everything in front of her eyes is taking place in silence, as though she were observing it through some thick and isolating glass barrier or like TV with the voices turned off.

The priestesses are clad in pale mauve smocks. They glide and dart, the movements perfectly assured and smooth, no wasted effort. A heavy woman with heavy grey hair sinks down into a chair in front of the grapefruit-yellow basin. With a visible sigh of pleasure, tweed-covered bosom lifting like hills in a minor earthquake, she leans back her head to receive the benediction of the shampoo. The priestess's plastic-sheathed hands administer to her scalp, the fingers updrawn like yellow talonless claws. In a chair facing the wall-to-wall mirror, a young woman laughs soundlessly up at her priestess, who is twirling the strands of black hair rapidly around yellow rollers. An ammonia whiff and a conglomeration of humid perfumes come to Stacey's nostrils.

Not Earth. Somewhere else. Quite a small planet, but with a very advanced technology. The whole process is absolutely painless, here on Zabyul. The silver mechanism is simply fitted over the head, creating an impression of gentle warmth. Soon she will emerge from the Chrysalis. That is what the mechanism is called. One of the butterfly priestesses comes over, checks the controls. All set—the transformation is complete. She steps out.

The entire room is made of a substance which reflects softly. She stares. Her? This very young woman has her features, but altered, made finer, the shape of the bones incredibly beautiful under the cream-textured skin. Quick—Jartek will be waiting. And there he is, strong and supple, his sex discernible under the sleek tight-fitting uniform of a galactic pilot. Then they are in one of the life-domes. He is a senior pilot, so naturally his life-dome is a relatively spacious gracious one, furnished with golden-foam couches that grow organically out of the walls at a flick of the Environator on his steady-boned yet now trembling wrist. He puts his hands on her breasts, then slides his fingers down to her willing sex. Now quickly

Okay, Mrs. MacAindra? If you'd like to come over here, Lenore will comb you out.

Thanks.

—— No wonder I'm afraid of having an anaesthetic or under-going hypnosis. What if I talked? I'm a freak. Or maybe I'm not, but how can you tell? There is only one thing you have to remember, Stacey, doll. Tonight, drink tomato juice.

Outside the door of the hotel banqueting room, Mac touches Stacey's arm. Half surprised, she glances at him and finds that he is smiling.

Now just don't worry, Stacey. It'll be all right.

Gosh, I hope so. I'm kind of nervous.

There's nothing to be nervous *about.* Just don't argue or I won't   I swear it

The room is large, old-fashioned, plush, velvet-draped, and full of people. Stacey straightens her black cocktail dress with perspiring hands. At one end of the room there is a long bar, be-hind which three waiters are being kept busy. Stacey pats at her hair. In the middle of the room is a bandstand, from which mem-bers of a small and bored-looking orchestra are dispensing waltzes and slow foxtrots. Stacey resists the desire to look behind her and make sure her waist-slip has not edged disastrously downwards. Across the room, corner to corner, stretches a white banner with one word in cerise, gold-edged.

RICHALIFE

Standing with a group of laughing girls, all lissome and blond with good teeth and no waists, is Thor, dressed in midnight-blue evening suit and drinking tomato juice. His silver hair glimmers phosphorescently. Stacey checks by running one finger along her outer thighs to make sure her panties have not by any chance suddenly lost their elasticity and begun to descend. Thor waves and grins, and Mac lifts a hand in a return salute. Stacey unobtrusively puts one hand behind her and touches a thumb to the small of her back in case her bra has become unhooked. The orchestra goes into the droning circles of a Viennese waltz, and before Stacey and Mac can reach Thor, he is dancing with one of the girls.

C'mon, then. Let's get a drink, eh?

You think we should, Mac?

Don't be ridiculous, Stacey. He's not intolerant. He doesn't try to foist his opinions on other people.

Not much, he doesn't.

Well, if you're going to take that line, you better stick to Coke.

No—I'm not. I mean I won't.

—— Resolutions, where have you gone? All night on Coke and I will be a raving lunatic. Two, though. Only two. Then stop. Spirits of my dead forefathers, strengthen me. They should strengthen you, nitwit? They probably all died of whiskey. Mac, don't leave me. I can't cope with this crew.

Stacey, this is Mickey Jameson. Mick, I'd like you to meet my wife.

Pleased to meetcha.

Hello—glad to meet you

91

And this is my wife, Priscilla—dear, this is Mac Mac-
Aindra and Stacey.

Hello there

Glad to meet you

What'll it be, Stacey?

Oh—Scotch and water, please, with lots of ice.

—— Maybe gin and tonic would be better? Mother's ruin.
No, that's for home. Mac prefers gin. Scotch for the crises. Up,
the clans.

Mickey Jameson is short, young, blue-eyed, pink-faced.
His wife is similar in feminine version. Stacey contemplates the
girl, wondering if she really is not perspiring or is only pretending
not to. The girl's dress is short and white but not virginal, and
her eye make-up is a work of abstract art. The long false eye-
lashes glow diamondly with a touch of what appears to be the
instant-snow spray that Stacey associates with Christmas trees.

—— Can't be. Must be some other gloop. Must ask Katie. If
I would only read articles on make-up instead of those epistles
telling me all the harm I'm doing, then I'd know. I can't read them.
I look at them from the edge of one eye, at a distance, but they
always scare me off. It looks so complicated. Things used to be a
hell of a lot simpler, in my day. Cream, lipstick and powder.
Finish. *In my day*. Lovely phrase, that.

Been with Richalife long?

Who, Mac? Oh, not so very long. What about your husband?

Just a month or so. But he loves it. It's the greatest, isn't
it?

Yeh. It's fine.

Mickey says he was just marking time, before. Just simply
marking time. He was in house paints. What was your hubby in,
before?

He was in essence—I mean to say, the essence of his work
was kind of educational. Encyclopedias, like.

92

Oh, say. Well, think of that, now. What made him switch?

Oh you know   go-ahead firm and that

Yeh   well   that's just exactly what Mickey said, too.

Mac and Mickey are standing shoulder to shoulder. Stouthearted men.

Yeh, well, like I said, Mick, I used to do the Okanagan—up and down the whole valley—with my previous firm, so that's why I wanted to keep the area for the time being. I know it like the palm of my hand.

Sure, boy, I can see that all right. I would've figured you for the city, though.

You could be right, there. Maybe it's time I changed territory.

A change is as good as a rest, I always say.

Well, you could be right.

At this point, Thor saunters up and joins the group, or rather, the group re-forms around him.

Hi, Mac. Hi, Mickey. Good to see you. Well, he*llo* there, Priscilla. You don't mind if I call you Priscilla, do you?

Why, certainly not. I'd just love you to, Mr. Thorlakson.

Thor's the name, sweetheart. Just Thor. And who have we here? Stacey, isn't it? Well, and how are *you*, Stacey?

Just fine, thanks.

I'm glad to hear it. Have you got all those nice kids of yours on the Younglife Program yet? Oh yes, you have. I remember the charts now. And if I remember correctly, they're doing just dandy, too. Just great. Well, that's splendid, Stacey. You have any trouble getting the whole brood to line up for the Program every morning, Mac?

Nope. None whatsoever.

—— Like fun. He leaves it to me, and sometimes I give them one and mostly I forget, or forget on purpose, thinking the stuff is probably subtly addictive, or will ultimately be found to contain traces of arsenic, and then I flush the baubles down the john when no one's around, and probably Katie will rat on me one of

93

these days. I don't know when Mac takes his. It is not a subject which is discussed between us.

Well, that's great. Say, you know, Mickey, this guy's got four children. Brave fellow, eh? You going to try for a baseball team, Mac?

Not yet awhile

Well, let me know when you think of trying, and we'll give you an extra ration of Richalife. How about that? Only save enough energy to get the product across, won't you, Mac? If possible, that is.

—— What's going on? What are you getting at, you slimy bastard?

Four kids aren't many these days

What's that? Oh—yes, you're perfectly right there, Stacey. Yes, indeed. Large families are coming back in, all right. Personally I've got nothing against large families. Provided people can look after them and educate them adequately. No, not adequately –properly. I would say *properly*.

We aim to.

Of course you do, Stacey. I'd never doubt that for an instant. Well, if you good people will excuse me, I see one of the office girls over there and I think I really must go and dance with her.

Thor skims shiningly off. Stacey goes to the bar and gets another Scotch by herself.

Mac?

Yeh?

What was all that?

What was all what?

Oh for heaven's sake, *you* know. He was needling

He was kidding. Can't you take a joke *yet*, Stacey?

Nope. No sense of humor. Me, Tess and Queen Victoria.

Look, I gotta go and see Stewart Essex for a minute. He mentioned he'd like a country circuit. I think it's time I got onto a city run. You okay here?

Sure. You go ahead. I'll find somebody to talk to.

The evening grinds along. Stacey discovers several other aimless wives whose husbands are in essential conference together.

Hello. Mind if I join you?

Oh, do. I'm Clare Gallagher and this is Joanie Storey.

Hi. Glad to meet you. I'm Stacey MacAindra.

Your old man's talking shop, too, I suppose?

What else?

Boy, I really love it. I was saying to Joanie, here, they take you out about once a month and then what do they do? Dance with you? Not on your sweet Nelly they don't. You got kids?

Yeh. Four.

Yeh? How old?

Daughter fourteen, son ten, son seven, daughter two. You?

I got only the two, but believe me, that's plenty. My little boy just turned five, and my girl is eighteen months. They're sure a handful.

I know, but they get easier. It makes a lotta difference when they're at school.

I suppose. But then again, I think the house'll seem awfully empty.

Well, I guess so. My youngest isn't at school yet, of course, so I don't know.

——— How to get out of this? They're thinking the same, maybe. Funny thing—when I'm with those know-everythings in some evening class or other, I think the hell with intellectual pursuits and all I feel like doing is gabbing about my kids. But when I'm with women who are gabbing about kids, I think the hell with it. Powder room—that's it.

In the course of the next hour, Stacey visits the Ladies' twice, on each occasion slipping a small cake of the provided pink soap into her evening bag. She repairs her make-up, stares gloomily at herself in the antiseptic-looking mirror, smiles stiffly at the other women who clank in and out of the toilet cubicles. She then goes back to the bar and obtains another double Scotch. She dances once with a corpulent youngish man who pumps her hand up and down and maneuvers her around the corners by swiveling her on his belly. After that, nobody asks her. She decides to stay within easy reach of the bar.

—— Who would want to dance to that dreary music, anyway? Not me. I used to love dancing. I used to be a good dancer. I said to Katie and Ian once, *You may not believe it, but I used to be a good dancer.* What kind of music in those days, they wanted to know. *Boogie-woogie,* I foolishly said. They damn near killed themselves laughing. They went around for days saying it—*Boo-oo-gie–woo-oo-gie*—and collapsing in mirth. Ha bloody ha.

Double Scotch, please.

—— Come on, doll, be sociable. Don't want to be sociable. Don't know anybody. What did Thor mean, needling Mac like that? He *was* needling him. And saying like that, *Who have we here?* Like I was something that just crawled out from under a stone. The bastard. Who does he think he is? How dare he talk to Mac like that? Listen, you thunder god, you, you double-dyed snake-in-the-grass, you refugee from the discards of Lucifer's army. Let me tell you one simple thing. Just one. Do you want to know why Mac didn't reply? Do you want to know why he didn't wipe the floor verbally with you? I'll tell you. I'll tell you straight. Because he is a gentleman, that's why. Because he cannot be bothered to stoop to your paltry jesting, you sick clown, that's why. Believe me, I'd say it to your face.

Thor's face. Immediately in front of her and somewhat above. His height. Very tall man. Surrounded by a circle of anonymous others. Stacey sees only Thor—the white opalescent skin, the eyes like turquoises, opaque blue, the silver mane. She realizes she has walked all around the room in search of him, and now she has found him.

96

Excuse me

Why, hi there, Stacey. You enjoying the party?

Yes. Yes, thanks. There was only one thing I wanted to ask you about.

Go right ahead. What is it? It isn't—ah—private?

Oh hell no it's not private it's only about that quiz

Quiz?

Quiz. Why'd you do it?

You mean the Richalife Quiz? I don't think I quite see

I said why'd you do it? What can you gain? Who's gonna tell you anything on a thing like that?

You don't think so?

Hell I know so. I mean if I feel guilty or anxious, like let's say I stabbed my dear old grandmother in the back for her money or I find I got stigmata on both palms and I gotta wear gloves everywhere I go, you think I'm gonna *say?*

Titters of general laughter. Thor reaches out and takes Stacey's hands.

Here—let me see. No, you're all clear, Stacey, I'm glad to say. You didn't strike me like the type. Well, about the quiz, now.

—— I got to stop. Stacey, girl, shut your trap. Change subject. Now. Essential. Get a grip on yourself. Think of Mac.

No, it's only that it's an intrusion or do I mean infringement? I mean infrusion, that's what I mean but I guess I shouldn't have brought it up

One of the circle, a slender man in glasses, puts a hand on her rump.

As long as that's all you bring up

Hey the party's getting rough

We've all got good manners here

Stacey lets the talk flow away from her. She glances around to find Mac, knowing she must focus on him. Finally she sees him. He is standing near a window, his face turned away from her. He is talking with a tall brown-haired girl whose face

97

is a medieval tomb carving, elongated, drawn in subtle lines of earnestness and prayer. Stacey quickly looks away.

—— Don't be ridiculous. He's only talking to her. Yeh, but that look on her face. What is she *saying?* None of your business, Stacey. None of your damn business. She looks so much more sensitive and that, than I look. What about one for the road? Stacey, kid, you're stoned. I am not stoned. All right, so even if I am, so what? I don't give a fuck.

She spins around to face Thor again, and in doing so, her evening bag spills open and two pink soaps slither down onto the polished floor. Stacey looks at them as though she has never seen them before. There is a small moment of silence and uncertainty. Then someone laughs, a high fluting. Stacey discovers with some astonishment that it is herself.

I always take them home for the kids. I do it with those wrapped sugar lumps too

Thor picks them up for her.

Think nothing of it. I know I used to like things like that, as a kid.

Yeh? Well, I'm certainly glad to hear it. Were you—were you always called Thor?

Except when I was called late for supper ha-ha. Yes, it's an Icelandic name.

That's what I figured. Lots of people of Icelandic descent where I came from. Not exactly where I *came* from, but same province. Manitoba. Prairie girl, that's me.

Really? How interesting.

He looks bored almost to the limit of endurance, and she recalls too late that she told him once before where she came from, as though compelled to flaunt her small-town background.

Yeh, and you know what? The only joke I can ever remember is about Thor.

Well, in that case, it must be a pretty good joke.

It's so-so. The great god Thor comes to earth once, see?

And I guess this would likely be in some Scandinavian country, eh? Anyway, he meets this lovely country girl. So he—he—persuades her. You know, he persuades her. To go into a hayfield with him. Well, he seduces her, see? But later on, he feels kind of bad, being as he had an advantage. I mean, he is—like—a god, see, so who could resist him? You know? So he says to her, *Look, there's something I oughta tell you. I'm Thor.* And she says, *Tho am I, but it wath worth it, wathn't it?*

Laughter. Ripples, extending outwards. Thor's uninterpretable face. The young henchmen, simpering in spectacles. Women's shrill braying giggles. Men's deep-voiced guffaws. Then Mac's arm on her elbow, pressing hard enough to bruise.

C'mon, Stacey. We promised the kids we'd be home by twelve.

Did we? I don't remember

Good night, Thor.

Thor is talking to someone else.

Oh—good night, Mac. Good night, Stacey.

G'night

The car is flying, and out in a blackness of sky, when the city lights have gone away, the moon is also flying, descending the hollow hill of night, climbing again to the center of everything, in trails of moonstone light. Stacey, leaning her head against the back of the car seat, can see it happening.

You know what they called the moon in the Highlands, Mac?

(No reply)

Mac, you know what they used to call the moon, there? They used to call it MacFarlane's lantern. You know that? And you know something else? That was because the MacFarlanes were a pretty sneaky lot, see, buncha thieves, actually, and they used to go around on these raids, see? Banditti. That's what they were, the MacFarlanes. Buncha banditti. So the moon was their lantern. And you know something else? The MacAindras belong to the MacFarlane clan. How d'you like that? That's you, kid.

99

Banditti. MacFarlane's lantern. Only that isn't you, is it, Mac? That isn't you at all. *Au contraire,* as we say in Quebec.

Dry up, Stacey. You've said enough tonight.

Dry up, Stacey. Shut up and simmer down, Stacey. Do this do that. I would like to live on a desert island. What would you like?

Don't ask me. I might tell you. No use in your condition.

What d'you mean, in my condition? You make it sound like I'm pregnant.

C'mon. We're home.

Home Sweet Home. Oh boy.

C'mon, Stacey. Just get to bed.

Okay okay okay okay

She is lying on a magic carpet. Must be a magic carpet, what else? It is moving very rapidly, in upward and downward swooshes. Each swirl leaves a color in its path   jet-trails of color smoke   one for each day of the week   pink purple peacock blue   tangerine green leaves greensleeves bird-feather yellow raspberry no not raspberry that's an essence the essence of the whole matter is is is

Blackness.

—— Help. Water. Water. I'm dying of thirst. Bathroom. Oh man, that's one degree better at least. What time is it? Half past seven. Morning. Can't be. Is. Oh perdition. Am I going to throw up? Nothing to throw except two glasses of water. Back to bed. No. Got to get up. Impossible. Not impossible. Got to.

Stacey goes back to the bedroom. Mac is almost dressed. He looks at her silently. Then she remembers.

Stacey, tottering over to Thor's court. Stacey, arguing in a loud harridan voice, her hair disarranged, her make-up long since vanished. *It's a-a-inf-infrusion, tha's what it is, so there, see?* Oh God. Two pink soap tablets tumbling out of her handbag. The gusts and shrieks of pointing laughter. Thief, thief—takes the soap from the ladies' john. Stacey, regaling the company with corny slightly low joke about—what? Joke about Thor. Oh God. Stacey, believing they were laughing *with* her.

— Oh no. It couldn't have been. It was. Was it that bad? Am I exaggerating? No. No, I'm not. It was probably far worse than that, even.

Mac—oh Mac, was it awful?

Look, Stacey, there's no point in discussing it.

It *was* awful. I can remember everything. Every word. Oh Mac, I'm sorry.

Yeh. Well.

I don't know what got *into* me.

Allow me to tell you, then. What got into you was Scotch.

Mac   please don't look like that

Oh Christ. Like what?

Grim. Like ice. I can't stand it

Look, Stacey, it's nearly eight o'clock. Can we just get breakfast?

Mac, I'm sorry. Honestly, I'm terribly terribly sorry.

Yeh. So you said.

I was kind of nervous anyway, and then you left me on my own

Great. So now it's my fault.

I didn't say that.

Stacey, there is absolutely no use in talking. I got to get to work. I don't want to discuss it.

I think we should. I think we should discuss everything

Oh God. Look, Stacey, I'm not asking much. I'm only suggesting that breakfast would be a good idea. Is that asking too much?

Okay okay okay I'm going downstairs right this minute. Mac, do you think you should tell Thor I'm sorry?

If he doesn't mention it, I most certainly will not bring up the subject. Now if you don't mind

Okay okay I'm on my way

Clutching her housecoat around her, Stacey rushes down to the kitchen. The motions of getting breakfast are automatic. The minutes are eternal, the voices piercing.

— Hush. Please. Just be quiet for once. I tell you, my eardrums will crack. How'd you like to have a mother with cracked eardrums?

She says as little as possible. At last they are all out of the house, and Stacey is alone with Jen. She pours her coffee and begins to sip at it cautiously.

— Oh my guts. When this coffee hits them, they will rebel into convulsions. Slowly, that's it. There. That's a bit better. Why did I do it? I'll never live it down. Mac will never forgive me. I'll never forgive myself. It isn't as though it's never happened before. No, Stacey, girl, don't think of the other times. Not that many. No, but all dreadful. Don't *think*—I command you. You do, eh? Who're you? One of your other selves. Help, I'm schizophrenic. Oh God, why did I do it? I was so damn scared of not doing well, and then I didn't do well. Maybe if I hadn't been so scared—don't make excuses, Stacey. *Mea culpa.* It must be wonderful to be a Catholic. Pour it all out. Somebody listens. Not me. I'm stuck with it, all of it, every goddam awful detail, for the rest of my natural or unnatural life. Mac scares me when he's like he was this morning. Why can't he ever say? Maybe if he ever did, he'd throttle me. I wouldn't blame him. My God, maybe he *will* throttle me one of these days. "Salesman Strangles Wife" —it could happen to anybody. Nobody is an exception. What would happen to the kids if that happened? Oh my guts, churning around like a covey of serpents. Covey? Nest? Medusa does in summer wear a nest of serpents in her hair. Joyce Kilmer. I can't seem to focus on anything. Whatsamatter with my eyeballs? When I close my eyes, something flickers across them. Jangled nerves. Feels like that tropical worm in that article—lives under people's eyelids and crawls over the eyes when so inclined. Charming. I'm sick. I'm ill. Have I ruined Mac's job? Was it as awful as I remember?

> Stacey, face distorted into a swollen mask like the face of a woman drowned, the features blurred. The lunatic laughter, hers.

—— I am exaggerating. I must be. Am I? I can't tell. It seems worse every time I think of it.

NINE-O'CLOCK NEWS PELLET BOMBS CAUSED THE DEATH OF A HUN-
DRED AND TWENTY-FIVE CIVILIANS MAINLY WOMEN AND CHILDREN IN

C'mon, flower. The least we can do is clean this house.

Duncan can play alone, for when he feels the world's aloofness he goes inward to more satisfactory countries. After school, he is not to be seen and Stacey finally discovers him in the basement, not in the playroom but standing beside the automatic washer, spinning the dials.

Duncan—what are you doing? Don't you dare
It's okay, Mum. It's not switched on.
Well, all right. What is it? A spaceship?

Duncan looks at her, half surprised and half pleased, a short stocky figure in jeans and striped T shirt.

Yeh. Sort of. I'm taking it to Venus. That's a neat planet, you know, Mum? It's very bright, all surrounded by these gases that they don't know what they are. Miss Walsh said.

How you going to get through all the gases, then?
This ship has a built-in-gas-goer-througher.
Well, that's great. But shouldn't you be outside, nice day like this?

I don't want to.
Why not?
Ian just tells me to scram.

Well, it's your yard, too. Come on, I'll speak to Ian.

I don't want to, Mum.

Oh, okay, but you ought to be out in the sun.

Stacey goes upstairs to the kitchen to begin dinner. Ian is standing beside the long low window, breaking small pieces of leaf off the potted plants.

Hey, my African violets! Cut it out, Ian. What's the matter?

There's nothing to do around here.

Why don't you play with your bug?

It's no fun. The wheels keep coming off.

Why don't you find somebody to play with, then?

Ron's gone with his mum to see his aunt. Terry's playing with Robert and they don't want me.

What about TV, then? Not that you should, this early.

Nothing on I want to see.

Well, what about going to see if Peter can play? He doesn't live that far. You could go on your bike.

Ian swings around slowly to face her.

Who?

Peter. Peter Challoner. You haven't played with him for quite a while.

Ian's grey eyes turn hard, hooded almost, and Stacey can see the small vein along his throat pulsing, as it does sometimes when he is more than usually tense.

What is it, Ian?

Peter's dead. I thought you knew.

Stacey looks at him, unbelieving. Ian's face prohibits questions, but she has to speak.

He can't be. What—what happened?

He got run over. It was that day you came home late for lunch.

Oh Ian—I didn't know—I must've missed it in the paper
                    The *scree-ee* of brakes. A white Buick. The
                    driver getting out slowly, as though unable to

104

look. The slight quiet figure under the front wheels. Stacey, running along the sidewalk towards home, heels snagging on the cement.

You didn't tell me, Ian. I didn't know. Oh honey. Why didn't you tell me?

Ian's face is pinched and rigid with its control, its go-away quality.

What would've been the use? What could you have done?

I could've

—— I don't know. For you, maybe nothing.

Stacey makes a tentative move towards him, one hand out to his shoulder. Ian breaks away, his thin strength arrowing past her, and reaches the back door. Then he turns upon her, a flame-furred young fox cornered, snarling, self-protective.

Can't you just shut up about it? He was dumb, see? Nobody but a moron would run out into the avenue after a football. It doesn't happen that easy unless guys are pretty dumb.

Ian, wait

But he is gone, out to his lair, the loft of the garage.

—— What's he been having nightmares about these past weeks? Why can't he ever say? How did he get to be that way, or was it born in him? God, how should I know? He gets further and further away. I can't reach him at all. Was he always that way, only I never noticed so much when he was younger?

Ian MacAindra, age four, marching around and around the kitchen table, to the martial music on the radio. Stacey, amused. Aren't you tired, honey? *Yes.* Why don't you stop, then? *I can't stop till the music stops.* So she turned off the radio when she saw he wasn't joking.

Mac has just come in, when there is a wail from the basement, and pounding footsteps. Duncan runs up the stairs into the kitchen, one hand bloodily scarlet. Stacey goes to him.

What happened?

Duncan's voice is barely discernible through his fear-sobbing.

Nail sticking out of the wall—didn't see it—it was rusty too will I die Mum? Ian says you die if it's rusty

No, you won't die. I'll fix it up. It'll soon be better. Don't worry. It'll be all right.

Duncan continues to sob, the tears runneling through the dust on his wide youngly plump face. Mac comes in from the hall, running his fingers distractedly through his brush of hair.

Duncan, for goodness sake shut up and quit making such a fuss about nothing.

Leave him, Mac. He was scared. Ian told him a rusty nail would

Scared, hell. He doesn't need to roar like that. Shut up, Duncan, you hear me?

Duncan nods, gulps down the salt from his eyes and the mucus from his nose. His chest heaves and he continues to cry, but quietly. Mac clamps a hand on his shoulder and spins him around.

Now listen here, Duncan, I'll give you one minute to stop.

Duncan stares with wet slit-eyes into his father's face. Stacey clenches her hands together.

— I could kill you, Mac. I could stab you to the very heart right this minute. But how can I even argue, after last night? My bargaining power is at an all-time low. Damn you. Damn you. Take your hands off my kid. Oh, God, I know, Sir—I know. Mac's probably spent the day placating Thor. And I haven't forgotten pitching Duncan and Ian to the floor either. What right have I got to say anything? But I can't help it. I can't stand this.

Leave him, Mac, can't you? Please just leave him alone.

Listen, Stacey, if he doesn't begin to learn some control now, when *is* he going to learn? Duncan, you just listen to me. You can't go through life bawling your head off, the slightest thing happens. What a mess you'll be if you go on that way. You'll

never get to first base if you can't learn to control yourself. Okay
—you're going to get hurt; you're going to get bashed around;
that's life. But for heaven's sake try to show a little guts.

—— All useless. Everything anybody says to their kids is
useless. Kids don't go by that. Or do they? Who is right, Mac or
me? Maybe we're both wrong. All I want to do is hold Duncan
so he isn't afraid. Is that wrong? What if Mac's dead right? Duncan did make a lot of fuss, I have to admit. How to stop myself
ruining him?

Later, when Duncan has gone upstairs, Stacey follows
him, first making sure that Mac is watching the news on TV in
the basement playroom.

Duncan?

He is sitting on his bed, holding one of his model cars
in one hand, turning it over and over without seeing it.

You okay now, Duncan?

He looks up at her, his eyes tearless, almost passive.

I never do anything right.

He didn't mean that, Duncan. He only meant

Well, I *don't*, Mum. I just don't do anything right

—— What words? I haven't got any. It isn't mine he wants
anyway. It's Mac's and Ian's, and those he won't get. I'm far from
him, too. Far even from Duncan. How did it happen like this?

After dinner, Katie is doing her homework in her room. Stacey
is bathing Jen. Mac has gone with his briefcase into the study.
Duncan is looking at TV, and Ian is prowling. Then Katie's in-
furiated shrieking voice.

Mother! Tell Ian to get out of here!

—— Heavens. She's started calling me Mother instead of
Mum. How long? I never noticed before.

Ian! What're you doing?

He barged right into my room without knocking. I can't
stand people doing that. Scram, you little creep!

Quit shoving me, you, or I'll

Ow! That hurt! Boy, I'll show you

Yeh? Well, how d'you like this then

Crash. Scream. Slam. Stacey flies out of the bathroom, hands soap-slippery, and along the corridor. She pulls Katie and Ian apart and pushes them into their respective bedrooms.

Okay, Ian. Just leave her *alone,* eh?

I was only

All right all right—you know what I told you about knocking before you go into people's bedrooms. And do not throw the hall chair *any more,* see?

Stacey carefully knocks and enters Katie's room. Katie is gathering up the littered textbooks, her long hair trailing on the floor as she stoops.

Katie, I know it was wrong of him. But he's been in a pretty low mood today. Try to be patient with

Patient! What good does that do? He never pays any attention.

Well, try

You try. That's your job.

Yeh, well just wait, sweetheart, till you've got your own kids

I'm not going to have

Oh? Why not?

Because it's for the birds, that's why.

What is?

The whole deal. You saying we get on your nerves all the time. You and Dad yakking away at each other—*Whatsamatter? Nothing's the matter. No need to talk to me in that tone of voice.* Man, not for me.

> Stacey Cameron, sixteen, watching granite-eyed while her mother retreated softly and billowingly into temporary but recurring nerves, meaning the solace of flowing eyes and codeine for the headaches. *I won't argue any more with you, Stacey—it hurts me too*

*much when you're so stubborn, and it isn't as
though I could even ask your father. You wait,
you just wait until you have your own children.* (I'll have them, all right, but it won't
ever be like this, my setup.)

Stacey stands in the doorway, unmoving, staring.

Katie—does it really strike you like that?

Katie does not reply. She cannot, because she is crying.
Stacey moves towards her, but Katie turns and faces the wall,
her voice low and muffled.

Go away, can't you?

—— It's her age. They're all like that, at about this age. Of
course I know that. Katie—talk to me.

Mac, talk to me.

Oh Christ, Stacey.

I know I know it's late—time for sleep—work tomorrow
—but please

It is eleven thirty and they are in bed. The light is out.
Mac has just butted his last cigarette and replaced the ashtray
on the bedside table. He sighs, and Stacey can feel him edging
a little further towards his own side of the bed.

—— You'll fall out of bed in a minute, Mac, if you're not
careful. What do you think it would do—pollute you, if you
touched me? And yet if I said that, it would be a terrible thing
to say. Unforgivable. Like what I did last night at the party.
Nothing is ever looked at and torn up and thrown away like
scrap paper. The abrasions just go on accumulating. What a lot
of heavy invisible garbage we live with.

Mac, about last night

Look, I told you. Let's drop it, eh? No use talking about
it.

Okay. But you don't seem to drop it.

What do you *mean,* I don't seem to drop it? It's you who

109

Well, you go around being gloomy and not talking—naturally I don't expect you to *like* what I did but was it really so terrible? I'd rather you got mad and yelled at me and then it would be all over maybe and we could forget it.

If I did yell at you or beat you up, would you really like that any better?

I only meant saying something, to clear the air. I didn't mean beating me up, for heaven's sake. I'd walk out on you if you did that.

—— Would I? With four kids? How could you walk out on him, Stacey, whatever he did or was like? You couldn't, sweetheart, and don't you forget it. You haven't got a nickel of your own. This is what they mean by emancipation. I'm lucky he's not more externally violent, that's all. I see it, God, but don't expect me to like it.

Stacey, I don't care to discuss it. Is that clear?

Yessir.

Cut it out, will you?

Cut what out?

That act.

Oh Mac, please

She has turned to him, and put her hands on his shoulders. For a moment he lies still, while she undoes his pajamas and begins slowly touching him where she knows it will have effect. Her hands move across the hair on his chest and down to his sex. He stirs then, and suddenly, abruptly, almost roughly, begins making love to her.

—— Strange that the hair under his arms and on his chest is auburn but between his legs dark. Can't see the color but I know it. The mole on his right shoulder. The scar on his thigh—right here—where he got gashed playing hockey when he was a kid. I know every inch of his skin. Mac? You want me? Yes, now he does.

I do too, Mac.

You do what?

Want you

Yeh, I know I know. Now, Stacey?

Yes. Now.

Stacey rises to him, her legs linked around his, and cries out as she always does without knowing it. He comes in pain-pleasure silence as almost always, telling her only through veins and muscles and skin that he is with her. When it is over, they separate because his weight on her ribs always makes her cough after a few moments, and anyway he always has to get up and go to the bathroom.

—— Did I take that christly pill this morning? I was feeling so grim—can't remember. Yes, I did take it. Along with the blue Richalife and four aspirins, with second cup of coffee. All these considerations.

> The apartment was cramped and dingy, and they had hardly any furniture. *It's ours, Stacey —just think of that—fantastic, eh?* And they slept in each other's arms and legs all night, with peace, and wakened whole.

You okay, Stacey?

Oh yes.

Good night, then

Good night

Within minutes she can hear Mac breathing deeply in sleep. Sometimes he moans in his sleep and she always asks him the next day if he had a dream but he can never remember. Tonight he is quiet. Stacey turns over on her right side, and pulls her legs up so she is lying Z-shaped.

—— Tonight I'll sleep. Let us be thankful for mercies, whatever.

The rain forest is thick, matted, overgrown with thorned berry bushes, the fallen needles from the pine and tamarack bronzing the earth. Smell of moss, wet branches, mellowly rotten leaves. It is very difficult to walk through. The wild brambles stretch out their fish hooks to tear at exposed skin. The ground is spongy underfoot, for the moss tops centuries of leaf mold. She has to continue, bringing what she is carrying with her. The thing is bleeding from the neck stump, but that cannot be helped. The severed head spills only blood, nothing else. She has tunneled at last through the undergrowth. Now she has the right to look. She holds it up in front of her. How is it that she can see it? What is she seeing it with? That is the question. The head she has been carrying is of course none but hers.

FIVE

)∿∩∿∩∿∩∿∩∿(

EVER-OPEN EYE BOUGAINVILLAEA BURGEONING, EDGING STREETS
WHERE BEGGARS SQUAT IN DUST. A MAN BURNING. HIS FACE CANNOT
BE SEEN. HE LIES STILL, PERHAPS ALREADY DEAD. FLAMES LEAP AND
QUIVER FROM HIS BLACKENED ROBE LIKE EXCITED CHILDREN OF HELL.
VOICE: TODAY ANOTHER BUDDHIST MONK SET FIRE TO HIMSELF IN
PROTEST AGAINST THE WAR IN

> Bloody fools. What do they think it'll accomplish?
> I know. But they believe
> Any coffee left, Stacey?
> Yeh. I'll heat it up.

Stacey comes back from the kitchen and hands Mac his
cup. He is sitting in the old chintz-covered armchair which was
their second piece of furniture, the first having been their bed,
and which has now been dismissed to the basement TV room.
Mac's legs are stretched out full length, and the frown lines between his eyes are still there even after an entire evening of no
work.

113

EVER-OPEN EYE A HILLSIDE AND SMALL TREES SEEN FROM HIGH AND FARAWAY. THE SMOKE RISING IN ROLLING CLOUDS. VOICE: AC-CELERATED BOMBING IN THE AREA OF

Mac?

Yeh?

Oh—nothing. I just thought it was kind of flickering for a minute, there.

—— Why talk? Mac doesn't like to, and he's right. What good does it do? Can we do one goddam thing? No. And what are my reasons, anyway? I said to Jake one evening two three years ago that I had this feeling like the fall of Rome and he said *You're not afraid it'll happen; you're afraid it won't*. Since then I always wonder. Anything for a little excitement? Goddam you, Jake Fogler. It's a lie. There are still a few things I do know. At least, I think there are. But even those are mixed now. Like laughing amid the desire to puke re: that newspaper interview with that woman somewhere in the States. *He came home on leave and it's like all his reflexes have been changed, sort of. His little sister jumped out at him from behind the door, just for fun, like, and he only just stopped himself in time from karate chopping her.* Little sisters of the world, watch it, eh? Never mind the broken-hearts bit. Broken necks are the concern these days. But I laughed as well. Conditioned into monsterdom, like the soldier. The look on Ian's face that time I pitched them both to the floor. And my eyes, covered with blood that wasn't there, so I couldn't for a moment see anything but rage. *Stop the noise, just stop the noise.* That's what I thought. How can I ever make up for it? What if it happens again? That precise thing won't, but something else may. In God's name, what is *Mac* like, in there, wherever he lives?

EVER-OPEN EYE THE SON OF ROBIN HOOD IS CANTERING ALONG THROUGH SHERWOOD. LUCKILY THERE HAPPENS TO BE A SIGN ON A ZIGZAG PIECE OF BOARD AS IN NORTH AMERICAN NATIONAL PARKS. NOTTINGHAM $3\frac{1}{2}$ MILES.

Boy, this one's as old as the hills. You ever seen it before, Mac?

Yes, I think so. May as well watch it anyway.

Yeh, may as well.

Ian nineteen, in love with the uniform he is wearing. Jen, eleven, talking by this time, suddenly startling him and yelling as she jumps out from behind a something. Ian's lifted hand caught by himself in mid-strike. His face not his own, and yet his own, belonging totally to the embryonic cougar which has always been there.

— No. No, Stacey. Do that one over again.

Ian nineteen in plain well-cut business suit, having just graduated (early, admittedly, but he is bright) from university, now entering his first job. There is a great future in the sale of nasal contraceptives, tapes of apes and rapes, instant-color chameleon embalming fluid and deep freeze for cancer patients who will be melted and resuscitated when a cure is found. This year a Volkswagen; next year a Jaguar. Like a mighty army moves the unbesodden; brothers we are treading where saints have been introdden.

— Very funny, doll. Try again.

Ian nineteen quitting university. I am a dropout. I opt out. Let the maggots crawl. I believe in peace, love, expanded consciousness and nonviolent violence. Ian, poet, artist, musician, going his own way.

— Nuts. Never Ian. Duncan, maybe. Anyway, what's the use in opting out? Maybe there is, but it's beyond me. I can't reach it. I'm in forevermore, like it or not.

Mac?

Mm?

What shall I put on those charts for Richalife? Where it says energy snap-up and that.

You mean you haven't put anything?

Well, no

115

Oh for Christ's sake, Stacey. Well, give them all to me, then. I'll do them.

For all of us?

Somebody's got to.

Yeh, well, I guess that would be the best thing. Mac, I would've thought you wouldn't have to work quite so hard now you've got a city area.

It's the exact opposite.

I thought maybe I'd ask Tess and Jake in on Thursday. Will you be home?

No. I have to go to a rally.

A what?

Rally. R-A-double L-Y.

Oh for heaven's sake. Well, can I come, too?

You wouldn't find it interesting.

How do you know?

Now look, Stacey

Okay okay. You don't want me to see Thor. You're afraid I'll disgrace you. Well, I wouldn't.

I did not say that. Did I say that?

Not in so many words. But that resigned tone of yours

Good God, Stacey. I can't say anything right, can I? If I have to check on my tone every time I open my mouth

Oh, I know. That's how it sounded. But I didn't mean

What precisely did you mean, then?

I don't know. I've lost it.

This is the first evening I've taken off in weeks, and now you

I'm sorry. Honestly, Mac. I know. I don't know what's the matter with me.

Look, Stacey, are you feeling okay?

I don't know. I've been getting these headaches

—— Is that true? Or did I just make it up? I say I am not much in love with the lies, but they don't get less—they get more. How can this be? God forgive me a poor spinner.

116

Well, you better see the doctor, then.

No—I think I'm exaggerating. It's nothing. It's just from looking at the TV all evening. I'll take a couple of aspirins.

—— I haven't got a headache at all. Yes, I have. As a matter of fact, now that I notice it, it's excruciating.

Maybe you need glasses.

Yeh, maybe

EVER-OPEN EYE THE SON OF ROBIN HOOD STANDS BEHIND KING JOHN AT RUNNYMEDE, MAKING THE RELUCTANT MONARCH SIGN THE MAGNA CARTA

—— Sometimes a person feels that something else must have been meant to happen in your own life, or is this all there's ever going to be, just like this? Until I die. What'll it be like to die? Not able to breathe? Fighting for air? Or letting everything slide away, seeing shapes like shadows that used to be people, nothing real because in a minute you won't be real any more? Holy Mary, Mother of God, be with me now and in the hour of my death. If only I could say that, but no. My father's dead face, looking no different except the eyes closed, and I thought his face had been dead for a long time before he died, so what did it matter, but I didn't believe that. Something should happen before it's too late. Idiot-child, what more could happen? What more do you want? You've got—yeh, I know, God. No need to write me a list. And I'm grateful. Don't take me seriously. Don't let anything terrible happen to the kids.

Click.

Well, c'mon, Stacey, it's getting late.

Yeh, so it is

Doctor Spender's waiting room is walled with plants—tall rubber plants with leaves slickly green as though varnished, ferns drooping like miniature willow trees, needled cacti. They are real, not plastic, and this, obscurely, gives Stacey faith in Doctor Spender's medical abilities. Stacey is the only person waiting. She riffles through magazines, looking only at the pictures. She is wearing her black skirt and a yellow tailored blouse, so it will be easier to strip to the waist in case he wants to listen to her lungs.

— Should I tell Mac I've been? I don't think so. If there *is* something wrong, it would only worry him, and if there isn't, he'd think I was neurotic. Boy, he'd sure be right about that. I shouldn't have come. There isn't a darned thing the matter with me. I wish I'd worn my blue suit instead of this skirt. Katie's right—it looks like Victoriana. Does it, hell. Why should it? I only bought it last year. What does Mac think about Thor? What does Mac think about? What are you thinking about, Mac? *Oh, nothing much.* Well, what sort of a nothing? *For heaven's sake, Stacey, what does it matter?*

Mac recounting, once, something that happened a long time ago. *Don't know why I did it, but when I was a kid I got mad one day and shoved my fist through a pane of glass in the kitchen window.* You did? It doesn't sound like you. What did your dad say? *Oh, he was furious, but he didn't strap me. He said that even if I had lost my self-control, he wasn't going to lose his.* What did he do, then? *Made me pray with him, for self-control.* Sounds pretty funny, likely. Well, not all that funny. *The prayer bit didn't do much good, but he was right about the other.* Yeh, I guess so.

— What really happened? How was it for him?

Mac, about Ian's age, listening to his mother's softly chiding voice. Must remember you are a minister's son, dear, and set a good example. It isn't asking very much dear and of course a BB gun is out of the question and it hurts me so when I hear you using swear words and. Mac, maybe only the once, when it was

*too much, his face like Ian's face, inheld, bitterly uncommuni-
cative, lashing out, not knowing he was going to smash the window until he had done it. Matthew, towering like Moses, bearing
in his eyes the letter of the Law. Kneel down, Clifford, kneel
down right here in the study with me, and we will both pray.
Mac, longing for any whip rather than this one, knowing this
occasion would never arise again, must not, looking at his father's
clamped-shut eyes, listening to the flat voice calling upon the
lord of all the galaxies to bear witness to a fragmented square of
a brittle substance called glass by some of the users of it who
lived on a small planet and who must learn not to break, not by
not wanting to, but by some other reinforced and steel means.*

—— Was it like that? If it was, how come we've got a window left? But how do I know? Mac, I'm a rotten guesser.

Okay, Mrs. MacAindra—you can go in now.

Oh—thanks.

Doctor Spender is youngish, overworked, soft-spoken,
perpetually tired-looking. He looks up from the file card on his
desk and smiles.

Hello, Mrs. MacAindra. What seems to be the trouble?

Well, it's these headaches I've been getting. And there's
this place right at the back of my head, and it sort of goes
kaboom-kaboom when I'm trying to get to sleep. Not really an
ache—just a dull throbbing, but it bothers me. Then I get neurotic
and start thinking I've got a tumor of the brain.

—— That's right, clown. Make yourself sound like a nut case.
Yes, but what if it *is* a tumor? These things happen. Oh God,
dead at thirty-nine. What kind of a death would that be? You'd
be incoherent long before it happened; the kids would see you
mindless, dribbling, maybe shouting all the four-letter words
you've decorously never said in front of them. No, I wouldn't
let them see me. If I was incompetent, Mac wouldn't let them
see, I hope. What would happen to the kids? Who'd bring them
up? My sister? But she doesn't know them, what they're like. I
don't want anybody else to bring them up.

119

We'll see, now. Show me exactly where the throbbing comes, Mrs. MacAindra. That's fine.

The examination goes on. Heart and lungs. Blood pressure. Any other symptoms? Finally the doctor looks at her, mildly inquiring.

Can't find anything wrong, superficially. Not worried about anything, are you?

Oh no. Everything's all right. I mean, at home.

—— How can I say anything else, without making it sound foolish? I can't put my finger on it, anyway. Too many threads. I can't say it, and who would believe me if I did? It's like being inside a balloon made out of some kind of glue, and when you try to get out, you only get tangled and stuck.

Well, I think I'll send you for an X ray, just to make sure there's nothing wrong.

I'm sure there isn't. It's probably just my imagination. I probably need to have my head examined.

Doctor Spender smiles.

That's exactly what you're going to have.

The X-ray results are negative. Stacey does not have tumor of the brain. She thanks Doctor Spender and puts down the phone. It is early afternoon, and Jen is asleep. Stacey moves around the house without knowing in advance what she is going to do. She goes upstairs to the bedroom and looks at herself in the full-length mirror. She is wearing a blue-and-pink-print dress, bought on sale last autumn. The pink is in the form of small clocks, all of whose hands indicate five minutes before either noon or midnight. She removes the dress and her slip, and puts on a pair of tight-fitting green velvet slacks and a purple overblouse which has been hanging in the cupboard for some months, as yet unworn. She then rummages at the back of the cupboard, on the floor, and comes up with a pair of high-heeled gold-strapped sandals.

—— Okay, so of course I know you shouldn't wear high heels with sandals. But I love high heels. I just do. All right, Mac, I know these are vulgar, especially with slacks. But I like them, see? And I can do with the extra height.

She listens at Jen's door. No sound. Let sleeping kids lie. Stacey in golden high-heel sandals tiptoes downstairs to the kitchen, collects the gin bottle and two bottles of tonic, and goes down to the basement room, leaving the door between the kitchen and basement open in case Jen calls.

—— This calls for some slight celebration. Reprieve. I'm not a goner yet. Did I really think I was? Well, it's in the middle of the night I start thinking about it, and then it seems pretty certain. Really, it's only what would happen to the kids. Yeh? It doesn't matter about you, Stacey? Well, it shouldn't matter. Why not? Because I'm thirty-nine and I can't complain. But they haven't begun yet. That's not how you feel about yourself, though. It matters. Okay, but so-what? I think of Katie—maybe Ian, now, too—thinking of me like I'm prehistoric, and it bugs me. I'm sorry, but it does. I'm not a good mother. I'm not a good wife. I don't want to be. I'm Stacey Cameron and I still love to dance.

The floor is dark-red linoleum tiles. Stacey kicks aside the numdah scatter rugs with their rough embroidery of magic trees, trees of life flowering unexpectedly into azure birds, green unlikely leaves. She pours a gin and tonic, drinks half of it and tops it up. The records are kept in a mock wrought-iron stand. Stacey shuffles impatiently through them and finally finds what she is looking for. She changes the record player to seventy-eight and puts the old disc on. The needle skids a little, complaining at the scratches on the surface.

Tommy Dorsey Boogie. The clear beat announces itself. Stacey finishes her drink, fixes another one, drinks half of it quickly and sets the glass down on top of the TV. She looks at her gold sandals, her green-velvet thighs. She puts her arms out, stretching them in front of her, her fingers moving slightly, feeling the music as though it were tangibly there to be touched in the air. Slowly, she begins to dance. Then faster and faster.

> Stacey Cameron in her yellow dress with pleats all around the full skirt. Knowing by instinct how to move, loving the boy's closeness, whoever he was. Stacey twirling out onto the floor, flung by the hand that would catch her when she came jazzily flying back. *Tommy Dorsey Boogie.* Stacey spinning like light, whirling laughter across a polished floor. Every muscle knowing what to do by itself. Every bone knowing. Dance hope, girl, dance hurt. Dance the fucking you've never yet done.

—— Once it seemed almost violent, this music. Now it seems incredibly gentle. Sentimental, self-indulgent? Yeh, probably. But I love it. It's *my* beat. I can still do it. I can still move without knowing where, beforehand. Yes. Yes. Yes. Like this. Like this. I can. My hips may not be so hot but my ankles are pretty good, and my legs. Damn good in fact. My feet still know what to do without being told. I love to dance. I love it. I love it. It can't be over. I can still do it. I don't do it badly. See? Like this. Like this.

—— I love it. The hell with what the kids say. In fifteen years their music will be just as corny. Naturally they don't know that. I love this music. It's mine. Buzz off, you little buggers, you don't understand. No—I didn't mean that. I meant it. I was myself before any of you were born. (Don't listen in, God—this is none of your business.)

> *The music crests, subsides, crests again, blue-green sound, saltwater with the incoming tide, the blues of the night freight trains across snow deserts, the green beckoning voices, the men still unheld and the children yet unborn, the voices cautioning no caution no caution only dance what happens to come along until*

The record player switches off.

—— Was I hearing what was there, or what? How many times have I played it? God it's three thirty in the afternoon and I'm stoned. The kids will be home in one hour. Okay, pick up the pieces. Why did I do it? Yours not to reason why, Stacey baby, yours but to go and make nineteen cups of Nescafé before the kids get home. Quickly. Jen? Lord, she must've been awake for hours. Oh Stacey.

The black coffee washes around in her stomach like a tidal wave. She gets Jen up, murmuring carefully, and then goes to her own bedroom and Mac's and changes into her blue silk suit. She puts on a pair of medium-heel navy-blue shoes. She holds the gold sandals for a moment in her hands, then delves into the clothes cupboard and buries them under a pile of tennis shoes and snow boots. She brushes her hair, back-combing it slightly, then slicking it down into neatness and spraying it so it will hold. She applies lipstick and powder. She examines herself in the full-length mirror.

—— Am I okay? No lurching hemlines, protruding slip straps, off-base lipstick or any other sign of disrepair? I think I'm okay, but how's my appraisal power? Shaken, no doubt. Remorse—overdose of same. I'm not fit to be in charge of kids, that's the plain truth. God, accept my apologies herewith. He won't. Would you, in His place? No. Come on, be practical. Dinner. Mac won't be here. Dinner downtown for him, the lucky bastard. When did I last have dinner downtown? Precious lot he cares. Goddam him, some night when he comes bowling in at ten o'clock expecting me to have kept dinner hot in the oven since six, I'm gonna say *Now listen here, sweetheart, want me to tell you something? There isn't any bloody dinner and if you want any, why don't you just go along and scramble yourself an ostrich egg? Why don't you just do that little thing?* Oh Stacey, this is madness. Get a grip on yourself. Yeh, well let's see now—pork chops, cauliflower with cheese sauce, mashed potatoes, and what for dessert? It'll have to be ice cream. Got half a carton in the freezer.

123

Maybe I should make apple Betty. What a slut I am, not a cooked dessert for those kids. No, I can't. I'm incapable of peeling an apple. Sometimes I want to say—*Listen, if all of you never had another dessert for the rest of your lives, would that kill you?* Answering chorus of *It sure would,* spoken with conviction. Come on, bitch. Another cup of coffee.

Stacey prepares dinner primly and with caution. When the children arrive home, she talks as little as possible. The meal is finally over and the noise begins to subside. The mist is beginning to clear. Stacey washes the dishes and then bathes Jen, reads two Little Golden Books to her, and puts her to bed. After some considerable time, Duncan and Ian are also in bed. Only Katie remains. Katie has finished her homework and is down in the TV room. Stacey goes down but does not go in. She stands near the doorway, looking, unnoticed.

Katie has put on one of her own records. Something with a strong and simple beat, slow, almost languid, and yet with an excitement underneath, the lyrics deliberately ambiguous.

Katie is dancing. In a green dress Katie MacAindra simple and intricate as grass is dancing by herself. Her auburn hair, long and straight, touches her shoulders and sways a little when she moves. She wears no make-up. Her bones and flesh are thin, plain-moving, unfrenetic, knowing their idiom.

> Stacey MacAindra, thirty-nine, hips ass and face heavier than once, shamrock velvet pants, petunia-purple blouse, cheap gilt sandals high-heeled, prancing squirming jiggling

Stacey turns and goes very quietly up the basement steps and into the living room.

—— You won't be dancing alone for long, Katie. It's all going for you. I'm glad. Don't you think I'm glad? Don't you think I know how beautiful you are? Oh Katie love. I'm glad. I swear it. Strike me dead, God, if I don't mean it.

At ten thirty, Katie is in bed at last. Stacey is now off duty. Mac is at a conference and will probably not be home until mid-

night. Stacey has a scalding bath, puts on a nightgown and housecoat, and goes downstairs again.

— What now? I should go to bed. Okay, Stacey, not more
than one gin, eh? Well, all right, if it's going to be only one, let's
make it good and strong. Too much has disappeared from this
bottle. I'll go to the Liquor Commission tomorrow and get another bottle and pour half of it into this one. So Mac won't think
it's odd. The other half strictly to be stashed away for emergencies.
Yeh, I can see it all now. Every other minute is an emergency.
Does he know? He must. Mac—listen. Just listen. I have something to tell you. No. It's not up to him. It's up to me. Any normal
person can cope okay, calmly, soberly. And if you can't, kid, then
there's something wrong with you. No there isn't. Everything is
okay. Everything is *all right,* see? Only I'm tired tonight and a
little tense. Why not try Ovaltine, then? Oh get lost, you.

Stacey takes her drink into the living room and sits on
the chesterfield with the lights off, looking out the window at
the city which is both close and far away.

> Stacey, naked with Mac three quarters of a
> year before Katherine Elizabeth was born.
> The cottage at the lake where they'd gone
> for the one week holiday they couldn't afford.
> The pine and spruce harps in the black
> ground outside, in the dark wind from the
> lake that never penetrated the narrow-win-
> dowed cabin. Their skins slippery with sweat
> together, slithering as though with some fine
> and pleasurable oil. Stacey knowing his mo-
> ment and her own as both separate and un-
> separable. Oh my love now

Going into the kitchen, Stacey swings the gin bottle out
from the lower cupboard and fills a jug with water from the tap.

— No use wasting tonic water. Of course this will taste
like essence of pine needles with a dash of kerosene, but then
my mother always used to speak very scornful-like of ladies whose

taste was all in their mouths. Couldn't say that about me. Nope. My taste isn't anywhere. Between my legs, maybe. Okay, doll, that's enough. So who wants to know?

Stacey returns to the living room and curls up on the chesterfield once more, her slippered feet underneath her. The big sliding door leads out into the hall and thence up the iron-banistered staircase to the bedrooms. Stacey leans around in the semidarkness to check. The door is closed. Should she put on the radio? She decides against it. If she uses her own voice, she can select the music.

> There's a gold mine in the sky
>   Faraway—
> We will go there, you and I,
>   Some sweet day,
> And we'll say hello to friends who said goodbye,
> When we find that long lost gold mine in the sky.
>   Faraway, faraw-a-ay—

—— Oh boy. Jen comes by her operatic tendencies naturally. Where did that song come from? Old man Invergordon used to sing it at local concerts in Manawaka when I was a little kid. Nobody knew how to tell him they'd rather he didn't. They weren't so bad, any of them, I now see. How I used to dislike them then, the Ladies' Aid and mother's bridge cronies and all of them, never seeing beyond their own spectacles and what will the neighbors think what will they say? But who here or anywhere, now, would put up with old Invergordon? *Drop dead,* that's what he'd get here and now. He stank all right but he had a lovely baritone. Only difference between Invergordon and Niall Cameron was that my dad was a private drunk and the old guy was a public one. It isn't the fact that there's no gold mine in the sky which bothers me. I mean who wants to say hello to people who are dead even if you happen to be dead yourself? It's the ones who say good-bye before they're dead who bug me. I start thinking—it's Mac. Then I think—hell, no, it's not Mac it's me and then I don't know.

Twelve thirty. Stacey takes the empty bottle into the kitchen and places it behind three bottles of wine and a bottle of vinegar. She takes the frying pan down from its hook and puts it on the stove. She takes the bacon out of the refrigerator and puts two slices in the pan. Cheese. Bread. The fried sandwich is made. She looks at it seriously, considering it. It does not look edible.

—— Must eat something absorbtive. Can't. Repulsive. Mac, talk to me. Mac? Katie? Ian? Duncan? Where are you or is it just me I don't know what the hell I'm talking about well what you should be talking about kid is coffee

Stacey makes herself a cup of instant coffee. She looks again at the congealing sandwich in the frying pan and decides to heat it up. She switches on an element but does not put the frying pan on until the circular coil is red. She reaches for the frying pan, stumbles, puts out a hand to balance herself. The hand lands on the edge of the electrical scarlet circle.

—— It hurts it hurts it hurts what is it

She has without knowing it pulled her hand away. She regards it with curiosity. Two red crescent lines have appeared on the skin of her left palm.

—— My brand of stigmata. My western brand. The Double Crescent. It hurts hurts

She takes the frying pan and throws its sandwich into the garbage pail. She switches off the stove, reaches into the cupboard for baking soda, mixes some with water and applies it to her hand. She then applies a light gauze bandage, one which can be removed easily tomorrow morning without anyone noticing. She walks upstairs and gets into bed. Blackness scurries around her in the room but within her head the neon is white and cold like the stars in the prairie winters.

—— How to explain this? Anybody can explain anything, if they put their mind to it. It's not difficult. I put the kettle on, and accidentally put my hand over the boiling spout. Mac— I'm scared. Help me. But it goes a long way back. Where to begin? What can I possibly say to you that you will take seriously? What would it need, with you, what possible cataclysm, for you to say anything of yourself to me? What should I do? I'm not sure I really want to go on living at all. I can't cope. I do cope. Not well, though. Not with anyone. Jesus I get tired sometimes. Self-pity. Yeh, I guess. But sometimes I want to abdicate, only that. Quit. Can't. What would it be like for one of the kids to come into the bedroom, say, one evening when Mac isn't home yet, any one of them, maybe waking up in the night and calling and me not an- swering, and coming in here and finding I'd gone away from them for good, overdose? Maybe they'd think it was their fault. I couldn't come back mysteriously and say *Listen, it wasn't any- thing to do with you, or not in the way you think, and I love you, see?* Even if I left one of those I'm-getting-off-the-world letters, saying *I care about you,* they wouldn't believe it. And they'd be right. Goddam you, God. I'm stuck with it. But I'm a mess and I'm scared. What if I had burned myself when one of the kids saw? Mac?

Stacey goes into half sleep, where the sounds of occasional cars and the light wind and the way-off ships can be heard but only in a way which needs no response.

Mac comes in at one o'clock.

It's okay, Mac. You can turn on the light.

Hi, I thought you'd be asleep.

Well, I was, sort of. How was it?

Okay.

Mac?

Mm?

I want to tell

Christ, am I ever beat. What?

Oh—nothing

You okay, Stacey?
Yeh, I'm okay
Kids all right?
Yeh, they're all right
Well, good night then.
Good night Mac

Stacey, neatly and matronly dressed, her gloves in hand, adjusts the despised veil on her white straw hat, pulling it down over her forehead and eyebrows as though she intends it to act as a disguise. She hesitates in the doorway of the large chair-filled hall, but the pressure of other people carries her forward and in. She chooses an aisle seat quickly, keeping her head down until she is sitting. But the precaution has been unnecessary. There are too many people around. Mac couldn't possible have noticed her. When she cranes her neck and peers over head tops, she cannot even see him. The platform at the front is decorated with gilded wicker baskets full of white roses. In between the baskets are tall white shields, each bearing one golden letter to form a word.

RICHALIFE

At the back of the platform there is a white velvet curtain, descending from the ceiling. A small gilt structure, a cross between a podium and a pulpit, stands in the middle of the stage, with microphone attachments.

Then Stacey spots Mac's auburn brush-cut. He is sitting in the third row from the front, with all the other salesmen. Stacey twists and squints, trying to see around the magnolia-covered hat of the woman directly in front of her. Finally she manages to focus on Mac. His tallness is hunched a little, and while she watches, he puts up a hand and runs it over his hair. Stacey turns away, unable to look.

—— When he does that, is it like me looking in the mirror to make sure I'm really there? What's he thinking? It may not be any of my business, but I'd like to know anyway. What if he starts coughing? Everyone will look at him. Maybe it would embarrass me more than it would him. Would he be livid if he knew I'd come? Well, come on, fellows, what are we waiting for? Let's get the show on the road, eh?

The audience is mainly middle-aged, half men and half women. They sit quietly, for the most part, not looking at one another.

— Maybe they'd all like to be incognito. I know damn well I would. I'd like to have a woolly muffler or a long trailing length of chiffon wrapped around my pan. If somebody like Bertha Garvey should chance to stroll in, I would crawl under the seat, so help me. Here we are—action at last.

The white velvet curtains part, revealing another section of stage on which six girls are gathered around a microphone. Their costumes are modest to a degree, long loose-fitting white robes, toga-like, with the Greek key design slanting diagonally across each bosom. The girls' hair ranges from white-blond to honey, all long and straight. The hall grows still, the whispers die, the ticking coughs are subdued, the feet compose themselves. When the audience is ready, the girls begin to sing, not loudly or jazzily, but in clear treble voices like a clutch of meadow larks.

> Richness is a quality of living,
> Richness quells the trouble and the strife,
> Richness is the being and the giving,
> Anyone can reach a Richalife.

Stacey surreptitiously slips out of her purse one of the tranquilizers Doctor Spender has given her for her pulsing-head condition, conceals it in her handkerchief and slips it into her mouth under the pretext of blowing her nose.

— Lucky for me I always could swallow pills without water. Well, well. Listen to that. They sure aren't what I would

130

have expected. I thought it would be all zing-twanging and go-go-go. But unless you go the the hangouts of the young, I guess you only find that kind of noisy stuff in churches now. Those little birds aren't even refined. They're refccned. Has Mac got his eye on them? Well, naturally, what do you expect, Stacey? All the same. You bastard, Clifford MacAindra, they're young enough to be your daughters.

The white curtain closes and the girls disappear. The audience sits uncertainly, not knowing whether applause is expected or not. Sporadic and nervous clapping breaks out like acne in isolated and obvious areas, then quickly fades.

Thor walks onto the platform alone and takes his place behind the gilt stand. A sprinkling of female exclamations can be heard, and he smiles a trifle, acknowledging them. This evening he is approximately seven feet tall. His newly laundered mane is accentuated by the spotlight which now comes to rest just above his head. He has abandoned his midnight blue in favor of a suit of silver, some luminous material that has the look of frost sheening on windows and pattering into faint ferns or snow flowers transferred from the farthest reaches of the polestar. But when he talks, his voice is not distant or unapproachable. The reverse. He talks with thc people, not at them. His voice is warm, friendly, sincere.

You heard the girls, here, singing about richness. Well, richness is something we all hear a lot about these days, don't we? Yes, we surely do, and sometimes we begin to wonder what it means, don't we? Well, sure do all know it means money in the bank. I guess there isn't one of us who doesn't know that. But that's not *all* it means. No, that definitely is not all it means, friends. It means response, happiness, a healthy mind in a healthy body. Wouldn't you agree? You, sir, right there, would you agree? You would? Well, you're right. Yes, richness means a healthy mind in a healthy body. But just how do we go about getting this? That's what I used to ask myself. That was in the old B.R. days —before Richalife. I'm not asking you to believe a whole lot of printed data. I only want to tell you what happened to me personally. I'm not trying to sell you anything, either. Believe me, the kind of person who feels he's being pressured into anything —we don't want him. We only want people who can believe that the human body and the human spirit can be changed, changed beyond belief, in the short space of one month. Amazing? Certainly it's amazing. But it can happen. I know. Because it happened to me. You know something? Once upon a time I could barely face the morning without three cups of coffee and as many cigarettes. Then I started reaching for a Richalife instead. And that is just what I got—A RICHER LIFE. Take my memory, for instance. My memory potential was hardly being tapped at all, before. Alertness-wise, the change A.R.—After Richalife—was really gratifying. I always had a good memory, mind you. Good, but not what you would call really excellent. Now I think I can honestly and truthfully say it's reached the excellent mark. I don't claim that the depth changes happened overnight. No, I wouldn't claim that. Even Richalife can't reach the deep cells of the mind instantly. When I began, just over a year ago, it took—oh, I should say about three or four weeks, approximately, before the depth changes were really well established. These very slight depression feelings I used to get—they were alleviated almost right straight off, definitely alleviated, but it must have been more or less a month before they totally disappeared. Yes, totally disappeared. Another thing, now

Stacey sits sifting her memory. Then it comes back.

Thor's apartment. Stacey with a thimbleful of sherry, feeling like a savage drinker, her feet slithering silkily on the skins of stillborn monkeys. *They were alleviated almost right straight off*

—— Well, I'm buggered. Does he just press his navel and the record switches on? No. Worse. It's the Martians. Must be.

We will begin with one creature, Zuq tells the assembled Council of Spirit Sires. He must of course look as nearly human

as possible. He must have a bloodlike substance (red, mind, not the proper polka-dotted purple to which we are accustomed), a substance which will flow if he is accidentally cut. The control shaft, in order to escape possible detection in case of severe and unpredictable wounding, must be buried deeply in what would be his left lung if he were an earthman. The first transmitted messages from his—as it were—mouth will be of a simple nature. We will then—I am speaking out of my many years of research and accumulated knowledge—we will then put into effect what I term the lemming syndrome.

Stacey squirms on her chair. The hall is growing sultry. She discovers to her surprise that Thor has stopped talking and is being loudly applauded. The white velvet curtains are sneaking apart, and the girls, with their arms lightly but not pervertedly around each other's shoulders, begin a soft humming which grows into a croon.

> *Peace of mind*
> *Can be combined*
> *With vigor*
>
> *Peace of mind*
> *Can be combined*
> *With fun*

Beside Stacey, an old man with a red neck like a retired prairie farmer looks hopefully and steadfastly ahead. His expression changes from concealed to open yearning, the yearning for rain in draught. Stacey glances quickly to the stage and sees the reason. The choir has vanished again, and now there is only one girl, a different one, on the stage with Thor. Her white dress is street-length but it bears the same Greek key design along the straight neckline. Her skin is extremely pale, and her features are delicate, severe, withdrawn, a girl from a medieval tomb carving. It is the girl Mac was talking to, or who was talking so earnestly to Mac, the night of the party. Thor takes her by the hand and leads her over to the microphone.

Now, ladies and gentlemen, it gives me real pleasure to introduce this charming young lady to you. Miss Delores Appleton.

He leaves her. The girl stands there, staring out at the upturned faces. Her hand goes up and she touches her visible collarbone. Then quickly she pulls the hand away and it returns limply to her side. A moment of silence. The audience is frightened, frightened for her that she may not be able to speak a word. She looks towards Thor, and he nods. Her face slowly unfreezes. She grasps the mike and begins to talk in a high bell-voice, rapid, tinkling.

Well, really, all I want to tell you is just about my own personal experience. I mean, that's all we can say for sure, isn't it, our own personal experience. I grew up in a small town, like, and when I came to the city I was sort of nervous. I mean I had never lived in the city before and I didn't know what might. I mean you never know who you might and what they might. And then it got so I couldn't sleep very well nights and at the office they started saying why did I look so tired out but it was only because I wasn't sleeping that well and so on. Well things sort of went from bad to worse, like, and then I heard about Mr. Thorlakson and Richalife and I thought why not so I tried it and it worked. I mean, my anxieties and this nervousness I had, well they just were so much alleviated and I went to tell Mr. Thorlakson about it and now I am working in his office and well that's about all I guess

Her voice ends in a small chime of laughter. The audience claps mightily. The girl walks offstage swiftly.

— Supposing that had been Katie? It doesn't bear thinking about. Who is she? What could *her* parents have been like? She can't be more than eighteen or twenty. Somebody ought to do something, but then again, she claims she's fine. Everything is all right for her now.

Stacey looks to see where the girl has gone. For a moment she cannot see, and then she finds the pallid hair and the Greek keys. The girl is sitting beside Mac, and he has one arm around her, not casually but tightly, like a wall against the world.

Dear Mother—Well here it is June and less than a month till summer holidays—horrors! Although I guess Rachel will be glad. Her free season starts when mine finishes. But I have to admit the kids are pretty good generally these days—the boys already making plans for putting up tent in back yard and sleeping there— mighty woodsmen and all that—perfectly safe, Mother, so don't panic—

Stacey puts down her pen and gazes at what she has written.

—— I wonder what would happen if just for once I put down what was really happening? Dear Mother—There must be some way of talking to kids but I don't seem usually to find it. Yeh, sometimes, and then I say *There there*, and they're partially restored, whatever was wrong. But Duncan said *I don't do anything right, Mum*, meaning it, and Mac was helping Ian with his arithmetic a day or so ago and bawled him out for carelessness but Ian is the opposite of careless maybe he didn't understand what he was supposed to be doing but then Ian all inclenched came out to the kitchen and said *Dad never makes mistakes*, believing it. I don't know what to do. I worry. I get afraid. I drink too much. I get unreasonably angry. The valleys under my eyes look like permanent blue-black ink even though I get enough sleep, and my hips are nobody's business. I think Mac has fallen for that girl and who could blame him I guess and I really think I wouldn't be so blamed mad about it if I could go and do the same thing myself with some guy but how and anyway I think this is a despicable reaction. After that evening at the rally I phoned the hairdresser and made an appointment to have my hair dyed. Bleached and then dyed fair, not ash blond, just fair. And when I got there, she said *You sure you really want to, Mrs. MacAindra?* And I looked in the damn mirror and said *Uh—well, I guess maybe not.* Not even the strength of my neuroses, if you would believe it. Please write immediately and let me know what was actually in your mind all those years because I haven't a clue and it's only now that this bothers me, now that I'm not seen either. Love, Stacey. P.S. Did you ever dance? No, that wouldn't be feasible, that kind of letter. She'd say to Rachel, *I can't think what Stacey can possibly mean.* She'd be upset for days.

Stacey picks up her pen again.

Oh, nearly forgot. Jen sings now. At least a step towards speech. Mac loves his new job and is doing awfully well. He's given me the old Chev. Everything is fine. Hope you are okay. Love, Stacey.

She puts the page in an envelope, addresses and stamps it, and goes out to the letter box at the corner. Julian and Bertha Garvey have driven out for the day to visit Julian's sister and have taken Jen along, ostensibly for the ride but actually because conversation is difficult there and Jen provides some possibility of amused distraction. Stacey is alone and it feels peculiar to her. She is wearing black slacks, a yellow sweater and sandals, and as she reaches the end of Bluejay Crescent, she looks back at it and feels disconnected, younger, separate.

— Hey, it's a nice feeling. Yet I feel I oughtn't to feel glad. When Jen goes to school, though, I could take a job. I used to be quite good. I guess my shorthand is rusty, but I could brush it up.

The chief architect's office is large but not at all flashy. No plastic plants or phony veneer for him. Andrew Delver, of Delver & Plumb, has designed every piece of furniture here, and it is all both functional and beautiful, sleek cool lines. She answers the bell's summons. God, Stacey, what a mess we're in with these contracts. Think you can make sense of my notes and get me four copies by lunchtime? Of course, Mr. Delver. Andrew, Andrew, for God's sake woman—it's about time you called me that—you're a love—I don't know what I'd do without you to cope

The truck hoots and draws up to the curb beside Stacey. She looks up and sees the grinning black-haired driver leaning out of the window. Buckle Fennick.

Hi Stacey

Hi

Where you going?

Just to the letterbox.

Hop in. I'll give you a lift.

It's not that far.

Where's Jen?

Bertha's got her this afternoon.

Hey, got a holiday? Climb in. I gotta take a few things out to Coquitlam. Coming right back. C'mon along, why doncha?

Stacey looks back at Bluejay Crescent, seeing it recede. Then, without thinking or knowing she is going to do it, she climbs into the truck beside Buckle.

Within seconds, it seems to her, they are in a mainstream of traffic and Buckle is manipulating the big truck in and out, weaving in a fast and inexorable pattern of sound and movement, intimidating the vulnerable cars, flying and swinging along the highway.

Haven't seen you for awhile, Buckle.

Naw. Want to know why?

Why?

Buckle increases speed. The highway shivers past, honking, obstacle-laden. Buckle crouches over the wheel, like a jockey.

Well, I thought Mac was kinda busy

He's always glad to see you. You know that.

Yeh?

What's the matter, Buckle?

Mac and me have known each other a long time.

I know.

Since the war.

Yes.

137

We went all through Italy together.

My God, Buckle, I know that.

—— Does that mean Mac's got to live with you on his door-step for the rest of his life? No, that's mean. Mac wouldn't say that. How many friends has Buckle got? One, maybe. How do I know?

Yeh, well I'm coming from Ace this day, see, on my way out and up north, and I happen to pass near where Mac's office is, see, and he's walking along the street with this Thor guy, so naturally I give him the old sign on the horn—beep beep beep BLAT, V for Victory. He looks up all right. That's all. No *Hi* or wave, nothing like that. He doesn't know me.

Buckle, he didn't mean

Shit, Stacey

Maybe he didn't see

He saw.

Well, I'm sorry. What can I say? Don't take it so hard. His mind was likely on the job. It's never on anything else now. He works all the time, like something was after him.

Stacey hears the vehemence in someone's voice that is coming from her mouth.

—— Traitor. How can you speak about Mac to anyone else? It's no one else's business. Not even Buckle's. Especially not Buckle's. Shut up shut up shut up. If you don't, it'll all come out and then

The house is burning. Everything and everyone in it. Nothing can put out the flames. The house wasn't fire-resistant. One match was all it took.

Buckle has momentarily taken his eyes off the road and Stacey sees him sizing her up.

Buckle, for God's sake the road

He laughs and looks again at the wheeling metallic ballet ahead.

Don't worry. I know what I'm doing.

So you say. I've never driven with you before, Buckle, you know that?

You should come on a long haul sometime just for the hell of it.

Yeh, I can see it all now.

The northern highway, uncrowded. Spruce and fir spearing upwards, and the high arched blue silences of the sky. When the truck stops, there are only small earth-close sounds—a few lethargic flies, the grass voices. Sun saturates and warms the moss and fallen bronze pine needles. He is poised above her—hard, ready, taut—and she can hardly wait for him to

— I must be berserk. I don't even like him.

Don't worry, Stacey. I wouldn't play chicken if you were along.

Play chicken? What? Oh yeh. You still do that?

It passes the time.

It'll pass it permanently one of these days.

I've never yet met a guy who didn't give way.

You never give way?

I don't have to. I know the other guy is going to.

That's crazy. You can't know.

Sure I know. I'm prepared to gamble that fraction of a second longer than he is.

You know all the truckers on the road, then? You know them all well enough to be able to tell?

I don't have to know them all. It's something I learned a long time ago.

You can have it.

It's better on the night hauls because then you've only got the other guy's lights to go by. Take a couple of weeks ago. I'm in the Cariboo, few miles past Hundred-Mile House, and it's about three in the morning and I'm getting kinda bored when I see these lights coming. From the spread of the lights it looks like a diesel job, about the same weight as mine and she'll do about the same speed. So I step on the gas just a little and pull out slightly. He does the same. He wants to play. I think it's probably Charlie Norton, Excello Cartage guy, does this run back on a Tuesday and never drives daytime. So I think, okay Charlie boy, we'll see. He's told guys in all the truckers' cafés from here to Fort St. John that he's going to take it away from me, see? Because they all know no one's ever beat me. So we're roaring along and he doesn't swerve and I'm starting to sweat a little but then I think Charlie Norton's the kind of guy who'll say he's going to do a thing before he's done it and that is a dead give-away. So I keep on, see? Well, when we're practically close enough for both of us to see the sweat on each other's foreheads, suddenly he gives a sharp right to the wheel and misses me by no more than a cunt-span if you don't mind the expression. He sort of swivels to a stop, and I pull up too. He gets out and whaddya know? It's not Charlie Norton at all. It's some young guy I've never seen before, and he's nearly drowning in his own sweat. We have a cigarette together, and he's leaning against the front tires all the time, holding his own elbow so I won't see his ciga-rette hand trembling away there.

You of course were perfectly calm.

I wouldn't say that but at least I wasn't shaking like a raped virgin. You can see what I mean about not having to know the guys. I'm okay while my luck's in and it's in because of what I know, see?

—— Here we go again.

No I don't see

Well it's simple but if you don't see it you don't see it. Here we are, kid.

Buckle pulls in and halts beside a warehouse. Men who have been expecting this arrival now rush out, opening the back doors of the truck, beginning to unload. One of the men, sloping past, looks up at Stacey and grins knifedly.

—— My God. It isn't possible. He looked at me like I'm a whore or something. And I can't say to him, *Listen bud I'm a respectable married woman named thus.* Because here I'm not.

They don't know what I am. They only see a woman in slacks and sweater, in the cab of Buckle's truck. My, my. Doesn't that seem strange. Do I mind? Am I offended? Hell, no. I'm delighted.

Buckle climbs back into the truck, waves to cohorts, starts up and they are off, back into the city.

How you doing?

Fine. Buckle, I think I should get home quite soon. I mean, if Bertha and Julian get back with Jen and I'm not there

Relax.

Yeh, well

Relax. How many days off do you get, Stacey? C'mon to my place. We'll have a beer, and you'll be home in lots of time to

I can't.

Why not?

Well, I don't think there's time

There's time.

Well

It's settled, then. I never wanted to ask you and Mac to my place after Julie took off.

Why not?

Well, it's not the same, like, is it?

Don't you have to take the truck back to Ace?

It can wait. They won't say anything. If they do, let them. They don't want to lose me.

Grenoble Street, finally, not far from the docks, and Buckle draws into an alley to park. He climbs out, goes around to the other side, and hands Stacey down. The alley is wet with leftover rain, and littered with chocolate bar wrappers, crumpled newspapers, a few purple paper squares from the discarded paraphernalia of quick love, an eggshell or two dropped from emptied garbage tins and resting fragile on the edge of mud ponds, a grapefruit husk from the beginning of someone's new day.

Okay, Stacey?

Yes.

The apartment is over a store which sells cut-price children's clothes. Honest Ernie's. The plastic raincoats glisten yellowly from the window, and the rows of rubber boots, black white or red, diminish from teen down to doll boots for creatures knee high to a grasshopper, who will plod purposefully through all the puddles of spring. Stacey looks away, reproached.

The stairs are covered with brown linoleum. On the second landing Buckle stops, takes out his key and opens the door. Stacey hesitates, smoothing her sweater down over her hips. Buckle takes her elbow gently, and they are inside.

The room is large. There is probably a bathroom and a bedroom or two elsewhere, but this room is for living and cooking. The window opens onto Grenoble Street, and the whine and wham of traffic curl upward and in. The floor is covered with the same brown linoleum as the stairs. A round oak table stands at one side of the room, covered in a white plastic lace-patterned cloth unrecently wiped over and yellow-flecked with egg yolk from the frying pans of the past. The gas stove stands in a corner, beside a sink which has a calico frill around its lower portions to hide the pipes. A chesterfield, once upholstered in grey, now worn to its cloth bone, stands gawkily in the center of the room. None of this creates more than a momentary flicker on Stacey's eye camera. All she is looking at is the big armchair positioned near the window.

Arbuckle—that you?

Yeh. Who else?

The woman is gigantic, outspread like rising dough gone amok, swelling and undulating over the stiff upholstery of the chair, gaping body covered with tiny-flower-printed dress huge and shroud-shaped, vastly numerous chins trembling eel-like separate but involved, eyes closed, and at the end of the Kodiak arms, contrasting hands neatly made, fine-fingered, encrusted with silver-and-gold-colored rings which might almost have been costly, from the way the hands flairfully wear them.

Beside her, on a low table within easy reach, is a brown teapot and a pink-pearl opalescent glass mug. The hand reaches out.

Stacey makes as if to step forward. Buckle stops her, holding her shoulders.

You don't have to. She doesn't know you're here.

What?

She's blind.

Then Stacey sees that it is true, for the hand searches for the teapot's handle, finds it, feels skillfully for the mug, and pours, the other hand slipped inside the rim of the mug to judge the rising height of the liquid. Stacey looks at Buckle. He is standing in front of her, her hands on his narrow hard-boned hips, and he is laughing but without sound. His voice is low, but not all that low.

She wasn't always blind. Another broad threw acid at her once. No doubt she deserved it, for whatever it was she did. After that she couldn't work her beat any more, but she was getting beyond it anyhow. It was only then that she put on all the tonnage, though. Don't worry, Stacey. She isn't listening. Did you think it was tea in the pot?

What? I don't know what you

It's port, the cheapest money can buy. She likes it to be in a teapot, that's all. She thinks it looks more respectable. Who sees it, but never mind. You gotta be respectable, maybe, if you're a retired

Buckle. No.

You don't want me to say it? Okay. I won't. Well, now you know why I never asked you here. She moved in the minute Julie left. Hey, I was forgetting. That beer. There's lots in the fridge. We got a fridge, in case you didn't notice. Then I think maybe we're gonna

I can't

Buckle opens two bottles of beer and hands Stacey one. She does not want it, and puts it aside on the table. Buckle's straight black hair falls over his eyes and he brushes it back. His face is brown, sharp, smiling.

You wouldn't have come here if you couldn't. So don't give me that line, eh?

He is wearing his usual jeans which proclaim his sex. His shirt is a black sports shirt, decorated with artificial gold threads, open at the neck. Stacey smells him, the clean sweat smell, the dust, the oil, the smell of man-flesh. She holds herself in hiatus, waiting. Waiting for the clue, the instructions which she will follow. She can feel his shoulder bones under her fingers although she has not touched him. She can almost feel his sex in her. In the chair beside the window, the undersea giant woman raises the pearl-pink heavy cup to her mouth and drinks un-speaking, listening or not listening.

Can she?

No. I told you. It's afternoon. She's away to hell and gone. So?

Stacey moves slowly towards him, not with the slowness of caution but the opposite. Then, as she is about to place her hands on him, his acute rasping voice.

Okay   that's it   don't touch me

What he is doing now concerns only himself, his sex open and erect in his hands. But although he retreats from her pres-ence, he watches her, needing to see some image in eyes, some witness to the agony of his pleasure.

You won't get it   Julie didn't like it when I did it this way   all she ever wanted was to take it   you're not getting it see

Stacey looks at him only for an instant. Then fear like tides. She turns for the door and finds beside her on the floor two silver coins, thrown.

There's your bus fare, lady.

She realizes that she has no money on her. She reaches down to the floor and picks up the silver. Then she runs. Down the stairs, onto the inhabited street, to the bus stop.

Saturday, and Mac arrives home midafternoon. Stacey is ironing a dress for Katie to wear to the school dance this evening.

You're home early.

Yeh. Where are the kids, Stacey?

Down looking at TV. Why?

Come on into the study for a minute, will you?

What's up?

Just come.

Okay. Wait till I unplug my iron.

She follows him into the study. Mac lights a cigarette and stands looking out the window.

Close the door, Stacey, will you, please?

Hey, what is it? Okay. There.

Mac turns to face her, and she sees in his eyes some nearly unbearable pain. His voice is steady, deliberately contained, exaggeratedly calm.

Buckle phoned me.

The nerves at the base of Stacey's stomach begin crawling.

Oh?

Yes. He told me.

He told you—what?

Everything. How you wouldn't take no for an answer. How he finally took you to bed.

He told you *that?*

Yes. Well? What've you got to say?

Fury floods in adrenalin bursts through Stacey's veins. She hears her voice, raucous.

What d'you *mean,* what have I got to say? Who're you? God? You don't own me. You believed Buckle, didn't you? It's a lie   I never did any such thing

Then, at last, she hears the outraged virtue in her own voice.

—— Oh God. No, I didn't do any such thing. But I would've, if Buckle had. No, damn it, I wouldn't. I wouldn't. I don't even

145

like Buckle. Even at that moment I didn't like him. I would've stopped. I would've found I couldn't go through with it. Wouldn't I? I don't know. I think I would have gone to bed with him. Even there. With her there. How could I? Buckle was smart—he found a two-edged sword.

Why would Buckle lie about a thing like that, for Christ's sake, Stacey?

If you don't know, then there's no use me telling you. But you'd take the word of a friend against mine, wouldn't you?

He's no friend of mine, not any more. Stacey—why? Why would you? Was it true?

No.

You went to his place, though, didn't you?

Yes. I went. I don't know why. I can't explain. You wouldn't believe me. But I went. All right, I went. But that's all. I never   I never   I never

For God's sake keep your voice down. No need to scream

I'm not screaming

You are. Now *cut it out,* see?

All right   I won't say a word   what's the use

Oh Stacey for God's sake don't go on like that. Quit crying. Okay. Okay. I believe you.

Do you?

Mac puts out his cigarette and lights another. His hands are not steady and his face is misshapen with a private grief.

I don't know what the hell to believe. I just don't see why you went to Buckle's place at all, that's all. It doesn't make sense. I would've thought I could've trusted both of you.

It would be the absolute end of the world even if it had happened?

Mac puts one hand on her shoulder and tightens it around the bone.

I won't have anybody else touching you   see

Stacey yanks away and looks at him, unbelieving.

—— He's really hurt. And I'd like to comfort him but how

146

can I—it's I who've caused it. And yet I hate him for feeling that way about me. I might as well be a car or a toothbrush. Damn him. Damn Buckle. Damn both of them. I want to go away by myself. Right away. Far.

What about the girl, Mac? Thor's secretary. That's different, I suppose. It's okay for you to touch her.

Pain changes to anger in Mac's eyes.

Yes, it *is* different, if you really want to know. It's not what you're obviously thinking.

I bet   I just bet

—— We go on this way and the needle jabs become razor strokes and the razors become hunting knives and the knives become swords and how do we stop?

Leave her out of it, Stacey. Just leave her out of it. You don't know a damn thing about it, so shut up about it, eh?

I will shut up. I'll just do that little thing. Don't worry I won't say a single word about anything from now on

For God's sake, Stacey, quit acting like a child.

I'm acting like a child? What about you? I suppose if a chance acquaintance told you I'd robbed a bank you'd believe that too

I told you   I don't know what in hell to believe

Well that shows pretty clearly what you *do* believe

Now listen here Stacey

Sh—the kids are coming upstairs.

That night in bed he makes hate with her, his hands clenched around her collarbones and on her throat until she is able to bring herself to speak the release. *It doesn't hurt. You can't hurt me.* But afterwards neither of them can sleep. Finally, separately, they each rise and take a sleeping pill.

The following day Mac's father arrives for Sunday lunch. Matthew is as scrupulously dressed as always, his dark suit clean and well pressed, his fine faintly lemon-colored white hair brushed neatly. But there is one difference. He is carrying a black silver-topped cane.

Hello, Stacey, my dear. How are you?

Oh, just fine, thanks. How're you? The cane is new, isn't it?

Well, not exactly new. My congregation gave it to me some years ago, and do you know, at the time I thought I would never have occasion to use it. But I've found a little bit of difficulty in navigating the steps at the apartment just recently, so I dug this out. It's most useful. Where is Clifford?

Out cleaning the car.

Oh yes, of course. And the children—at Sunday school, I suppose?

Yes. The boys are, at least. Katie got home rather late from the school dance last night, so I thought just this once

—— Katie got home at two in the morning and I was frantic and couldn't sleep despite sleeping pill and she was furious at me for being frantic. What if she gets pregnant? What if some guy is really cruel to her, sometime, ditching her? What if she takes drugs? Whatifwhatifwhatif? Then I think I'm worrying needlessly, just like my mother did, and Katie isn't stupid and she was with a whole group of kids. And I think she's probably a damn sight more principled than I am at this point.

Matthew is looking at her gravely, nodding his head as though with understanding.

Oh, I know Katherine doesn't miss going many Sundays, Stacey. I quite realize that. But a few weeks of not attending can develop into a habit, you know. Not that I'm implying it will, in Katherine's case. I'm sure you and Clifford are much too conscientious parents to allow that.

—— I and Clifford as parents you do not have one single solitary notion about. If I ever said that, what would Matthew say? Would he have a stroke? Or would he just be quietly wounded? Nothing ever can come out. I sometimes see us like moles, living in our underground burrows, with eyes that can't stand any light. Once I thought it was only people like Matthew and my mother who had that kind of weak eyes. Now I know it's me, as much. C'mon, Stacey, say something nice, something agreeable.

How was church?

Just fine. The text for the sermon was from Psalms. One I always find particularly—well, you know—particularly fine.

What was it?

Matthew smiles and his voice is even, gentle, the almost toneless drone of one accustomed to reading from the pulpit.

Save me, O God, for the waters are come in unto my soul

Stacey looks at him, but can find no clues anywhere in his apparently untroubled face. She walks out of the kitchen and goes upstairs. She locks the bathroom door and when she has stopped crying she washes her face with cold water.

S I X

)ᴠₒᴠₒᴠₒᴠₒᴠₒᴠₒᴠ(

The kids are in bed, even Katie. Stacey sits on the chesterfield, turning the pages of a magazine. "Salad Days—Here's How to Be Slim in the Swim." Stacey looks frowningly at the mound of edible vegetation in the color photograph, and quickly flicks the page. "Icings with Spicings." Flick. "A Nervous Breakdown Taught Me Life's Meaning." Flick. Finally she hears Mac's key in the door. But he does not come into the living room. He goes straight down to the basement TV room. Stacey follows him. He has turned on the set and is already sitting in the armchair in front of it.

    Mac?

    I'm looking at the news, Stacey, if you don't mind.

EVER-OPEN EYE A SMILING MAN READS PRINTED DISASTERS IN A VANILLA-FLAVORED WHIPPED-CREAM VOICE

    I *do* mind, as it happens. What about listening to a piece of news from me? I didn't go to bed with Buckle.

So you say.

You still don't believe me, do you?

Mac's voice is cool and steady, appraising the situation like a member of the legal profession.

How can I be sure?

Stacey's anger bursts away like blood from under a torn scab.

All right, okay, you can't be sure. Even if it did happen, is that the only important thing? Is that all that interests you about me? Not me, or even going to bed with me, but just making sure that I don't ever glance in any other direction? Because if that's all

Mac has risen and taken hold of her wrist.

You did go to bed with him, didn't you?

Stacey pulls away.

No I didn't   but I damn well wish I had

Go ahead then

Mac—this is crazy. Look, can't we just talk without getting all steamed up?

I'm not steamed up in the very slightest. You're the one that's doing all the shouting.

If we could just talk about everything I mean like everything

Mac looks at her from incomprehensible eyes. His voice begins low, then suddenly rises, becomes almost not his voice at all.

Leave me alone, can't you? Can't you just *leave me alone?*

Stacey stares. Then she turns and runs up the stairs to the hall and up the next flight of stairs to their bedroom. Rapidly, she changes out of her dress and into her dark green slacks. She puts on a green high-neck sweater, grabs her purse and goes quietly down the stairs.

The Chev is parked in front of the house. Stacey turns the key and starts. Before she has driven a block she realizes she is driving too fast but she does not slow down. She looks in the rear-view mirror, half expecting to see Mac's car, but there is nothing behind her at all. She has no idea where she is going. She heads into the city along streets now inhabited only by the eternal flames of the neon forest fires and a few old men with nowhere to go or youngsters with nothing to do. Then through the half-wild park where the giant firs and cedars darken the dark sky, and across the great bridge that spans the harbor, past the shacks dwelt in by the remnants of coast Indians and the apartments and garden-surrounded houses of the well heeled. Along the highway that leads up the Sound, finally and at last away from habitation, where the road clings to the mountain and the evergreens rise tall and gaunt, and the saltwater laps blackly on the narrow shore, and the stars can be seen, away from human lights. Only now does Stacey slow down, not because the road is too winding and hazardous to drive swiftly, although it is, but because she can now bring herself to drive more carefully.

—— Does he hate me? If so, how long? Where did it start? Everything goes too far back to be traced. The roots vanish, because they don't end with Matthew, even if it were possible to trace them that far. They go back and back forever. Our father Adam. *Leave me alone.* And maybe Eve thought *Okay, Sahib, if that's the way you want it,* and it was after that she started getting crafty. How did Mac get to be that way? How did I get to be this way? I can't figure it. But God knows we don't ever make much of a stab at figuring it. What's the matter with us that we can't talk? How can anyone know unless people say? How come we feel it's indecent?

> Stacey Cameron, eight or nine, back from playing in the bush at the foot of the hill that led out of Manawaka. There was this gopher on the road, Mother, and somebody had shot it with a twenty-two and all its stomach and that was all out and it wasn't dead yet. *Please,*

dear, don't talk about it—it isn't nice. But I saw
it and it was trying to breathe only it couldn't
and it was. *Sh, it isn't nice.* (I hurt, Mother.
I'm scared.) (Sh, it isn't nice.) (I hurt, you
hurt, he hurts—Sh.)

Another car has approached and Stacey edges over to
the cliff face just in time. It shoots past, but she is shaken. At
the next widened pass point she draws in, stops and lights a
cigarette.

—— Stacey, go easy. What if anything happened? What
would happen to the kids? Maybe Mac would marry Delores
Appleton. I could almost face the thought, and yet I know he
wouldn't. She is too young, too edgy, too somehow battered a
long time ago. I don't give a good goddam who he might marry
if I got wrecked, but I don't want anybody else bringing up my
kids. Yeh, you're such a marvelous mother. Great example to the
young, you. A veritable pillar of strength, I don't think. Listen
here, God, don't talk to me like that. You have no right. *You* try
bringing up four kids. Don't tell me you've brought up countless
millions because I don't buy that. We've brought our own selves
up and precious little help we've had from you. If you're there.
Which probably you aren't, although I'm never convinced totally,
one way or another. So next time you send somebody down
here, get It born as a her with seven young or a him with a large
family and a rotten boss, eh? Then we'll see how the inspirational
bit goes. God, pay no attention. I'm nuts. I'm not myself.

Stacey starts up again. The night is getting chilly and she
rolls up the window of the car, wishing she had brought along
her dufflecoat.

—— How could Buckle tell Mac that? Why ask? You know
why. Mac wasn't paying enough attention to him. Buckle is
like a kid. Oh? None of my kids could conceivably be that vicious.
Buckle, how could you? How do I know? I'd have to know everything that ever happened to him. I think I'm a crumby mother at
times, but what about his? Yet she kept him and brought him up

somehow. I can only guess, fragments here and there. Mac, can't I ever say how it was with me or what happened at all? You don't want to know. You want everything to be all right. *Is everything all right, Stacey?* Yes, everything is all right. Okay. I get the message. If that's the way you want it, that's the way it'll be. From now on, I live alone in a house full of people where everything is always always all right.

Ahead, the road is coming close to the shore of the Sound. Stacey pulls across the road and draws up on a flat stretch of grass. She climbs out, not bothering to lock the car, and looks around. She wants to go to the shore but is uncertain how to get there. A stretch of sparse forest is in front of her, and she can see the dim lights of several shacks or houses. She goes back to the car and gets the flashlight from the glove compartment. When she shines the subdued light, she can see a muddy trail, overhung with grass, leading at right angles from the road and towards the beach.

—— Hell. All private property, no doubt. Can I get past those houses? I'm freezing. It can't be mid-June. I'm scared. Where am I and what am I doing here? Okay, take it easy, Stacey. Where is the flask of Scotch you so providentially stuck in your purse? Here. Little tin flask. It was my dad's. Yep. Niall Cameron carried it with him in the First World War. Meant to be a water flask. When I went back for the funeral, it was with his things and she was going to throw it out. *I'll have that,* I said, and she looked at me with rank suspicions, all completely justified. Okay, Dad. Here's looking at you. You couldn't cope, either. I never even felt all that sorry for you, way back when. Nor for her. I only thought people ought to be strong and loving and not make a mess of their lives and they ought to rear kids with whom it would be possible to talk because one would be so goddam comprehending and would win them over like nothing on earth, and I would sure know how to do it all. So I married a guy who was confident and (in those days or so it seemed) outgoing and full of laughs and free of doubts, fond of watching football and

154

telling low jokes and knowing just where he was going, yessir, very different from you, Dad. Now I don't know. Perhaps it isn't that the masks have been put on, one for each year like the circles that tell the age of a tree. Perhaps they've been gradually peeled off, and what's there underneath is the face that's always been there for me, the unspeaking eyes, the mouth for whom words were too difficult. *No. No. No.* I can't take that. I won't. Hush. How to get through, just this minute, to the shore? What if there are dogs? Alsatians. Dobermans. Come on, Stacey. (I'm scared. What am I doing out here alone?)

Her feet squelch in the rain-wet earth of the rutted track. She walks slowly, brushing aside the thorned tendrils of blackberry bushes, past the dwelling half-concealed in the undergrowth, the light glowing uncertainly from one window. She makes her way slippingly to the shore.

The beach is not a proper beach. It is at most three feet wide, and the sand is pebbled over, knotted with rocks and with shells which crisp underfoot. The trees do not come down quite this far, but heavy-leafed bushes bend almost to the water's edge. Driftwood has been washed up, gnarled branches and fragments now seen as sea-bleached dead-bone grey in the glim of the flashlight. A log strayed from a boom is grey-white on the outside rounded edge but on the circular cut-through it is a water-deepened rust color. The log is half as high as Stacey, but she clambers onto it. She is wearing rubber-soled canvas shoes and her feet are wet. The log is only slightly damp on the surface, although sea-soaked at its core. Stacey opens her purse and gets out a cigarette. In front of her, the black water dances lightly, glancingly, towards the shore, sending the little stones skeltering down in thin ridges after each retreating wave. Out deeper, the water is more rough, breaking in wind-stirred crests. No night clouds, and the sky is as black as the water, but shot through with stars which one instant look close, earth-related, lights provided for us, small almost cozy nightlights to keep us from the dark, and the next instant look like themselves and alien, inconceivably far, giant and burning, not even hostile or anything identifiable, only indifferent. Stacey smokes and lets the silence exist around her. The sounds are only the underlying steady ones of the water and wind, and the occasional pierce of water birds.

— How good to hear nothing, no voices. I thought you were the one who was screaming about nobody wanting to talk. Yeh. Well. How good it feels, no voices. Except yours, Stacey. Well, that's my shadow. It won't be switched off until I die. I'm stuck with it, and I get bloody sick of it, I can tell you. Who is this *you?* I don't know. Shut up. I'm trying to be quiet and you won't let me. If only I could get away, by myself, for about three weeks. Joke. Laugh now. The only time I can ever get away is when all the kids are in bed. And this period of rationed time is rapidly diminishing. It's because we had the kids over so many years. Jen's there all day, and so okay she's in bed by seven, but then the boys and Katie are home and Katie doesn't get to bed until halfway through the night now or so it seems. You can't tell a fourteen-year-old to go to bed at seven. I don't have any time to myself. I'm on duty from seven thirty in the morning until ten thirty at night. Well, poor you. Let's all have a good cry. What would you do if you weren't on duty, bitch? Contemplate? Write poetry? Oh shut up. I would sort out and understand my life, that is what I would do, if you really want to know. You would, eh? Well, you're alone now. You're off duty. Start sorting, brain child.

A water bird cries, a far eerie ululating.

Diamond Lake, that one year when Niall Cameron managed to take them all there for two weeks in the summer, Stacey ten and Rachel five. Stacey, sturdy-legged, curious, energetic, flashing along the shore day and night, gawking up at the spruces and down at the moss sprouting with wild-pink bells

156

which looked like lilies of the valley but with no leaves only deep-pink stalks and mild-pink waxen flowers. Stacey listening at night on the beach alone, frightened but having to stay, listening to the lunatic voices of the loons, witch birds out there in the night lake, or voices of dead shamans, mourning the departed Indian gods, she not thinking of it like that then, only wholly immersed in the unhuman voices, the begone voices that cared nothing for lights or shelter or the known quality of home. But when she went back to Diamond Lake, eight years later, the birds had left. When the people came in numbers, the loons went away, always. She never discovered where they went, but she thought then, that eighteenth summer, of where they might be, somewhere so far north that people would never penetrate to drive them off again.

—— There *isn't* any place that far north, that far anywhere. There must be. That's where I'd like to go, very far away from all this jazz. If only the kids could be okay.

The lake is not large, but in the daytime it shines a deep oil blue. It is somewhere in the Cariboo. The Cariboo country. Up there. Somewhere. The barns are made of logs (Mac has told her, so she knows; he has been there). The boat she owns is only a rowboat, but she can manage it very well, skilfully in fact, and Ian and Duncan are good with it, too. The house is made of logs, but tightly chinked so that it is extremely weatherproof. It is an old converted barn. Two floors. With careful planning, she has organized five bedrooms. One for each of the kids, and one for herself. She teaches school. It is a small community, and naturally everyone knows everyone else, but the farmers and Indians and (? etc.) are glad that at last a teacher has come who wants to settle here and

—— Doll, let me ask you one simple question. Can you add more than two and two? Great teacher you'd make. Ian says *How do they expect me to do these problems when Mr. Gaines won't explain?* And I say, *Wait until Daddy gets home from work, and maybe he can help you with them.* And Mac looks at the damn things and I guess braces himself and tackles it, because there's nobody else to shove it off onto and then I have the gall to wonder why he bawls Ian out. He probably doesn't know how to do them any more than I do. Teacher. Oh boy. But the lake the lake the lake and the way the trees looked, spearing up there into the sky and the loons' voices and everything mysterious waiting to be discovered

Stacey pulls her sweater sleeves down around her wrists, and lights another cigarette. The wind is rising and she is cold. She resists the urge to look at her watch.

—— This erstwhile piece of the forest hurts my ass more than any pew in church when I was a kid. Go home, Stacey. You've got to, sometime. That's for sure. Got to be there to get breakfast—the immutable law of something or other. Where's the flask? Here. There. One more swallow and that's it. I don't want to go home. I want to go away. A long way off. I'm bloody sick of trying to cope. I don't want to be a good wife and mother.

Diamond Lake, and Stacey, eighteen, swimming outward. She was a strong swimmer, and when she reached the place where she could see the one spruce veering out of the rock on the distant point, she always turned back, not really accepting her limits, believing she could have gone on across the lake, but willing to acknowledge this arbitrary place of reference because it was further out than most of her friends could swim. This summer they had come here on their own, at last, without parents. Stacey, swimming back to shore,

158

coming up for air intermittently, knowing with
no doubt that she would make it fine, thinking already of the dance she would go to that
evening, feeling already the pressure on her
lake-covered thighs of the boys

—— Okay. I see it, Sir. I didn't see it before, but I see it
now. Thanks for nothing. That's the place I want to get away to,
eh? The Cariboo? Up north? No. I've never been any of those
places. I only think of Mac or else Buckle, on the road, up there
somewhere. When I imagine it, it always looks like Diamond
Lake. Like, I guess I mean, everything will be just fine when I'm
eighteen again. Come on, Stacey. Home.

Hi. Do you mind me asking you what in hell you are
doing there?

Crash. Out of the inner and into the outer. Stacey peers
through the darkness. At least he is not accompanied by an Alsatian. Presumably this is the occupant of the dimly outlined
dwelling she weasled past some time ago.

I'm sorry. Is this your property?

Not exactly. I'm staying up there. It belongs to some
friends of mine—they're away at the moment, so I'm caretaking.
The beach is supposed to be everybody's property. Only this one
being about a quarter of an inch wide and not that accessible,
we don't often get people here. Especially around midnight. You
contemplating a swim?

Well no

Don't drown yourself, that's all I ask. Guy drowned himself here not long ago and we haven't heard the last of it yet. By
all means do it, but not right here, eh?

I didn't intend

Hey, sorry. Want to come up and have some coffee?

I think I should be getting home

Yeh, sure. Well, come and have come coffee first. Aren't
you cold?

Well

159

Stacey's eyes, now accustomed to the darkness, examine him. He is shorter than Mac but not that much shorter, brown indifferent hair slightly too long and with an uncombed look, broad square face with outjutting chin and thick eyebrows, face supposed to be clean shaven but not all that recently, body solid but too young yet to have accumulated any extra fat around the belly or chest, dressed in paint-splashed brown corduroy pants and a brown-and-off-white Indian sweater in thick wool with Haida or something motifs of outspread eagle wings and bear masks.

—— He doesn't look like a murderer. Oh doll. You have a great eye for a sweater or a muscle, but how in hell do you know what a murderer looks like? If it was Katie, going to this guy's shack or whatever, for coffee, what would you think? I'd have a fit, that's what. And yet right this minute I couldn't care less. Maybe he *is* a murderer. "Salesman's Wife Stabbed on Sound." Should I go?

The young man is standing beside the log on which Stacey sits, and his eyes look amused.

You coming or not?

Well, it's very nice of you

C'mon we don't live on manners here if you're coming, come

She follows him up the mud-soft trail to the house. The raw plank steps lead into the kitchen. It is an A-frame, fairly large but as yet unfinished, the boards unpainted, the lumber still yellow-brown and smelling of pinegum. The ceiling of the main room stretches pointedly upwards, and from one rafter is suspended a looped cord from which hangs an exposed bulb, alight. The room is filled with assorted junk—coarse-webbed fishnets in grey piles on the floor, the big smoke-green thick glass bubbles used as weights on nets, suitcases imperfectly closed and half spilling their underwear and shirts, teetering stacks of books in corners, books outspread or dog-eared on a low table made out of a polished pine slab glowing and golden but with roughly tacked-on uneven do-it-yourself wrought-iron legs, somebody having got sick of the job of an artisan. The half-finished grey-stone fireplace has no mantel and bears deep eyeless cement pits where future hand-selected stones will possibly one day go. Ten-foot-high unhemmed and floor-trailing curtains of moss-green sackcloth veil the huge front window. An open and beauti-fully illustrated child's ABC rests on a rumpled loose-weave green and grey wool rug, Arabic-patterned.

— Heavens. A semiclassy pad. If people have to safety-pin up the hems of their curtains—well. Okay, so a bourgeois I may be, but that kind of a slob I'm not. Still, all the books. What right have I to say? The hell with that. They're trying to intimi-date me with the superiority of unhemmed curtains.

The man points out a black canvas chair, and Stacey tensely sits on the edge. Then, seeing his smile, she slopes back. The stove in the outer region is kerosene—she can smell it. He returns in a little while with two mugs of coffee.

Sugar? Cream?

Well, thanks. Both.

He sits down on a hassock and looks at her. He is still smiling, but when he questions her she feels unprepared.

So, okay. What's the bad news?

Stacey cradles the hot coffee mug between her hands.

What?

He grins now, but whether mockingly or not, she cannot tell.

The bad news. What's with you? Why are you here?

I   it's nothing   I just drove out

Oh. You just drove out? At this time of night? Here? Look, if you don't want to level with me, don't level with me. Go home. But don't sit here and drink my coffee and tell me you were out for a little fresh air. By the way, my name is Luke. Luke Venturi.

Stacey mumbles her own name and he laughs.

161

Hey, you're really scared, aren't you? Whatsamatter? Think I'm gonna strangle you with one of your own nylons? Come on. Why you here?

Stacey does not look at him.

I didn't want to stay at home any longer. I took off.

Her hand is too unstable to light her own cigarette. Luke takes it from her, lights it, hands it back.

You took off. Well, well. That's all right. Don't worry. Sometimes people do.

She can look at him now, but she feels her own eyes apologizing.

They don't. They don't. Not where I come from.

Luke laughs again, but it does not strike her as cruel, only removed from her, as though he were looking at things from some very different point of view.

Well, maybe not, where you come from. Wouldn't know. You know, once I was up in the Cariboo, hitching, and I stopped off at this farmhouse in the middle of, like, nothing, this goddam broken-down old house, huge actually it was, and the usual pump and cows outside and all I wanted was a meal and only this one kid came out, see, kid about twelve he must've been, and I asked where was his dad and mum, and he said *My dad's out there he'll be back at five. Mum, she took off, two-three months ago.* And you thought, Christ, no wonder she took off. But there he was, though. Hey, Stacey? What did I do? Is that where you live?

She has put her coffee mug on the floor and her head is in her outfolded arms. She does not know where the crying began or when it can end.

I'm sorry I'm sorry

It's okay, Stacey, you don't have to be sorry. It hurts?

Yes.

Well go ahead and bawl. No shame in that. You're not alone.

She lifts her head and looks at him.

162

That's where you're wrong.

Luke picks up her coffee mug and goes to refill it.

No, baby, that's where *you're* wrong.

She takes the coffee mug from him.

You're real? You're not real. I'm imagining.

He smiles.

You're not imagining. But maybe I'm not *that* real, so don't count on it. You drive far?

Not that far. What do you do?

Luke lights another cigarette for her, and takes one himself from her package.

Do? What do I do? Well, that's a good question.

I mean, what work do you do?

Yeh, that's what you have to find out, first thing, eh? Well, I think I'll get on with a fish boat this summer, go north.

You're lucky

Lucky?

I always thought I'd like to go somewhere up there. But I've got four kids.

Now we come to it, eh? Four kids. Well.

Don't you do anything else, the rest of the year?

Sure. Work here and there. Sawmills. Sometimes I sign on as cook, lumber camps. Wouldn't think I'd be a good cook, would you? But I'm not bad, if I do say so myself. Pastry is my downfall, though. I make pastry which is—not to put too fine a point upon it—like porcelain. Well, nobody wins them all. You make good pastry, Stacey?

Not bad.

I thought as much. I said to myself, there is a woman who looks like she makes good pastry.

Stacey has been drawn into his laughter.

It sounds like an insult to me.

What? You give someone a compliment and they interpret it in reverse. It's a semantic problem we have. I do other things, too, sometimes. I write.

163

Oh? What?

Luke shrugs and bends his head.

Science fiction. SF. Not space opera with sex. Allegory, more, and all happening on this planet. The bug-eyed monster bit is dead. Don't get me wrong. Asimov, Bradbury, Blish and all the old brigade don't have to lie awake nights worrying about competition from me. Not yet, anyhow. I've had precisely one story published. Want my autograph? It's free.

I like SF. I sometimes

Yeh? You sometimes what? You started to say it, then you quit, like I'd think you were way-out for mentioning it. How funny you are, merwoman. Who held you down? Was it for too long?

Stacey examines his face, unable for the moment to believe the easiness of his words.

Maybe. I never thought of it that way. Or—yeh, maybe I did, but I'm not sure any more. I was only going to say I sometimes you know like imagine that kind of situation SF I mean

Luke now cannot withhold his laughter, but it encompasses her as his hand encompasses her wrist.

Like it's the secret of the confessional? Oh baby. You're unbelievable. It's so sensational?

She takes her wrist back and drinks her coffee, saying nothing. Luke accepts it but after a moment comes back again.

I'm sorry. Four kids, eh? What are you trying to be? A good example?

I can't be.

Well, that's good. So why try? Why don't you come out a little?

What?

Come out. From wherever you're hiding yourself. See— if I look very hard, I can just about make you out in there, but miniature, like looking through the wrong end of a telescope.

I can see what you mean, sort of. But it's odd

164

Everything is odd, merwoman, everything

That's what I think. Only

Only what?

They don't think so

Luke's eyebrows, heavy over the square quizzical face, now lighten purposely.

Well, I'm not them.

Stacey gathers her purse, gets out her car keys.

I have to go home. Thanks for the coffee.

That's okay. And cheer up, eh?

I'll try. Thanks for noticing I wasn't so cheerful.

That's me—perceptive to a degree. It only stood out all over you.

Stacey hesitates in the doorway, not wanting to go, wanting Luke to suggest that she might like to drive out again sometime. But he only smiles at her, so she finally turns.

Well, so long.

So long.

Stacey pulls up the Chev on Bluejay Crescent and goes with extreme quietness into the house. She tiptoes up the stairs. No sound. She creaks the bedroom door open.

Mac is sitting up in bed, smoking. He looks at her.

Great. You've decided to come home? Where in the bloody fucking hell have you been, Stacey? I damn near called the police.

I have been out driving.

Out driving? At this hour?

Yes.

All right. Did you go to Buckle's place?

No.

That's what you say.

If you don't believe me, hire detectives. Who cares? I went out driving, that's all.

If you had stayed out half an hour longer I would have called the

Why?

Because I have some sense of responsibility even if you don't.

Yeh, well maybe you're right. But I'm back in time to make breakfast. I'm not totally lacking in a sense of

Look all right I believe you what else can I do for God's sake get to bed will you please it is two A.M.

Okay right away

Stacey pussyfoots into the bathroom, washes her face, puts on her nightly cold cream and steps back into the silent hall. There, in front of her bedroom door is Katie, in her yellow lace nightie, long red hair along her shoulders, not saying anything, just looking.

Katie—

Katie turns and goes back into her bedroom. Her words are on purpose not loud enough to wake the younger kids.

Just don't ever bawl me out again, eh?

For three days Stacey housecleans compulsively, lugging the vacuum cleaner savagely from room to room, washing and ironing curtains, turfing out boxloads of broken toys from the boys' room, straightening her dresser drawers. In the evenings, she goes to bed even before Katie is in bed, and tries to read. She leaves Mac's dinner in the oven for him, and when she hears his key in the door, about ten, she switches off the light on the bedside table. Their bedroom is at the front of the house and he drives in the back lane to the garage so he cannot see the bedroom light as he approaches. Her eyes are closed by the time he comes upstairs and she does not open them. She listens each night to Mac's daytime breathing turning into sleep. She lies stiffly, far to her own side of the bed, not moving in case she wakens him and speech becomes unavoidable. In the mornings they are protected from each other by the presence of the children.

On the fourth morning, Stacey phones Tess Fogler and asks her over for coffee. The high-pitched girl-voice comes back at her.

Why thanks Stacey I'd just love to

Stacey replaces the receiver and looks at herself in the hall mirror. She is wearing her dark-green slacks and green pullover. The day is too warm for them. It is only now that Stacey realizes she has been wearing them for the past four days as though they were the one contact with what she now does not believe actually took place.

—— How can I get out? Evenings are out of the question. If Mac is home it's impossible; if he isn't home it still is impossible. Katie would be okay with the other kids for a few hours in the evening. Sure, but where am I going? Out to see a sick friend? Days. I can't ask Tess to mind Jen again. I've already imposed on her too much. I'm not going to ask her. I simply am not. What you ought to do, Stacey, is ask Tess over more often, no strings. I know, I know. But she never has anything to talk about. Yeh, and you're such a brilliant conversationalist yourself? Oh shut up. I will ask her over more often. I swear it. And I won't ever ask her about Jen again. It would be different if it could be reciprocal, but what can I do for her that would be any use? Let her pour out her woes? She never does. Maybe she hasn't got any, not really to speak of. I look at her, done up like a Christmas present, and I wonder what's actually inside. Maybe nothing. How can you tell unless people say? He didn't mind talking, Luke. He took it for granted. *What's the bad news?* As though it were to be expected, to mention it. Okay, God, say what you like, but I damn well wish I could get away just sometimes by myself. But no. It's a criminal offense, nearly. What makes any of them think they've got the right to tell me own me have me always there not that they notice when I am only when I'm not

Katie, four, almost as chunky as Stacey had been as a child, Katie with then-short auburn hair, sitting beside Stacey on the chesterfield, gravely turning the magazine pages, coming to the picture of the ever-alluring Girl in White Lace. *Do ladies wear it then, Mum?* Wear what when? *Their bride dress when they go out to find the husband.* Well, no, not just then. *I'm going to.* Sure, you do that, gorgeous—you'll be a knockout. And they laughed conspiratorially together. Ten years later, Katie in the upstairs hall outside her room, eyes fully aware, unforgiving. *Just don't ever bawl me out again, eh?*

—— Katie, wait. Let me explain. No, I guess I can't. And if I did, it might be worse for you than not trying. Katie, I promise —never again. I won't leave even for an hour. I swear it. How could I go out there again, anyway? He didn't ask me to come. What do you imagine he'd do, Stacey? Greet you with a vast shout of joy? Like hell he would. He'd stare at you aloofly, and say *Oh, it's you.* No—he'd smile politely but it would be only that, just politeness. And what would you say, dream girl? *I need to talk to you please please talk touch me even if it's only your hands on my shoulders.* That would go down wonderfully. Have a little pride, Stacey. Why?

Jen is warbling beside Stacey, running up and down the hall with her short arms extended around a multitude of dolls. She drops them and reaches for Stacey's arm.

What is it, flower?

Yatter-yatter

You mean your doll carriage? Okay, let's get it. I'm going to phone Doctor Spender this week and have him have a look at you. No—I'm just impatient, aren't I? You're perfectly okay, aren't you? Daddy's right—I just get worked up over nothing. Don't I?

R-r-ring.

Stacey opens the front door and Tess comes in, fawn-graceful in new dull-orange dress, carrying in her hands a number of swan-necked gilt-headed bottles and portly drum-bellied jars, like a collection of princesses and frogs.

Look, Stacey, my new facial stuff. It's fabulous. Just simply amazing. I've only been using it a few days but I can really notice the difference already. You can't buy it in the drugstores—it's only sold door-to-door. This awfully nice woman came around and I asked her in more out of politeness than anything you know and then we got talking and well I mean I don't usually buy cosmetics door-to-door but this sounded so interesting. They're all natural products.

Tess deposits the bottles and jars on the kitchen table and Stacey picks up a squat translucent jar filled with a green perfumed ointment. The label reads HATSHEPSUT—Avocado Wrinkle Cream.

Natural products?

Yes, I mean, like, they don't contain any animal substances.

Is that good?

Tess nods.

It's much better for your skin. All natural vegetable substances.

What's so unnatural about animals?

Tess laughs trillingly.

Oh Stacey, you're just like Jake. Well, there's nothing I guess what you would exactly call unnatural about animals except they are animals aren't they and creams and that made out of animal fat well there's something sort of *unfresh* about it, isn't there? It never struck me until Mrs. Clovelly—that's her name— pointed it out and then I could see it right away. You take natural vegetable oils, now, and there's something sort of, well, *nicer* about it, you know? Also, it's much more compassionate. I mean, you don't have to have all those animals killed for their fat.

Yeh. Well, you could be right. What all kinds you got, Tess?

Tess displays them one by one, cuddling them between her long smooth fingers.

Well, this one's *Geranium Leaf Skin Astringent,* for toning up the skin. This is *Pineapple Shampoo,* for restoring the natural oils of the hair. And *Rose and Rhubarb Night Cream*—this pale-pink one—rhubarb may sound a little funny, but it's so refreshing, really, and just smell it—the roses are for the perfume, and the rhubarb juices are for the skin-cell restoring process. And *Violet-Rosemary Hand Cream*—smell—isn't it lovely? And *Strawberry Under-Eye Lotion,* and you've seen the *Avocado Wrinkle Cream.*

—— My God, does she apply them or eat them? Sh, doll, don't offend her. Sale on at Eaton's—remember? No. Don't. You're not to ask.

Gosh, they make quite an imposing array, Tess. What does it mean—HATSHEP—whatever it says?

HATSHEPSUT. Pronounced Hat-shep-*soot.* Mrs. Clovelly said. That's the name of the whole line. They're called after an ancient Egyptian queen. Queen Hatshepsut. She was very famous. She ruled as pharaoh in her own right.

Gee. Well. How interesting.

Jake had to look her up, of course, in a book. He came downstairs laughing like crazy and saying she was famous for her cruelty and she dressed as a man and married her stepson or some such relative and he hated her so much he had her name chiseled off all the monuments after she died. But I bet that's not true. Jake gets a big bang out of jokes, I mean. But anyway, I like the name, don't you? I think it's sort of cute to name them after an ancient Egyptian queen.

Yeh it's very

No sugar or cream for me, thanks Stacey. I just have it black.

Oh sorry. Absent-minded. I don't see why *you* diet.

I just feel I mustn't ever let myself go, that's all. How's your diet coming along, Stacey?

Lousy. I haven't got the perseverance of a grasshopper.

Well, you *do* so much. You must burn up a lot of energy.

Yeh, I guess. Things get on top of me every so often. I been doing spring cleaning these past couple of days. Haven't had a minute. I meant to get downtown while the sale's on at Eaton's. If I don't get those kids some new pajamas soon, they'll be going to bed bare.

Why don't you go this afternoon, then? I'll take Jen.

Oh, I couldn't, Tess. You've been so good

It's nothing. I like having her. We get on famously, don't we, sweetie?

Jen, arranging her young in the doll carriage, looks up and nods agreeably.

Well, it's terrifically nice of you, Tess

I don't mind. She may not talk but she talks to me, at least I feel she's talking. You go ahead, Stacey.

Thanks a million. I really am grateful. Listen, if there's ever anything I can do for you, Tess—anything—please let me, eh?

There isn't, honey, but thanks.

I'll tell Katie to pick Jen up after school if I'm not home yet.

Sure. Okay.

After Tess has gone, Stacey begins making the kids' sandwiches for lunch. Then she realizes it is only ten minutes past eleven, and they will not be home for another hour. She leaves Jen playing in the veranda and goes upstairs. She shuffles rapidly through the coat hangers in the clothes cupboard and finally pulls out a cotton dress, slightly shabby, not belonging to any identifiable age group, printed in blue and dark green, like seawater and fir trees.

When Katie and the boys have gone back to school after lunch, Stacey takes Jen over to the Foglers' house. She then gets in the Chev and drives downtown to Eaton's, where she purchases the first pajamas she sees which are the right sizes. Back to the car, and out of the city along the winding road that leads up the Sound.

— He won't be home. Or he'll be home and he won't even recognize me. Or there'll be a girl there—long fair hair, about twenty. Why did I come? I'm off my rocker. It isn't me, it's somebody wearing my appearance, my face, takeover by aliens from out there. My real mind is in the deep freeze in their spaceship. Why would he want to see me again? He wouldn't. Otherwise, he would've asked me to come out. Just for half an hour—that won't take up much of his time. It shouldn't have been so easy, with Tess. All right, don't rub it in. Stacey, you're a monster. Am I? Am I? I don't care if I am. All I know is I have to get out. *I have to get out.*

The A-frame in the daytime looks more obvious than it did at night. Unpainted, the timber a cool light brown, it juts up among the green-needled trees and the welter of bushes like a small strange cathedral with a rubble of trodden timothy grass, paint tins and splinters of kindling wood at its feet. Uncertainly Stacey walks up to the steps and looks at the door, which is open. Luke appears in the doorway. He is still dressed in the thick wool Indian sweater and brown corduroys. He flicks his coarse slightly too-long hair away from his forehead, wipes a hand over his mouth as though he has only just finished eating, and stands looking down at her. He has not shaved, and his jaw is now beard-brown as though he intended it that way. Then, mercifully, he grins.

Hey, how about that? It's the merwoman. I had a hunch you'd come back. It was in my horoscope, more or less.

Stacey walks up the wooden plank steps.

Your horoscope? You don't believe in

Well, it's as certain as anything else, isn't it? I'm Cancer. Cheerful sign to be, eh? The forecasts are always telling me my artistic temperament is due for a surprise, and it never fails to happen. Come on in.

I—thanks. I mustn't stay long

Sure.

I used to work for a guy who did horoscopes. Before I was married, that was. I mean, it was sort of a sideline with him. He was really in the import business. Stuff from Hong Kong, like fried bees and chocolate-covered ants. Tinned, naturally. But maybe the horoscopes were his real business. He used to get me to mimeograph them. He had a big mailing list. I always wondered if it was legal. His name was Janus Uranus, not his real name of course, the one he put on the mimeographed horoscopes. His real name was Curtis W. Forrester. Probably that wasn't his real name, either.

—— Was it really me, wondering then if it was legal? Or was it Mac? The first time I met Mac, he definitely stated *It doesn't sound legal to me, Stacey.* What if I'd stayed on with the old guy for a while longer? My whole life would've been different. I might have married—who? (Whom?) A fortune teller, an artist, a master mariner, a prophet. Yeh?

Stacey, bringing in the supposedly individual horoscopes in job lots for the old man to leaf through. The fifth floor one-room office heavy with abandoned paperwork, tribes of spiders, decrepit carved-oak desks from a gaudier era. The old guy, short and blue-eyed, bald but sideburned like her imagining of the Wizard of Oz. *We won't disappoint them, Stacey. These must go out tonight—think of the people who are waiting for the ineffable Word, Stacey, waiting to be told what life holds and withholds, the inalterable soul movements, stately as orchestral or bowel. Think on it, girl, I implore you.* Yes, Mr. Forrester. *Call me Janus. What kind of a reply are you fobbing me off with, anyway, girl? What is your young brain doing in there?* (Thinking you're off your rocker, you mangy old coyote, that's what.)

Luke is laughing and bringing the coffeepot and two pottery mugs into the main room. Stacey sits down on the Arabic-patterned rug and tucks her feet underneath her. He hands her one of the cups.

Janus Uranus? That's a terrific name, Stacey. Why did you ever leave?

He scared me. And embarrassed me. Eccentrics always do. I don't want them to, but they do. It has something to do with the way I was brought up, I guess. Actually, I left to get married, so it wasn't only Janus. I was relieved to get out, though. I don't know how much that had to do with how I felt about Mac. Maybe it did. I never thought of it until now.

Timber Lake sixteen years ago had hardly any cottages. Jungles of blackberry bushes and salmonberry. Spruce trees darkly still in the sun, and the water so clear you could see the grey-gold minnows flickering. You know something, Mac? *What?* I like everything about you. *That's good, honey. I like everything about you, too.*

Stacey reaches out and touches the sleeve of Luke's Indian sweater.

Luke—that's not true. Janus didn't have anything to do with the way I felt about Mac.

Mm? Janus, the two-faced god. Uranus, the frozen planet, farthest from our sun. Combined with the recurrence of *anus* in each word. He sounds a great guy. Do you reckon he's still alive?

Stacey withdraws her hand.

—— He collects people, maybe? Sure, Stacey—fine collector's piece you'd make. Still, he didn't hear what I said this time. Idiot

child, why should he want to discuss Mac? I don't want to, either.
That's just what I don't want. So okay—don't, then.

I wouldn't know if he's still there or not. It wasn't quite
a century ago.

Luke turns to her in amazement.

Hey—that supersensitivity. It's too much. You waiting for
the verbal cracks, or what? It wasn't meant

I'm sorry

Don't be sorry, Stacey. People should never be sorry—it's
a waste of time.

Aren't you, ever?

Nope. You keep on communicating your own awfulness
to yourself, and nothing changes. You just go on in the same old
groove.

How old are you, Luke?

He takes the cigarette packet from her outheld fingers
and lights one for each of them. He hands hers to her, and looks
at her, directly, as though purposely not evading her eyes.

How old? What's that got to do with anything?

I was just curious

Well, to be precise, I was twenty-nine on my last birthday. But being Cancer I'm due to age another year soon. You
seem to be waiting for me to ask you how old you are. Okay.
How old are you Stacey?

I wasn't   I didn't mean   well, I'm thirty-five, actually.

—— My kingdom it extendeth from lie to shining lie. I was
the one who nearly flipped when Mac pared off a few years from
himself with Thor. Well, I only took off four. Luke's nearly thirty.
Nine years younger. So what? I'm only talking to him.

Thirty-five. You make it sound like about eighty. Does it
bug you?

No, not really. Only I guess I've changed somehow without realizing it. I worry more. I scare easier.

What scares you, merwoman?

175

You don't want to be bored with hearing that kind of thing.

Hey, don't be coy, Stacey, or I may just throw you back on the beach. It's okay. Don't worry. If I get bored, I'll let you know. The things that scare people are hardly ever boring. You could be an exception, of course.

It's about the kids mostly, I guess. What'll become of them? How'll they end up? I can't face the thought of anything awful happening to them. But I can't do anything to prevent it happening, either. Everybody's living dangerously—that's how I see it. What if they got hurt, killed even? That seems the one thing I couldn't bear. But everybody feels that way, or nearly everybody, and that doesn't stop it happening. There was this newspaper picture of this boy some city in the States kid about twelve Negro kid you know shot by accident it said by the police in a riot and he was just lying there not dead but lying with his arm cradled up in a dark pool his blood and his eyes were wide open and you wondered what he was seeing. His parents cared about him as much as I do about my kids, no doubt, and worried about what might happen to him, but that didn't stop it happening. You think I'm silly to think about it I can't help it

Luke refills her coffee mug and comes down from his perch on the canvas chair to sit cross-legged beside her on the rough wool rug.

No. *Silly* isn't the exact word I would have chosen.

A strange thing happened seven years ago—that was the last time I went back home I mean to my home town Manawaka. My mother and sister live there. My sister hasn't got any use for going through all the old rubbish in trunks in the attic, but I kind of get a bang out of it and so does my mother and I never got on well with her when I was a kid but after I had my own kids I felt different I guess I could see more why she used to fuss—it was mainly because she was scared about us. So we went up to the attic this day, my mother and I, and among the junk I found a revolver which used to be my dad's—he died some time before this—and I said to my mother *I'll have this as a souvenir*. She didn't know there were any bullets for it, but there were. When I got back home I mean my home here I hid it in the basement on a little shelf under one of the rafters.

Yeh? What did you plan to do with it? Or rather, whom? Yourself, when the Goths' chariots and the final bill came in, or when some evangelist corporal decided this is the way the world ends not with a whimper but a bang?

I didn't—I wasn't thinking of it exactly like that. I didn't have all that wide a view, to tell you the truth. It was at that time —remember—when people from California and around there were saying they planned to come up here for safety and I had to laugh, living here, because it didn't feel that much better here to me. It sounds crazy, even to me, now. I've never told anyone. I thought—*if anything happened*—that's the way I always thought of it—*if anything happened*—that phrase only, just like my mother could never bring herself to say anyone had died—they had always passed on—anyway, if anything did, and the kids got—you know—damaged or like burned so they couldn't recover and I didn't know where to take them and there was no place to go anyway, then I'd

Luke puts a hand over hers to steady it.

Sh. It's all right. It didn't happen. Hush, Stacey. Have you still got it?

No. I thought about it and thought what it would be like to have to do a thing like that and after awhile I realized that I couldn't not even if they were even if I couldn't do anything except wait I'd just have to do that and look at them and hold them whatever they were like or I was like because I couldn't do anything else. Maybe I'd have to keep telling them everything would be all right. We went to Timber Lake that summer with the kids. I took the revolver along and went out one night by myself and threw it in the lake. I never told Mac. He always used to say I shouldn't worry—that it was useless, and of course that was right. Maybe he worried, too, for all I know. But he never said.

That's not good.

No. But it *is* useless to worry. What can you do?

Luke shrugs.

I don't know, baby. I always walk along in the right-intentioned marches, but I don't tell myself that the face of the world is going to be altered that way. My mother believes in the power of corporate prayer. She's still an Italian farmwoman at heart. She was blessed once by the Pope—it was just before she and my dad came over to this country and I was about two months old—she had me when she was fifteen, great for her, eh? Anyway, it was in the big square of St. Peter's, and the Holy Father stood on the balcony and lifted his arms and there was this huge crowd milling around. To hear her tell it, you could feel the radiance as though there were hosts of angels swooping around like so many pigeons. I never bought that, but then again, there could be something in it. So I plod along. It makes as much sense as anything else.

You know something, Luke? The other thing worries me just about as much. I sometimes think in the end it's me who's hurting them the most, after all.

You could be right. You probably are. I'm not much of an authority on the subject.

Stacey eyes him alertly, hearing the faint drawl of boredom only just now in his voice.

— Enough, doll. Enough about the kids. They're not real to him. Why should they be?

Luke—I should be going. Did I interrupt your work?

My work? Well, not exactly. I don't work that hard. I was put off it as a kid by having parents who never quit working.

What do you do when you're not writing?

I putter, sort of. Look

He jumps to his feet and pulls Stacey by the wrist, taking

her to the far side of the room, cluttered with books and pieces of driftwood.

I did these this morning—bookshelves. The old brick and plank method. These friends who own this place won't ever get around to making any for themselves, but they could sure do with some. Other times I go fishing. I'm no hell of a fisherman, but it makes me feel good if I can catch something I can live off. Frustrated pioneer instincts, too well known to be detailed here. We've got a boat. It's a terrible boat—leaks like a senile gent, but we patch it up. Only a rowboat, not one of those fiber-glass speedboat jobs that all the salesmen have.

Not all the salesmen

What?

Not all the salesmen, I said. My husband is a salesman.

Yeh?

He used to sell encyclopedias. Then he sold essences. Now he sells—never mind. He's doing well at it   very well really

Look out there, Stacey, eh? I like going out when the Sound isn't all that quiet, when it's talking to itself, and the water goes slap-crash against this feeble little boat and you wonder who is down there like that prehistoric undersea creature in that story and after ten million years or something it rose up to answer the mating call only sad to tell what it actually heard was the foghorn from a lighthouse

I got married sixteen years ago and I thought he was like Agamemnon King of Men except I'd never heard of Agamemnon then only later when I took all those goddam night courses like in Ancient Greek Drama but that was how I thought of him only of course that view couldn't last all that long how could it if you are with somebody all the time and see how they go to sleep with their mouth open or something and I wouldn't have minded about that except he doesn't talk any more hardly at all can you imagine what it's like to live in the same house with somebody who doesn't talk or who can't or else won't and I don't know which reason it could be

179

I go out there in the boat and I don't mind being absolutely and utterly alone in fact I like it that's when I get ideas for whatever it is I'm going to write and when I was a kid it was impossible ever to be alone

Stacey all at once recognizes the parallel lines which if they go on being parallel cannot ever meet.

Why couldn't you be alone when you were a kid, Luke?

Because after me came my five sisters and the house was also always full of cousins and aunts or somebody. Funny thing—I liked them all, and yet I used to wish they'd all get the hell out sometimes so things could be a trifle peaceful. Our house was the noisiest for miles around. Still is. You should've been there the night of my sister Angela's wedding about six months ago. My dad and two of my uncles set up an orchestra in the kitchen—an accordion, a guitar, and my dad on drums, actually a well-chosen selection of frying pans and soup kettles. Everybody dancing all over the house. At about four in the morning, people bawling their eyes out over great classical airs like "Santa Lucia." It was murder. The police finally arrived, and my dad offered them some of his homemade wine. I thought I'd rupture myself laughing.

Stacey gazes at him enviously.

I wish   I wish

What? You wish what, merwoman?

I wish I'd had that kind of family

Luke smiles.

Everything looks both better and worse from the outside, I guess. You think—*How lucky they are* or *How in hell can they stand it?* Maybe they're not so lucky, but they can stand it. Want some of my dad's wine?

He really makes his own?

Of course. I would not say he was the most skilled wine-maker in North Vancouver, but he must be in the top brackets. None of this chemical slop for him, he says. He gets half a truck-load of California grapes every year. Then the crusher comes in.

You ever seen a grape crusher? You hire it by the hour. Nothing unprofessional for my old man. He puts the brew down in oak barrels in which whiskey has been made. Fermentation—and then you rack it and bottle it and six months later you got a good rough red, like Chianti.

What's he do, your dad?

People always want to know what a guy does. I wonder why is that?

I take it back.

No, don't. He works for a building contractor. He believes you have to work very hard in this life, just to keep your head above water, or to escape whatever it is that's waiting to crush you like a grape. And even then you may lose at any moment. Like *Christ in Concrete*. Only he couldn't visualize himself in a star role. One of the lesser apostles, you might say. I'm not sorry he hasn't got anywhere. Where is there to get, that you would all that much want to be? I'm only sorry he doesn't see it that way. He thinks he's a failure. How much better, I think he tells himself, if he owned four apartment blocks like my mother's brother. Here—try the wine.

It's good.

Not bad, is it? I'll put the bottle between us. Help yourself.

Thanks. I mustn't stay much longer

Sure.

Tell me about your SF stories.

Luke pulls his Indian sweater down around his wrists and leans back, propping himself on an elbow.

I've written mostly short stories, but the one I'm trying to do now is longer, like maybe novel-length. I won't talk about it—it'll go away if I do. Superstition. Sometimes I think it's great —or, well, let's say not bad, anyway. Other times I think it's pure crap. It's called *The Greyfolk*. Takes place some thousand or so years hence, when this continent is all desert and the few remaining people are governed by African administrators who fol-

lowed the First Expedition which was sent from Africa centuries
after the Cataclysm here, when the radiation danger had finally
disappeared, to see if there were any survivors. There were. A
few small creatures looking almost human crawled out of their
hidey holes in the dunes. They'd evolved over the years into
wizened grey-scaled folk who lived on sand lizards and water
from dew ponds. They'd lost their language and all knowledge
of their past, although they had a few dim racial memories and
some bizarre quasi-religious cults. The Administration taught
them basic Bantu, and after a hundred or so years, the greyfolk
are producing some brilliant students, but none of them will do
anything except invent gimmicks like the Cacophonoscope,
which gives out with lamenting greensongs in color, or the
Ululator, which is the sob machine, and you take your pick for
whatever variety gives you your kicks. Story really concerns the
dilemma of Kwaame Acquaah, the Chief Administrator, who is
deeply against Africa having colonies and who wants the greyfolk themselves to discover how to restore their soil et cetera, but
who can't think how to overcome the mental block that obviously
exists among them. The educated greyfolk have developed the
belief that their ancestral culture was harmonious, agrarian and
ideal until the disaster, which some believe to have been an act
of nature such as multitudinous volcanic eruptions and others
believe to have been an outside attack by unnamed destroyers.
Acquaah's problem is whether to let them continue in these com-
forting beliefs or to tell them what really happened. In the end,
they have to know, of course. Trouble is, I'm not sure what happens when they find out.

     He laughs and turns towards her, refilling both their
glasses. Stacey cannot think of anything intelligent to say, but it
does not seem to matter. Luke drinks and goes on, and she
realizes it is not her opinion he is seeking.

     Goddam, Stacey—I've gone and talked about it, haven't
I? Not much, though. I could've gone into a lot more detail. I
haven't given away much. Anyway, maybe it'll all get changed.

I know the basic situation's been done before, but not by me. What kind of remark is that? Egotistical? Or just self-protective? I can't think of any way to end the story, and I guess some sort of ending is required, although sometimes I wonder why. Why not just stop and let the reader make up his own ending? Don't get me wrong. I don't expect you to say. It's my problem. Sometimes I wish

Wish what?

That I had less imagination or more talent. I don't wish that often. Mostly, it's okay just to *be*. Only sometimes you get these delusions of purpose. But we don't have to mean anything.

I'm not convinced.

Aren't you, merwoman?

I don't think you are, either.

Don't you, Stacey?

Stacey puts her fingers on the hairs of his arm. He glances at her, unsmiling. Then, after a moment, he begins to stroke her wrist.

—— He seems so damn young. And he wants me to say *Everything's all right*. He, too. Even though he knows I can't. How peculiar. Luke, hold me. Stacey, don't beg. Am I?

Luke's hands are on her shoulders, pulling her inward towards him. Then his tongue is in her mouth. She is surprised by the force of her own response, the intensity and explicitness of her pleasure.

—— Stacey, ease up. Not so fast. Now I see what the trouble is. I've grown unaccustomed to the ritual of the preliminaries. I'm out of touch with the rules. I've only gone to bed with one man for a hell of a long time, when the byplay was necessary. Rein in, Stacey, or Luke will think you're a whore. Well, he'll be wrong, then. Whores don't want it that much. Only women like me, who think there may not be that much time left. Luke—Luke? Am I begging? All right, so I'm begging.

Luke withdraws slightly and looks at her, questioningly.

Stacey—if you want to go home, now's the time

No

So okay, eh?

Yes

Her thought processes switch off, and she is momentarily saying nothing inside herself. She reacts as she once did to jazz, taking it as it was told to her unverbally, following the beat. Luke takes her hand and puts it on his sex. The surge in her own sex is so great that she presses herself hard against him, urging him. Luke laughs.

You really want it, don't you?

Yes

But when they are taking their clothes off, thought returns unwelcomely to her.

—— I don't want to expose myself to him. I'm not perfect enough. He's too young. I've got on me the stretchmarks of four kids, the lines of dead silver worming across my belly. Will he notice? He'd have to be blind, not to. I can't help it. I'm not twenty any more. The padding of fat on my hips and on the inner reaches of my thighs. Goddam. I never knew it would be like this. It's different with Mac—he's seen me alter so gradually that he hardly notices, or if he does at least it doesn't make him want to throw up. Or so I like to think. Mac knows what I looked like when I was twenty-three, and I didn't look bad then, in fact I looked pretty good. I don't want Luke to see me as I am now. I want him to see me as I was then. He hasn't been knocked about that much yet. Men preserve themselves for longer than women, anyhow. Mac's got life's scribblings under his eyes, and his belly isn't so absolutely taut as it once was, but it is a damn sight tauter than mine, let's face it. Four kids have ruined me. It's not their fault. It would have happened anyway—at least I've got something to show for it. Oh God I wish I looked better. What you need, Stacey girl, is a kaftan with a small zipper. Does he think I look too terrible?

Luke   I'm not twenty

He puts his fingers across her mouth, gently but also reprovingly.

Sh

He is certain, assured, unscarred. The hair on his rib cage is dark brown, almost black, and his thighs are dark-haired, his sex hardsoft long eager to be in her. He puts a cushion under her head on the Arabic-patterned rug, and kneels above her.

Merwoman   you're trembling

Am I? I guess it's because I want

What you want is this

Then she takes his sex in her hands and guides it into her. She comes before he does, but she is still there when he reaches it. She feels him shudder, return to himself. Then he rests on her, and she explores his skin. His voice is barely audible.

Stacey. That was

Yes

You really loved it, didn't you? You wanted it for a long time, didn't you?

Yes

—— But that's not true, either. It makes me sound like I was deprived for lo these many years. It wasn't like that at all. It was something else. It's too complicated to explain, and anyway, he doesn't want to know. Maybe it gives him something, to imagine he's like the rain in a dry year? And in a way, he is. But not in quite the way he thinks. What does he think? I'll never know. Was he only being kind? Did he want me? I'll never know. So accept it, doll. I can't. I want to know. But you can't. I know. It might be worse, really to know. I know that, too.

Luke is looking at her in what appears to be astonishment.

Hey. Whatsamatter?

She has drawn up her left arm and is trying to see her watch.

I have to go home. My God, what time is it? I should've gone home long ago.

185

Luke shuts her eyelids with his fingers. She can feel his relaxation, his sleepiness.

You don't have to go. Stay the night.

Stacey's hands take in his jawbone, his collarbone, the brown hair under his arms.

Luke   I'd like to   but I can't

Why not?

Because   because

You want to sleep with me, all night, so why don't you?

I can't. I can't stay away all night. It's not possible.

You're a strange woman.

That's not being strange. The other would be.

Okay. That's your problem, I guess.

She dresses swiftly, and by the time she has her hair combed, Luke is also dressed and standing by the door. He kisses her lightly.

So long, then. Stacey.

—— I actually want to thank him. I want to explain myself to him, make myself real to him. I want to say—look, this is what I'm like. It would take too much time, and he's been patient enough.

So long.

The drive home is endless. Stacey hazards quick glances at her watch and each time finds that it is later than she imagined it could possibly be.

—— I should've been home two hours ago. Okay, so Mac won't be home, but the kids will have been home for ages. What'll I say? What'll they think? I don't care. I don't give a damn. I do, though. Katie? Ian? Duncan? Jen? What if they think I've had an accident or something? What if they phone the police? They wouldn't—they'd phone Mac. God, just don't let them phone Mac. Okay, Sir, so that's not a proper request—you don't need to remind me. I refuse to feel guilty. Be patient, God. I will, no doubt. Just give a little time. Don't begrudge me a couple of free hours. I feel marvelous, if you really want to know. I feel set up. Luke.

His is a little wider than Mac's but not quite so long. Bitch. Only a whore would compare. That's not true. Who could help it? It's not a qualitative difference, anyway. It doesn't matter a damn to me. That's not what is important. Would a guy think of it that way, though? I don't suppose so. They'd see it as a personal assessment or—how do I know what they'd think? Wouldn't it be strange if I could ever stop thinking in terms of *them* and *me?* Luke Venturi. I don't even know who he is. I know he's too young. Nine years—well, okay, nearly ten, then—that's not so much difference. Luke—you did want me. Didn't you? Did you? Well, nobody makes love with someone who absolutely repels them—he couldn't have, if he'd felt that way. He wanted me. He wanted *me.* Do we deceive ourselves by any chance, Stacey, doll? Very well, then, we deceive ourselves. Bugger off, voice. I'm happy as I am, at least momentarily. If only I could get out to see him more often. Luke, I couldn't get enough of you. I'd like to go to bed with you for seven days and seven unbroken nights. I'd like to start again, everything, all of life, start again with someone like you—with you—with everything simpler and clearer. No lies. No recriminations. No unmerry-go-round of pointless words. Just everything plain and good, like today, and making love and not worrying about unimportant things and not trying to change each other.

> Stacey, touching him too urgently—now, now, no time to waste, I haven't got all day. Stacey lacking any merciful robe.

—— All right, all right. Don't tell me. I don't want to know. My God, I actually made love with someone other than Mac. *How could I?* I'm not like that. What do you mean—*that?* I feel just fine, to be truthful. I feel like about a million dollars or so. Let us not speak in such crude terms, kid. God, I feel set up like anything. My heavens, it's six fifteen. Faster, Stacey. The kids will be frantic.

SEVEN

꙳ꙮ꙳ꙮ꙳ꙮ꙳ꙮ꙳ꙮ꙳

Stacey pulls up in front of the house on Bluejay Crescent and scrambles out of the car, her arms filled with parcels of pajamas. Inside the veranda, Katie is standing, slowly rocking Jen in the old hammock. Jen is nearly asleep. Katie has been crying and has fairly obviously only recently stopped.

—— What's the matter? I shouldn't have stayed away so long. It's worried Katie. Or is she just angry? How can I ever make up for it? Is Jen ill? Is that it? God, let Jen be all right. Don't let it be that. Please. I'll never go away again. I swear it.

Katie—what is it?

Katie leaves off swinging the hammock and goes to Stacey, stumblingly, putting her arms around Stacey's neck and her head on Stacey's shoulder.

Oh Mum

What *is* it, Katie? Please, honey, just tell me.

Jen

What about her? Is she all right? She isn't sick? Katie,

I'm sorry I'm so late. I stopped in for coffee and then the traffic —— How can I lie to her like this and expect to hear the truth from her? Sure, so tell her the truth—would that make the situation any better? What's *wrong?*

No, she's not sick. She's okay. I think she was just scared. Let's go into the kitchen, Mum. I don't want to tell you in front of her.

Okay, honey. Hush, Katie, love. Don't cry. Just tell me what happened.

In the kitchen, Katie sits down, her head bent, the flames of her hair covering her shoulders and breasts. She has stopped crying, but her voice is strained and there is a kind of bewilderment in it.

Well, I went over to Mrs. Fogler's to pick up Jen, like you asked me to. The door was open, see, and I was just going to ring when I heard Mrs. Fogler talking to Jen. It seemed kind of strange, what she was saying, so I listened for a minute. She was saying *The little fish doesn't want to get eaten up but she's silly, isn't she? She doesn't run away and hide. So the big fish catches her, see? Watch now—look what he's doing to her. Nasty—he's nasty, isn't he?* Maybe I shouldn't have done it, Mum, but I tore inside the living room without thinking, and Mrs. Fogler was kneeling beside the table where the fishbowl is, and she was holding Jen on a chair, I mean she had her hands on Jen's shoulders and wouldn't let her get down, and Jen was sort of squirming to get away and Mrs. Fogler was making her look. And the big goldfish had killed the other one and it was

Oh Katie

Then Mrs. Fogler looked up and saw me. Mum—she looked sort of—I don't know—frightened. I just grabbed Jen and brought her home and didn't say anything. I couldn't. I didn't know what to say.

Stacey puts her arms around Katie.

There, honey. You did right.

But what *is* it with her, Mum?

189

I don't know. I don't know. I should never have left Jen with her.

Katie looks up.

No—it wasn't your fault. You didn't know. How could you?

—— Yeh, how could I? Maybe I should've, though. If I hadn't wanted so much to go out. Katie doesn't know any of that, or she wouldn't be so sympathetic. What's it done to Jen? Maybe nothing; maybe something I'll never know, something concealed, some unknown fear that'll be part of her mental baggage from now on.

I suppose not, but I'll never forgive myself all the same.

You shouldn't feel that way, Mum. Listen, don't worry, eh? Jen's okay now. I think this trauma thing is exaggerated, anyway.

Well, we won't leave her there again.

No. What do you think we ought to say, though? To Mrs. Fogler.

Gosh, Katie, I don't know. What could be said? Maybe it's better not to say anything. Maybe she'll say something.

Yeh. Maybe.

Stacey recognizes all at once the way in which she and Katie have been talking. *We.* They have never before encountered one another as persons. At the same time, Katie has been unwittingly calling her *Mum* instead of *Mother.*

Katie—thanks

For nothing. I thought I made a mess of it. I just snatched Jen and ran.

I would've done the same.

Really? No, you would've known what to say. You always do. I never do.

I don't always, either. Sometimes I think I hardly ever do.

Really?

Yeh.

Stacey makes the dinner and puts Mac's in the oven for him. She cannot eat, but when the kids have eaten, she takes Jen upstairs for her bath. Jen has wakened up fully by now and insists on having her entire collection of plastic ducks, cups and teapots in the bath with her. Having soaped and rinsed her, Stacey lets her play for a while, and watches while Jen scoops up the bath water and pours it out again. Jen sings to herself, unaware that she is doing so.

—— Flower, you're beautiful. Is she really fragile or is it just my imagination? Her arms always look so thin. But Ian wasn't ever plump as a very young kid, either. Katie was, and so was Duncan, but that doesn't mean anything. Probably Jen's okay. Surely she'll talk soon. What's she feeling now? If only she could say. She doesn't look upset. How can you ever tell what's going on in anybody else's head? Maybe it was worse for Katie than for Jen. Or maybe not. Jen was squirming to get away, Katie said. Jen—I'm sorry sorry sorry. I shouldn't have gone out. I shouldn't have stayed away so long. I never will again. Oh? You won't, Stacey? You won't ever go out to Luke's again? Luke—I want you. I want to talk to you. I want to make love with you again—and again and again. I thought at the back of my head somewhere that I could do it only once, and then all demons would be laid to rest, laid in both meanings. I would know just once again the feeling of another man, and I would have done something that belonged only to me, was mine only, related only to me, nothing to do with any of them. Did I want to get back at Mac? Yes, that too. If it hadn't been Luke, it would've been somebody else, sooner or later. But it was Luke, and now I want him again, even now, already. Better to marry than burn, St. Paul said, but he didn't say what to do if you married *and* burned. I can't leave Jen with Tess any more. What is it with Tess? What can I do about it? You can't say to somebody, pardon me but maybe you ought to see a good headshrinker. Should I tell Jake? Probably he knows. He brought the damn things home. Should I tell Mac? Yeh, and have him say I'm making a fuss about nothing. He doesn't want to know. He doesn't want to know anything difficult about me or the kids. Nothing. Okay, and now I don't want to tell him, either, so we're even. I can't ever get away alone now. Bertha, maybe? With Julian on her hands all day long, crabbing away at her, she's got enough to worry about. *I can't go out alone.* That's what it amounts to. Jen, honey, I love you. I love your thin arms and your wide grey eyes and that fine red-gold hair of yours. I love the way you sing without any words that nutty song you learned from Duncan, "I'm Bringing Home a Baby Bumblebee." I love you—and resent you. No, I don't. That's an awful way to feel. It may be, but I feel it all the same. I can't get away by myself because of you. And I have to get away sometimes. I have to. I'm trapped. I have to see Luke. *I have to.* Too many people here, too many crises I don't know how to deal with, too much yakkity-yak from all of us, too few words that tell any of us a damn thing about any of the others. With Luke, everything is simple. He doesn't complicate things. He says what he's thinking. Luke—you make love beautifully. It was lovely. Luke, it was lovely. I can still feel him in me. Goddam Tess. Stacey, that's barbaric of you. I don't care. I don't care. I want to get out of here and I can't and one day I'll forget that Jen was scared and I'll get mad at her for something that isn't her fault, for holding me here. God, Sir, don't let it happen that way. It may though. I have a terrible temper. I always have had. My mother used to say *Stacey, you have a terrible temper— you must learn to bank your fires.* How right she was, not that I saw it then, only thinking she'd never had any fires so couldn't know. But they're not that easy to bank. What if I slap Jen one day, suddenly, hard, without knowing I'm going to do it, just because she's here and young? God, don't let me. Stay my hand. I scare the hell out of myself when I think this way.

Come on, flower. Time to get out of your bath. C'mon— that's it.

Newspaper story. Young divorced mother found in bathroom in catatonic state beside

the body of her three-year-old son. A broken
wine bottle had been plunged deeply into the
child's chest. Photograph showed girl being
led away, her face dull, absent, her hands
darkly blooded up to the wrists.

—— She was a hophead, for heaven's sake, Stacey. Yeh.
Nothing like that, nothing even remotely like that could happen
here. And then again, anything that could happen to anybody
could happen to anybody. Anything. When I think that way, my
guts turn over. Even if I never lay a hand on Jen in anger, never,
what if I become temporarily deranged some day, some day
when I'm feeling the trap worst, and yell and scream at her? Just
because she isn't yet school age and she needs me. You want to
know something, God? Sometimes all I want to do is sit down
quietly in a secluded corner and bawl my goddam eyes out.
Okay, so you don't want to know. I'm telling you anyway.

Want some pretty-smelling powder, Jen? That's right—
you sprinkle it on, yourself. Hey, how about that? Now you smell
like a flower as well as looking like one.

Stacey hugs Jen tightly and gently, wanting only to be
aware of Jen's warmth and perfection. But as she does so, she
recalls that *Hey, how about that?* is Luke's phrase.

Mac still is not home. Stacey puts Jen to bed and goes
downstairs to round up the boys. Duncan is in the kitchen, his
face pressed against the screen of the back door, his shoulders in
an attitude of dejection.

Hi, honey. What's the matter?

Ian's upstairs and he won't let me in the room. It's my
room, too.

What's the matter with him?

How should I know? He's mad at me. He's always mad
at me.

Okay, I'll go and see.

Stacey goes upstairs again and tries the door of the boys'
bedroom. It is locked.

Ian?

The voice that reaches her is sullen and suspicious.

Whaddya want?

Why won't you let Duncan in? Come on, open that door right this minute. What's the trouble, anyway?

He's a dumb moron and I don't want him in here. Why can't I have my own room? I'm sick of sharing with him.

Because there are not enough bedrooms for you to have your own room, that's why. As you very well know.

Jen and Katie have got their own rooms. Why can't they share for change? I *hate* Duncan in here with me. He's always breaking my models and stuff. He hasn't got any brains.

Stacey feels her annoyance beginning, like a nettle sting in the mind.

Now listen here, Ian, you unlock that door, you hear? Duncan has as much right in there as you, and he isn't always breaking your models at all, and it's time for both of you to go to bed. All right. I'm going downstairs and I'll give you ten minutes. You open the door and we won't say any more about it.

Stacey goes back down to the kitchen. Duncan is still looking out into the back yard. Stacey sits down on a kitchen chair and finds to her surprise that she is crying.

—— For heaven's sake, what's the matter with me? I don't know I don't know I don't know

Duncan turns and sees her. He looks shocked.

Mum—you're not *crying*, are you?

—— Mothers don't cry. Only kids. Pull yourself together, Stacey.

No, not really. I just felt sort of tired for a minute, there. I'm okay now. Everything's all right.

Ian bawled today.

What?

He bawled. He never bawls, does he, Mum? But he did. I saw him. I guess that's why he's mad at me, maybe. He doesn't like people to see him bawling.

Duncan—tell me. What was wrong with him?

He—well, a bunch of us kids were playing out on the Crescent after school, and Ian went out on the road after the football, only he didn't see this car coming, and it just missed him. He said he didn't want to play any more and when I went to look for him, he was in the basement, bawling.

Oh Duncan—why didn't you tell me before? Before I went upstairs. I didn't know he was

Stacey rushes back upstairs.

—— I was away away away with Luke making love with Luke and Ian was here and he might have been hurt. He might have been run over. Stacey, don't be a fool. You couldn't have stopped it even if you had been here. Maybe not, but even so even so even so. And Ian cried. Ian. Who never cries. Because of what happened to Peter Challoner and because Ian thinks about death—how much? Some people don't know they're ever going to die until it happens to them, but Ian knows he's going to die. He knows it will happen to him some day. He's ten, and he knows that already. Was it Peter's death that taught it to him? Or has he known for a long time, in ways I don't know anything about? Maybe he thinks of it as I've always thought of it, wondering what form it would take for me, what face it would wear, what moment in my time it would choose for our encounter, imagining it as sudden severed or seared flesh and then again imagining it as something to be fought for in senility when there isn't any strength for even that battle and they keep you going against your will on tubes and oxygen, the total indignity, imagining it in order to defeat it, like as a kid I used to imagine the dead men below in the mortuary, conjure them up on purpose so they wouldn't take me by surprise, although in reality I never saw even one of them. I always thought that was why I thought about it, but Ian does too and *his* father deals in rejuvenating vitamins. Have I passed it on, along with the chromosomes and genes?

195

Ian?

Yeh?

Honey, I'm sorry I was cross. I didn't know—Duncan just told me—about the road—Ian, try not to let it upset you. It's all right now.

And from the bedroom, from behind the locked door, the sudden shrill desperate voice.

Can't you leave me alone? *Can't you just leave me alone?*

—— Ian. Mac's words. Ian, don't—I can't bear it. And you can't bear the way I try to know, the way I try to enter your locked room, can you? All your locked rooms.

Stacey goes down to the kitchen without another word.

Duncan—you go to sleep in Daddy's and my bed for now, and I'll move you after a while. Ian's kind of upset.

Mac has just come in and has overheard.

What's the matter with Ian?

Stacey tells him. Mac sets down his briefcase and prepares to go upstairs.

He'll open the door all right. I'm not going to have that kind of temperamental display.

Mac—leave him.

Now listen here, Stacey, it's perfectly ridiculous for Duncan to go to sleep somewhere else just because Ian doesn't choose to open the door. He's got to learn to consider other people.

Yes, but he needs consideration, too.

He's damn well going to learn to show a little responsibility.

—— My God, of course it's not Ian he's mad at. It's me. Only maybe he doesn't know it.

Mac starts out of the kitchen, but Stacey takes hold of his arm.

Mac, don't you dare go up there. Just don't. Ian has to be left alone for a while—he *has* to. Can't you see? You, of all people, ought to be able to see that. You got no business knocking Ian for wanting to be left alone occasionally.

Mac removes her hand from his sleeve. He turns and walks into his study.

Okay. Have it your way, Stacey. Do anything you like with them. Ruin them, for all I care.

Stacey looks at Duncan. His eyes are fixed on her face, but she cannot guess at all what he is seeing. Then he trudges upstairs. She hears him knocking very softly at Ian's door and after a few minutes, the door opens. The boys go to bed in silence, without speaking to one another.

— All right. I shouldn't have said that, in front of Duncan. But you shouldn't have, either, Mac. Damn you damn you damn you. Imagine saying *Ruin them, for all I care.* What in hell does he think Duncan's going to make of that? That I'm no good and Mac couldn't care less about any of them? Mac, how could you? Let me tell you one simple fact—whatever you're like, whatever you're thinking, whatever you're going through, I don't want to know, see? I just don't want to know. Not any more. All right, I don't have the guts to say it to you. But there it is. I hate you. I wish to God I'd never laid eyes on you. There it is.

Doorbell. Stacey answers it, and finds Julian Garvey standing inside the veranda. He is a small man, and with old age he has shrunken even more. He has a wispy tonsure of pepper-grey hair, and his seamed red-mottled face resembles a surly gnome. With Stacey, he is invariably courteous, even exaggeratedly so. He saves his salvos for Bertha.

Evening, Stacey. I trust this isn't an inconvenient moment? If you're busy, just say so.

No, not at all. Come in, Julian.

Well, actually it was Mac I wanted to see, really. Is he home?

Yes, he's just come in. I'll call him. He's in the study.

Oh—well, maybe I could go in there? I just wanted to have a private word with him. Get his advice, you know. I've been seeing these Richalife pills advertised all over the place, and I sort of wondered

197

—— Oh Lord. Sure. What else? You wondered if they'd restore your virility? Or prolong your life eternally? There's one born every minute. And Mac will sell them to you, too. Never doubt it. He's not the same guy as the one who told the pensioner on Grenoble Street that he needed encyclopedias like he needed a hole in the head. No. Mr. MacAindra has altered more than somewhat. Well, climb on the magic carousel, you stupid old bugger. Who gives a damn?

Sure, Julian. Come right in.

Stacey knocks.

Mac?

What?

It's Julian. He's here to see you.

Oh—okay. C'mon in.

The door opens and Julian goes in. Stacey pours herself a gin and tonic and saunters quietly near the study. Unfortunately the door is thick and the voices are not loud, so she cannot hear anything except a low mumbling. At last Julian emerges. Stacey sees him to the door. His hands are empty.

Mac said he didn't really think   man of my age, you know   well, I just wondered

Oh. Well, good night, Julian.

Good night, Stacey.

The study door is partly open and Stacey looks in. Mac is sitting at his desk with his head leaning against his outstretched hands, his palms covering his eyes.

—— Mac? Mac, I'm sorry. You did right—are you wondering if you did, or cursing yourself for it? You're still the same guy at least in some ways and I'm the same too in some ways. I don't hate you. Maybe you don't hate me, either. I'm just sorry sorry sorry. For us both.

For three days Stacey prowls the house, unable to settle to any work. She prepares meals numbly, almost without noticing. She intends to go over and try to talk to Tess, but she does not go. On the fourth morning the doorbell rings and Tess is standing in the veranda. Involuntarily, Stacey glances around. But Jen is playing in the back yard.

Hi, Stacey. Have you got a minute?

Sure. Come in. Have some coffee?

Well, thanks. Don't make it specially.

No, I was just going to have some anyway.

I thought I'd pop over and see if you wanted me to mind Jen. I mean, when you get your hair done.

— Tell her. Say something. I can't. I don't know how. I'm embarrassed.

Oh—well, thanks, Tess. But I'm not getting it done this week.

Are you okay, Stacey? There's nothing wrong, is there?

N-no. I've just been feeling kind of tired these past few days. It's nothing. Everything's okay.

— Coward.

Well, I just wondered, seeing as you usually get it done about this time of week.

No, I'm fine. I'm—getting kind of sick of going to the hairdresser's every week. And she never does it the way I want it, anyway. I'm thinking of growing it and doing it myself.

Well, it's a time-saver if you do. I've always done my own.

Tess?

Mm?

Are you okay? Are you feeling all right? I mean, there's nothing worrying you?

Tess's eyes grow wide with question and alarm.

What makes you say that, Stacey? Do you think I don't look all right?

No, it wasn't that. Well, maybe I thought you looked a little worried or something

Heavens, everything is all right. I don't know why you should think

— Tell her why. Say it. You've got to. I can't. She doesn't

199

want to talk. She doesn't want to say anything about anything. Maybe she believes everything is all right. Maybe it *is* all right, actually. Maybe it didn't really mean anything, that day. Maybe it happened sort of accidentally, and she didn't give it a second thought.

Well, I'm sorry. I just wondered

No, everything's fine. The doctor says my blood pressure's much better, and he's given me these new tranquilizers. Not that I really need them, but I'm very highly strung, as you know. I always was, even as a child. My father used to say *Tess, quit jumping around like a flea—you get on my nerves.* He was right. I always had to be doing something. I was always on the go. I'm thinking of taking up tennis again. What do you think?

Good idea. You probably need to get out more.

Oh, I go downtown a lot. I'm a great little bargain hunter.

Yeh.

Jake's got a part in a new six-episode series.

That's good.

Yes. He's playing opposite Fay Faulkner. She's a lovely girl.

So-so, I'd say.

Well, she's got that very dark hair and that absolutely white skin. Jake says she's very intelligent as an actress. He says not many of them are. He's trying out for TV again. It would be wonderful if he got in. They ought to take him on—he's got such an interesting face. He'd be so happy if he could. Not that he's not happy right now, in radio, but I mean he'd be even happier. Oh, I meant to say, Stacey, if you want any of the HATSHEPSUT line of cosmetics, I can give you Mrs. Clovelly's phone number.

Thanks. I'll let you know. I'm sort of overstocked at the moment.

I think they've made a lot of difference to my skin. I really firmly believe they have. Don't you think so?

Yes—I think they probably have. I always thought you had a marvelous skin, anyway, though.

It takes a lot of looking after, believe me. I've got one of those skins that has a tendency to be dry. It needs nourishment. I just have to keep at it.

Yeh, well maybe I should try the night cream.

—— Tess. What's the matter with us? Or maybe you really are only talking about the outer skin? I don't know. I can't get through the sound barrier any more than I can with any of them. Is it only me who wants to? (Is it only I who want to?) Goddam. I can only break through with one person. Luke Luke Luke

I should be running along now, Stacey. Thanks for the coffee. You'll give me a ring when you want to leave Jen?

Yes. Sure. Thanks, Tess.

—— I won't, though. Not ever again. And I don't know how to explain it. I'll have to quit going to the hairdresser's. I can't suddenly begin to take Jen along with me.

When Tess has gone, Stacey checks to make sure Jen is all right and then goes upstairs. She sits on the bed and looks at herself in the full-length mirror.

—— I can't get out. I can't. There's no way. Not now. I've got to. I've got to see him again. I can't help it. It's not a luxury, it's a necessity. Look at that face in the mirror. You're thirty-nine, kid. Well, I don't know. Maybe I'm not so terrible to look at. That's odd—I look better to myself now than I did a week ago. Sure, and guess why. I do look better, though. I'm not a bad-looking woman. I haven't got wrinkles—well, not many, anyway —even though I don't plaster on the *Avocado Wrinkle Cream*. My legs are good, and so are my breasts. All right, I'm no glamour girl, but strong men wouldn't necessarily flinch at the sight of me. Luke thought I was all right. He liked it. He loved it. Oh my God, it was marvelous. I've got to see him again. And talk to him as well. He can talk. He isn't clammed up. He's open and honest. He knows how to allow himself to speak. He doesn't tell lies. He doesn't need to. Okay, I know it's crazy. I am well aware that it is even ludicrous. If it were the other way around, Luke ten years older, it wouldn't seem peculiar in the slightest, so why should it, this way? It isn't the number of years that count, it's the way people feel about each other. I'm damn well going to see him again. You can't. I'm going to. How? I don't know—yet. That remains to be seen. Mac has a conference tonight. He won't be home until midnight, more than likely. Oh Stacey. The more you want to level with everybody, the less you do. I know. You don't need to tell me. Ease up on me, God, can't you?

That evening, when Mac has gone out again after dinner, Stacey puts Jen to bed and approaches Katie, who is doing her homework in her bedroom.

Katie—you remember Rosalind Ackerman? I met her at the Ancient Greek Drama course last winter, remember? She was over here a few times. Well, she phoned today and asked me to go over tonight—she's having a few women in for bridge. Would that be okay? You wouldn't mind? I wouldn't be late.

Katie looks up and smiles.

Sure, that's okay. You run along. Can you get the boys in bed first, though?

—— Oh Katie, you're stabbing me to the heart.

Yes, of course. I'll get them tucked in before I go. Thanks, honey.

That's okay.

As Stacey is saying good night to Ian, he props himself up in bed on one elbow and looks at her, frowningly.

Mum—I don't feel very well.

Stacey's heart turns over. She puts a hand on his forehead.

Where don't you feel well, Ian? I don't think you've got a fever.

It's my stomach, like. I got this sort of an ache, right here.

—— Could it be a reverberation from the car thing, the other day? Yeh, you think psychosomatic, and one day it turns out to be appendix, burst before anybody can do anything. They don't die of it any more. There's antibiotics. But I'm never convinced. Show me where.

Right here.

Well, that's your stomach all right. It wouldn't be your appendix that high up. Did you eat anything different from anybody else today?

No, I don't think so. Grant and me had some salted peanuts. He bought them with his money.

Maybe that was it. Gee, I don't know, honey. I wonder if I should stay home? It isn't a sharp pain?

More like a dull ache, kind of. But then it comes in twinges, you know, and gets sharper.

—— The old question. How serious? I never know.

Well, it doesn't seem all that serious to me, Ian. Listen, if it gets worse, you tell Katie, eh? If it got really bad, she could phone Doctor Spender. I won't be late. You settle down now, and try to sleep.

Okay. G'night, Mum.

Good night, honey.

Stacey calls good-bye to Katie and goes outside and into the Chev. The drive out to Luke's is interminable tonight.

—— Blasted traffic. And I've got to be home by eleven at the latest. It isn't fair to put that responsibility on Katie. Would she know when to phone the doctor? It's hard enough even for me to know. But I don't think it was anything much. He didn't have a fever. What if someone's there, at Luke's? What if he isn't there? What if some other woman is there? What'll I say? I'll approach quietly, and if I hear voices, I'll just go away, that's all. If only he had a phone. He's really bushed out there. I guess that's the best way for him to be able to write. I wish I could be there to make meals for him. To sleep with him all night.

Luke is home and alone. He stands in the doorway of the A-frame, still wearing the Indian sweater with the bear mask design, his beard now recognizable as such.

—— Too good to be true. Thanks, God. Travel now, pay later. Send me the bill at the end of the month. No—don't. Is he smiling? Or is he only trying to smile? I wish I hadn't come. It was madness. He's never yet asked me to come out. I've just arrived. What a situation to put him in. What can he do, short of ordering me off the premises? Luke, I'm sorry. I couldn't help it.

Hi. Luke—I hope you don't mind me—I mean, if you're busy

—— Worse. That makes it even worse. How can I humiliate myself and yet not stop doing it? Luke—please—just once more.

Hi, merwoman. How's life?

Life? Oh, not bad, I guess.

Nice dress—bronze, like those chrysanthemums in fall.

That's because I'm at a bridge party.

Luke laughs, but a little wryly.

Yeh. I guess that's necessary. Well, come in.

Thanks. How's your work?

Luke leads her into the main room and shows her a pile of typed pages.

It's coming on. Only I'm beginning to see a lot of flaws in the structure. And I'm not sure the inventions are sharp enough —you know, like the perambulating statues of African statesmen in the Residence garden, in lieu of trees. Well, the hell with it. I wish I could take you out fishing. Would you like to go out in the cockleshell that we jokingly refer to as a boat?

—— No. I'd like to go to bed with you, if you really want to know.

I'd love to, but honestly I can't stay very long

Well, let's have some coffee, then.

Luke puts the coffee on the stove, and she goes and stands beside him, putting an arm tentatively around him. He laughs, turns the stove low, and at last holds her tightly, his sex hard against her.

Who wants tea and sympathy? Let's have coffee and sex, Stacey, eh?

They make love on the rough wool rug, as before. Stacey's hands knead his shoulders, his ribs. She reaches a climax almost as soon as he is inside her, and again when he comes.

204

When it is over, he outlines her face with his hands and kisses her eyelids.

Luke

Mm? I'm feeling no pain

Me neither. Or is it—I'm not, either?

Who cares?

I'm illiterate, Luke.

Who cares? You're pretty good, you know?

I didn't know. Tell me again.

You're great. I like it with you.

Oh Luke   I like it with you too   I love it

That's good   the coffee's boiling over

Don't tell me. Let me guess. You're a romantic at heart.

Well, sure. But have you ever wiped up scorched coffee from a stove?

They have the coffee without getting dressed, but the evening has an edge of chill, so Luke drags in a blanket and drapes it over them both. Stacey touches his chin.

Your beard is coming along nicely.

Yeh, well it's only because I'm too lazy to shave, that's all. I won't need to shave where I'm going this summer anyhow.

Where you going?

I was going to sign on with a fish boat, but I think maybe I'll just hitch and see what happens. If I can finish this book for better or worse in a couple of weeks, I'd like to go north again. That's a great country, Stacey. Ever seen it? Up the Skeena River—Kispiox, Kitwanga, crazy names like that. In some parts, nearer the coast, you drive along the edge of a mountain and the trees are like a jungle, only it's mostly evergreen, but all this fantastic growth, bushes and ferns and moss and jack pine, all crowding each other, dark and light greens, northern jungle, rain forest, and the damn road's so narrow you swear any minute you're going to plummet over into some canyon or other.

I've never seen it.

There's this place where there's a ferry. Is it Kitwanga? Yeh, maybe. Anyway, this beat-up old raft crawls across the Skeena and it's attached to some kind of a cable, and you think —man, if that cable goes, that's it—the river is wild as hell. But the old guy who runs it is calm as anything, probably been there forever. Charon. He talks very easy and slow, and you think— maybe it wouldn't be such a bad death, after all. And there's this village near there somewhere, Indian village, a bunch of run-down huts and everything dusty, even the kids and the dogs covered with dust like they were all hundreds of years old which maybe they are and dying which they almost certainly are. And they look at you with these dark slanted eyes they've got, all the people there. They come out and look at you with a sort of in-choate hatred and who could be surprised at it? Because lots of people visit the place every summer, for maybe half an hour. The attraction is the totem poles. And there they are—high, thin, beaked, bleached in the sun, cracking and splintering, the totems of the dead. And of the living dead. If I were one of them, the nominally living, I'd sure as hell hate people like me, coming in from the outside. You want to ask them if they know any longer what the poles mean, or if it's a language which has got lost and now there isn't anything to replace it except silence and some-times the howling of men who've been separated from them-selves for so long that it's only a dim memory, a kind of violent mourning, only a reason to stay as drunk as they can for as long as they can. You don't ask anybody anything. You haven't suf-fered enough. You don't know what they know. You don't have the right to pry. So you look, and then you go away.

Is it really like that?

Luke turns to her, sharply, unexpectedly.

I don't know. That's the way it looked to me. Why don't you come along and see, Stacey?

What?

Come with me. See what you make of it.

I'd like to, more than I could ever say. But I can't.

Why not, merwoman? You want to get away, don't you? I thought that was the whole point with you.

I've imagined myself getting away more times than I can tell you

Then do it.

Stacey looks at him, appalled and shaken by the suggestion of choice. Then she turns away again.

If I had two lives, I would. You think I don't want to?

I don't know what you want. That's what interests me. What *do* you want? The most, I mean.

I want to go with you.

Okay. Then it's settled.

No. Luke—I can't leave

What can't you leave?

My kids and and

Luke nods and hands her her clothes. They dress without speaking. Then she lights two cigarettes and gives him one. He puts an arm around her.

It's okay, merwoman. I didn't really think you'd come along.

He withdraws from her, a little, and smiles. His voice has an undercurrent of mockery, but his fingers reassure her shoulder.

> *Ladybird, ladybird,*
> *Fly away home;*
> *Your house is on fire,*
> *Your children are gone.*

Stacey becomes tense, examining his face to discover his meaning, but not discovering it.

Luke—why did you say that?

He shrugs.

I don't know. It just came into my mind. Hey—how about that? I've scared you, haven't I? I'm sorry, Stacey. I didn't mean to.

I have to go home

Right now? You haven't been here long.

It's just that

—— It's something I can't tell you. Sure, you level with him, Stacey, you just go ahead and do that little thing. You thought you could.

You don't have to explain, Stacey.

Luke, I want to come out again.

I know, baby. It's a pity that you can't.

How do you know I can't?

My horoscope told me. Or else I've got second sight. That must be it. You wonder if there's a third or fourth sight, and how that'll work out, in a thousand or so years. Merwoman

What?

I'm not twenty-nine. I'm twenty-four.

In Stacey's bones the sword turns with slowness and pain. Her hand circles his wrist, but she does not look at him.

Luke   why

Let it be. Just let it be, eh? Ease up on yourself, merwoman. You going to be okay?

Me? Sure—I guess so. Well

Well

But neither of them can say anything more. Then she goes. The car responds to her tension, and she drives fast, hardly seeing where she is going, her inner automatic pilot having taken over.

> Luke, his Indian sweater bulking around him, recounting something. *She was once blessed by the Pope—it was just before she and my dad came to this country, and I was about two months old—she had me when she was fifteen, great for her, eh?*

208

—— I'm not old enough to be every twenty-four-year-old's mother. But I'm old enough to be his mother. She's the same age as I am. I can't bear it. You have to, Stacey. There isn't anything else you can do. And in the end, he said what was so, but I didn't. I didn't say I lied about my age, too, but in the opposite direction. But he knew.

Ladybird, ladybird

—— It's all right. He didn't have a fever, Ian. But what if anything developed? What if it did turn out to be appendix, this time? Would Katie call the doctor or would she just wait, hoping everything would be all right and I'd get home soon? Look, it's all right, Stacey. Don't panic. Why did Luke have to say that idiotic rhyme?

Ladybird, ladybird,

—— Luke. I can't not see you again. I have to. I didn't even ask you exactly when you were going away. It isn't so easy for me to organize, getting out to your place. Don't you see? Stacey, have you forgotten what he told you? Let me tell you one simple fact, doll. He's only ten years older than Katie. Lots of girls marry men who are ten years older than themselves. Okay, God. That's enough. That's enough for the bill. Aren't you ever satisfied? Ease up on me, eh? Why did he ask me to go north with him? Why? What if I'd said yes? Would he have backed down? He knew I wouldn't say yes.

Bluejay Crescent. Stacey pulls the Chev to a jarring halt and climbs out. Mac is coming down the steps out of the house.

Mac? I thought you

Mac runs one hand through his brush-cut hair. His tall lank frame communicates tiredness and something else which she cannot guess.

Mac? Is everything okay?

He looks at her then, and his voice is drab, drained, dry.
Stacey, he's dead

Stacey crumples, and he grabs for her, pulling her up.
Her eyes see nothing, not even Mac's face, and she does not
know she is speaking the one mourning word.

Ian Ian Ian

Mac takes her by the shoulders, to steady her, and she
suddenly can feel him trembling, trying to control it and not
succeeding.

Stacey—it's not Ian. Christ, why should you have thought
that? Ian's asleep. He's quite okay. It's Buckle.

EIGHT

ᗰᗰᗰᗰᗰᗰᗰᗰ

Buckle? It's Buckle?

Stacey cannot take in the reality of Mac's words, or quite believe yet that Ian is safe and she herself essentially unpunished after all. She pulls away from Mac and looks at him as though suspecting she may read in his eyes some insane and subtle deception. But Mac's face reveals only his open hurt.

Yes. They've just phoned me.

They?

The police. They want me to go to the   the   to identify
— He can't say *morgue*. Oh my God—Buckle is dead. And my first thought was only relief that Ian was okay. Buckle can't be dead. He can't be. But he is. I never cared for him, but I wouldn't have wished him any harm.

> Stacey, seeing Buckle approach her, feeling him already inside her although they were still apart. Stacey wanting him, even there, even in that room under the sightless eyes of

the she-whale. Then the words he spoke, and
the flung coins. Stacey, running down the
linoleum-covered stairs, hating hating hating
—— He won't be able to tell Mac any more lies about me.
That's over. Serves him right. No—I'm not thinking that. I can't.
That's terrible. I'm not like that. I'm not like that at all.

Mac, who never touches her in public in case somebody
might see, suddenly puts his arms around her again and holds
her cruelly tight, blind to the streetlights, blind to Bluejay Crescent, holding her not for her need now but for his own.

Stacey—he had an identification card on him and he
had he had put me down as his next of kin.

She can feel his enormous effort not to break down. This
one thing, the contrived kinship with its implications, he can
bear less, almost, than Buckle's death.

Mac oh Mac I'm sorry
—— Now he can't ever settle it with Buckle. They were
friends for a long time and then they weren't and that was my
fault. I can't bear that. No—yes, I can. I didn't do it all—it was
Buckle, too, and for reasons further back than mine. Why did
Buckle say that to Mac about me? Now Mac won't ever know, or
be able to say he's sorry he told Buckle to go to hell. If he is sorry.
He *is* sorry. But he wouldn't have been if Buckle hadn't got
killed. Got killed? I don't even know what happened. Yes, I do,
though.

Mac—how did it happen? It was on the road?

Oh sure. What else? Head-on collision. Both killed. At
least Buckle was driving alone on that run.

Collision with another truck?

Yes.

With another truck like his? One of the big diesels? I
mean I mean

I know. Yes. It was one like his.

I guess it would have had to be. He never played chicken except with

> The highway shivering past, honking, obstacle-laden. Buckle riding the truck like a jockey. Buckle, for God's sake, watch the road. His laughter, as he looked at the wheeling metallic ballet ahead. *I've never yet met a guy who didn't give way.*

—— I thought it was pure ego, superconfidence, when he said that. But maybe after all it was only disappointment.

Mac turns to go.

I told them I'd be right down.

Mac—why do you have to go tonight? Wouldn't tomorrow be

I'd rather go now and get it over with.

I'm coming with you.

For a moment, she thinks he is going to refuse. Then he nods, and it is almost like a need-admitting sigh.

Okay, Stacey. Would you   would you drive?

Sure. Of course.

They take the Chev instead of the Buick because Stacey is more familiar with it. They drive in silence. Stacey is on the point of speaking, several times, but she is afraid she may say the one wrong or fuselike word which may make something explode in his head or heart and break the control which he will need, which he would never forgive himself for not having in this final encounter.

A grey building, not far from the waterfront, where the cheap-wine and meths drinkers gurgle and cough out intolerable lives. Only one light burning. The courtrooms, coroner's office, all black, shut, nobody home. Only the chapel of the violent dead holding its eternal hours, crash and stab not knowing nine to five. Stacey parks, and Mac puts a hand on her arm.

213

You stay here, Stacey.

I'll come if you want me to. I mean it.

Yeh. I know. I—thanks. But no.

The car door opens and closes; the door of the building opens and closes. Stacey smokes and waits.

— I couldn't have gone in. Yes, I could have. No, I couldn't. Well, if I'd had to, I would have. And yet I'm curious as well. How do they stash them away? In grey-metal drawers like outsize filing cabinets, chilled for preservation? I don't want to know. And yet I think of it, and what it would be like to be lying there, among them, one of them, not in a hospital with fragmentary hope but there with none, everything broken, drained out, gashed. Don't be ridiculous, Stacey. As if you'd know, if you were. But somehow I always think I would know it, be able to see myself battered and wrecked, extinguished.

Cameron's Funeral Home was never entered into by children. Stacey and her sister were forbidden. After Niall Cameron's funeral, when Stacey was grown and had her own children, she went in, forced herself in, to banish the long-ago cold tenants once and for all, send them back to limbo or even heaven, put them under that dutifully flower-prinked earth where they had lain years. Everything was dusty and jumbled, bottles once booze mixed with the jars and potions of a profession old as the pharaohs. Her mother found her there. *He would never let me clean here, your father wouldn't. He'd never let me tidy up. He said it would be a violation—I've never understood what he could have meant, but then he was always a little well you know.* Yes. And they'd turned and exited, locked up again, and Stacey went to the Liquor Commission and bought a mickey of rye

214

but had to drink it in the bathroom and gargle with mouthwash after, and her mother said *You might consider that someone else might like to have a bath dear*. Sorry. Sorry. Sorry.

—— Buckle? Buckle—I'm sorry. I'm sorry. I shouldn't have gone with you that afternoon. It was only because because. I didn't mean. Did it hurt you that Mac's wife would? Naturally it did. What do I do about that? One more piece of baggage to lug along. I wish I could get rid of all of it. I wish I could start all over, with things simpler, really simple, none of this mishmash. Luke? I want to see him again. I can't. I can't want to. But I do. He's not fifteen years younger. He is, though. Even if he weren't, how could I get out? Out of where I am. All I want to do, God, is go away and throw all of this overboard. What about the kids? Yeh. And Mac? I don't know. Whatever he's feeling, I don't want to know. But I do know. And I can't get rid of that.

Mac opens the door and climbs in. He lights a cigarette and does not look at Stacey. She eases the car into motion as though she has to be careful not to have it jolt. They travel home in silence.

—— I can't say anything. God, don't let him tell me. I don't want to know.

Once home, they go to bed without yet speaking. Mac turns off the light on the bedside table. Then, almost immediately, he switches it on again and walks very quickly to the bathroom. Stacey, lying stretched straight and stiff as a brass curtain rail, hears him vomiting, flushing the toilet to mask the sound. Mercifully, no child wakens. Mac returns, crawls into bed, turns to her and puts his arms around her. He is crying now, the lung-wrenching spasms of a man to whom crying is forbidden. Shocked and frightened, she can only hold him, stroke his shoulders. Finally it subsides and he gets up and gropes for Kleenex and cigarettes. His voice is rough with self-condemnation.

Sorry.

Mac—you don't have to be

Well. It was just that

He returns to bed and lights cigarettes for both of them, something he has not done in a long time. They sit up in bed with the ashtray between them. Stacey cannot say anything to enable him to speak, because she is afraid of what he will say. But after awhile he tries again.

Stacey—you don't mind me saying?

Of course not. How could I?

—— I could. I do. But if he doesn't say, it'll be the worst thing that ever happened to him. What I lack is strength. Enough strength. Enough calm. Just give me enough to boggle through this one night, God, and I'll never ask for anything again. Yeh— I know. You've heard all of that before.

Mac speaks in an untoned voice, at least to begin with.

His back was broken, so he looked twisted sort of and his head was was

Buckle Fennick, prince of the highway, superstitious as a caveman, Buckle who could swagger standing still, now lying still once and for all, Buckle with torn eyes unsocketed, blood wiped boredly away by attendants but smears still on the dark skin of his Indian-like face

Sh sh it's all right

He hadn't changed the identification card, Stacey. Not even after he phoned me that time. He left it the way it was. Me as his nearest

I know

Why? How could he? I don't get it. You know, I never did that well by him.

You did so. You did.

I always kind of resented how much he came around.

You never said. He didn't know. I didn't, either.

Well, how could I say? It was something that happened a long time ago

216

It is a time they have seldom spoken about, Stacey and Mac. Their children will learn it from books.

> Preceded by pipers, the men of the Queen's Own Cameron Highlanders marched through the streets of Manawaka on their way overseas. Stacey, fifteen, watched them go, the boymen whom she soon might have known, perhaps married one if they had stayed. Nearly all the Manawaka boys of that age joined the same regiment. That was the war, to Stacey. She felt at the time ashamed of her own distance and safety. But after Dieppe, she could never again listen to the pipes playing *The March of the Cameron Men*. Even twenty years later, it remained a pibroch for them. The rough-fibered music forced mourning on her as though it had perpetually happened only the day before.

You mean in the war?

Yes. I didn't understand it very well and I thought maybe I was just imagining things

What was it?

In Italy. Quite near the end. At that point we were cleaning up. You know, sweeping all before us, like. And maybe careless. Anyway, there was this bridge—funny, I can see it right now, a little brick bridge, those Roman arches, been there for centuries, I guess. Buckle and I were on supply transport, truck full of rations, spelled each other off. He was driving, and you know how he drives. Bat outa hell isn't in it with him and how we got separated from the convoy I'll never know because I hadn't had any sleep the night before and he hadn't either but it didn't seem to affect him so much. I dozed off and when I wakened there we were on this godawful road all by ourselves and he said he had looked at the map and figured a short cut which I thought was lunacy but try to tell him anything. Anyway, there we were at this bridge and I said let's get out and have a look first and he said—God, Stacey, I can hear the way he said it—he said, *Okay, chickadee, you get out and walk because I'm driving across.* I was a kid—only just turned twenty, and I didn't like to be reminded. It made me bloody angry, because he always thought he was so goddam tough and all that, and I guess I thought he was being patronizing, but I wasn't going back on what I'd said, so I did get out. He went bowling on, not waiting for a check and

Go on—say it.

Well

Say it.

The bridge blew. Mined. It went before Buckle got properly onto it, or there wouldn't have been much of him left to pick up, but the truck was thrown and flung half into the river, which wasn't that deep. I hauled him out. He had three broken ribs and concussion—I only learned this later—at the time I thought every bone in his body was broken. He kept bleeding from his mouth and nose. He was unconscious. I thought he'd had it. I thought he'd choke with the blood in his throat, so I—but I didn't really know what the hell to do. After what seemed about a year, I found a farmer with a donkey cart, and finally we got back to the other road and met up with the last of the convoy. I don't know, Stacey—that trek in the cart, it was weird, like it was only being imagined or some such thing. It wasn't that I hadn't seen worse things—nothing like that. But Buckle kept coming to, just for a few seconds at a time, and from the way he looked it wasn't only because he was in pain   it was something else entirely

Mac—what bugs you?

Mac stubs out his cigarette and lights another. She can now see him, her eyes having adjusted to the dark. His face shows nothing. His voice is so plain as to be almost casual.

I couldn't figure it at the time. But later on I thought maybe it was just that I hadn't done him any favor. I hadn't done anything he wanted me to do.

So then you had to take him on for life? Because

—— Who is this guy? Why did I never know?

It sounds crazy I guess

It doesn't sound crazy. Mac—stop beating yourself. You're not God. You couldn't save him.

That's only too obvious.

Not obvious enough, maybe. Mac?

Yeh?

I never went to bed with him.

Mac reaches out and puts a hand tentatively on one of her breasts.

I believe you now. I wish to Christ I had before. I just felt   I don't know

Look—I might have. I guess I actually might have. But that wasn't what he wanted. I don't guess he was all that interested in women, Mac. That was why Julie left him. He liked it with himself but with somebody looking on.

Oh Jesus

Would it have been better if I hadn't told you?

No. It's better this way. It's   believable

Maybe he wanted you.

Mac involuntarily tenses.

Yeh   maybe

Did it scare you, that?

Christ, Stacey, we're talking a lot of bullshit. We better go to sleep.

Would it have been the end for you if I had gone to bed with him? In a way it wouldn't have mattered.

Maybe not. But you didn't.

No. I didn't.

—— But I did with Luke, and you don't know that and I can't tell you because would it do any good to tell you? I don't think so. I want to, but I can't. Maybe it'll come out twenty years from now just like this about Buckle has come out now. In the meantime, we carry our own suitcases. How was it I never knew how many you were carrying? Too busy toting my own.

Stacey?

Yeh?

—— What now? Whatever it is, I can't take it.

About Delores

Who?

Delores Appleton. That girl.

Oh yeh. Her. What?

I did.

—— What does he expect me to do? Throw a fit? I'm delighted. I'm not the only one

Oh?

Only once, though. And only after I thought you'd gone to bed with Buckle.

—— Thanks. Heap coals of fire on my head. I'm made of asbestos.

Oh?

Yeh. But it wasn't it wasn't well I could see it wasn't what she needed and what she needed I couldn't

How do you mean?

Well I guess she really needs to be cared about by some guy over a long time

—— Oh Mac. Like I have been, by you, come hell or high water, in some way or other. Go ahead—stab me to the heart. Maybe I'll undergo a change of heart. The new one will be plastic and unbreakable. And yet, goddam it, you did want her before, and couldn't admit it until I'd given you some kind of cause for permission.

Yes. I can see that. I guess she does. Mac—I don't mind honestly

Don't you?

Well

—— Does he *want* me to mind?

Mac—we'd better try to go to sleep   seven o'clock isn't that far off

Yeh   you're right

Good night, Mac.

Good night, Stacey.

After a while, he is asleep but Stacey still is not. Something remains to be done. Gingerly, she edges out of bed, so as not to waken him, partly because he needs to sleep and partly because she could not explain. She goes into the boys' room. Ian is sleeping, on his left side as always, his forehead slightly damp with sweat. Stacey does not touch him. She only listens to hear very definitely his breathing.

EVER-OPEN EYE   TROOPS PARACHUTING INTO ANOTHER COUNTRY   THE COMMENTING VOICE IS BUSINESSLIKE, INTERPRETING DEATH AS NUMERALS

How come you never take us to the beach, Mum?

I will, Ian.

Yeh, but summer holidays started one week ago—one whole week—and so far we haven't been down once.

Yeh, that's right, Mum. Ian's right. You *never* take us to the beach. It's not fair.

Okay, okay, Duncan. We'll go tomorrow.

EVER-OPEN EYE   POLICE TURN HOSES ONTO RIOTING NEGROES IN A CITY'S STREETS   CLOSEUP OF A BOY'S FACE   ANGER   PAIN   RAW THE WATER BLAST HITS HIM WITH THE FORCE OF WHIPS   HE CRIES OUT AND CRUMPLES AND IS SWEPT ACROSS THE PAVEMENT LIKE A LEAF LIGHTLY DISCARDED FROM SOME TREE

Is that a promise?

Yes. Yes, it is, Ian. I should've taken you before. I know. I'm sorry. We'll go tomorrow. Jen too.

Duncan and Ian last summer at the beach, wrestling and wisecracking, brown skinny legs and arms, the shaggy flames of their hair, their skin smelling of sand and saltwater. Sea-children, as though they should have been crowned with fronds of kelp and ridden dolphins.

—— Luke? I could tell you. I could talk. How can I with Mac? He's got enough to worry about. I can't upset him any more. I mustn't. If I could just talk, Luke, nothing else, just talk *The totem poles are high, thin, beaked, bleached in the sun, carvings of monsters that never were, in that far dusty land of wild grasses, where the rivers speed and thunder while the ancient-eyed boatman waits. Luke is walking beside her. Luke, I'm frightened to death of life. It's okay, baby—you're not alone —I'm with you there.*

Luke in his Indian sweater, his beard brown and beginning to be soft. *Merwoman—What? I'm not twenty-nine. I'm twenty-four.* Luke, before that, sitting cross-legged (was it?) on the Arabic-patterned rug. *She had me when she was fifteen—great for her, eh?*

—— I can't see him again. He doesn't want to. He knew I'd lied about my age. He probably thinks I'm older even than I am. Okay—big deal, Stacey. You've done what thousands of other women have done. Don't I know it? That's what hurts the most, maybe. Shameless shameful attempt at rejuvenation. Pitiful, really. By Christ, I loathe *that* thought. The only blessing is at least I don't have to worry about being pregnant. Sure, count your blessings, kid. Go ahead and do that. *I Was Pollyanna's Mum.* A ray of sunshine. Face it—he was only being kind. I asked, and he didn't say no. Was that all? Wasn't he lonely out there? Didn't he need a woman? He probably needed a girl, and that is precisely what he will get and maybe he will tell her about me. *There was this middle-aged old doll, see, and* No. I won't think of it.

Katie's voice shrilling from the kitchen.

Mum! Granddad's here.

Oh—okay, Katie. I'll be right there. The dinner's all ready. Where's Dad?

How should I know?

Stacey flicks off the TV and gathers Ian and Duncan.

Come on, kids. Go and say hello to Granddad.

Duncan eyes her doubtfully.

What'll we tell him about Sunday school? He won't like it.

You don't need to tell him anything. I'll tell him.

What'll you say?

Stacey's voice is sharper than she intended.

Listen in, then, why don't you, if you're so curious?

—— That was a hell of a thing to say. I take it out on Duncan, just because he's quite rightly concerned at how Matthew will feel that the kids have quit going. I told them they could quit, because I was sick of that particular sham, and I nearly fainted with surprise when Mac didn't even argue, but now do I feel good about being honest for once in my life? No. I reproach myself and wonder if I'm denying them something for which they'll later reproach me. And I don't know how to tell Matthew, either.

Sorry, Duncan. I didn't mean it to sound like I was mad. I don't know how to tell Granddad, either.

Duncan puts his hand in hers.

Well, you'll think of something.

—— Don't bank on it, boy. I wish I had your confidence in me. I'd be a world-beater. Your temporary confidence, that is. Ian's outgrown it, nearly, and Katie lost it long ago. And yet in some ways not. Look at how she was that day with Tess. She thought I would have known what to say.

Matthew is Sunday-dressed, immaculate as always, his eyes a little vaguer to Stacey's view than last week, his straight determined body held that way with a little more difficulty.

Stacey, my dear. How are you?

Just fine, thanks. How're you?

Oh, pretty well. I can't complain. The apartment's very hot these nights and I haven't been sleeping too well, but apart from that, everything's fine.

Why don't you ask Doctor Spender for some sleeping pills?

Matthew shakes his head firmly.

No. I'm sure that it's not a good idea to rely on external props of that nature.

Yeh. Well, you could be right

—— Praise God I finished off the triple-strength gin and tonic in the TV room and didn't bring the glass up with me. Well, I haven't been stoned since that time with the stove. I don't guess Matthew would think that sufficient cause for feeling heartened, though. He'd never be able to get over the fact that it happened at all.

I'm sure everyone sleeps as much as they actually require. I don't suppose I require quite so much sleep any more. All the same, it's nice to get away from the apartment. It's much cooler here.

—— He doesn't get out enough. I know it, and what do I do about it? Bugger all.

I—I'm taking the kids to the beach tomorrow. Why don't you come along?

Oh no—I couldn't do that. It would be too many for you the car too crowded

No it wouldn't. Katie's not coming. She goes with her friends by bus. The boys and you can go in the back seat.

Well, it would be very nice, but

—— Look. Either come or don't come but please for mercy's sake don't make me persuade you because I just may not do that little thing.

Oh come on. It'll do you good.

Well, perhaps I will, then. It would be very nice

Good. We'll pick you up about two.

Well, it's very nice of you, Stacey.

—— No, it damn well isn't. You don't know. Don't kid your-self—I'll regret it. You'll fuss like fury every time a kid puts a foot in the water, and I'll get silently to screaming pitch. Oh boy. I can hardly wait.

Stacey goes to the study door and knocks.

Mac?

Yeh?

Dinner's ready. Your dad is here.

Okay.

—— What's he doing in there? Accounts? Sales reports? Mourning? I don't care, whatever it is. Or I don't want to care. All I want to do is get dinner over with. Why we have to change from Sunday lunch to Sunday dinner, every summer, I do not know. It's supposed to be so we can go out for long relaxing drives in the day. Mac has been in that goddam study since eleven this morning, emerging only for a sandwich at one. Let the kids scream and roar. Let me go out of my mind, nearly. Fat lot he cares. Damn you, Mac, don't you think I might ever like to get away by myself? But no. Oh Stacey—ease up, can't you? Buckle was his best friend. Strange—I told the kids, and they said hardly anything and they haven't mentioned it since. I don't know how they feel, or if they know that Mac is feeling anything at all.

Mac unlocks the bolted door and comes out of the study. He brushes past Stacey without looking at her and goes upstairs to the bathroom. But his face has passed close to her, close enough for her to be able to see that he has been crying.

—— Mac listen tell me

But it is not the time, and there are too many people around, so nothing can be said even if it could be said.

The following evening, Mac is home from work earlier than usual. Stacey pours him a drink, expecting him to go down to the TV room. She drinks her own while getting the dinner. Mac stands in the kitchen doorway, glass in hand, propping his height against the doorframe, and now Stacey notices for the first time that his brush-cut is growing out and the auburn of his hair looks almost like itself again. She does not know whether to mention it or not. If she says it is an improvement, he may take it as a criticism of his previous appearance. Alternatively, he may realize that if he intends to keep a brush-cut he ought to have it trimmed. She decides not to say anything.

— He's got something to say to me. What's the bad news now? Oh God, I didn't mean that. The way his face looked yesterday

Stacey?

What?

Thor's giving a party. At his place.

Oh God. When?

Tomorrow.

Tomorrow? My hair's a mess. I went in the water with the kids today. And I can't get it done.

Why not, for heaven's sake? The hairdresser can't be that booked up. If so, find another one.

It's not that. It's

— Doesn't he ever get himself in these fixes? Is it only me? How can I explain? I still don't know what to do about Tess. If she sees me going out, I could say I'm taking Jen downtown for clothes. Yeh, but then later she'll notice I've had my hair done. Hell.

Mac is frowning.

Honestly, Stacey, why you have to make everything so complicated I just do not know.

It's okay it's okay I'll get my hair done don't worry. Do we really have to go?

Naturally we have to go. What do you think? What would Thor think if we didn't?

Search me. What would he think?

He'd think—oh, for Christ's sake, Stacey, why do we have to go on like this? You know damn well what he'd think.

—— His voice. Tired. Beat. And I go on and on about nothing. I don't want to go to Thor's. I don't want ever to see that character again.

I'm sorry.

And look—this time please don't

I won't I won't I won't. I'll drink tomato juice, like him. Yeh, I can see it all now.

Ease up on me, Mac.

Me ease up on *you?* I was only

Okay. I know. Listen, could you call the kids for dinner?

In the morning, Stacey washes and sets her own hair. When it is dry, she brushes it out, sitting in front of the dressing-table mirror in the bedroom, with Jen on the floor going through the large morocco leather jewelry case which contains Stacey's earrings. Stacey flings down the brush, grabs her comb, re-combs and back-combs, squirts hair-spray thickly over the total effect, then angrily runs her hands through, tousling and disheveling.

What a sight. Why wasn't I born with beautiful fine red hair like you and Katie, flower? Thor will take one look at me and say *Who let her out of the zoo?* Well, I won't go, that's all. How can I? No—the heck with it—I will so go. I'll say *Oh Mr. Thorlakson how do you like my new wig? On sale at Woolworth's.* Yeh. Laugh now. What am I going to do?

Babble babble mutter

Look, sweetie—if you don't want to talk, don't talk. But just don't give me that halfway stuff, eh?

—— That's marvelous. Blame it all on her. For a second, there, I really wanted to swat her.

It's okay, honey. Everything's okay. C'mon—I'll have some coffee and you'll have some juice and we'll feel a lot better.

—— Everything's okay. Everything's just dandy. Oh Luke. I want to go home, but I can't, because this is home.

By that evening, Stacey has managed to tame and subdue the tangled jungle of her hair. Jen is in bed. Duncan, Ian and Katie are looking at TV. Stacey is wearing her black sheath dress, supposedly slenderizing. She tugs at the waist, trying to straighten the wrinkles in the material, but her hips are against her.

Do I look okay, Mac?

Mac is looking at his watch.

Fine fine you look fine. Aren't you ready *yet?*

Coming coming. Right this minute.

—— Still the same. Same drill, same marching tones whistled by us both.

Thor has not risked his apartment. The party is being held on the roof of the building, an extensive patio-like square, which has been prudently fenced in with chicken wire to a height of some eight feet, for the area is habitually rented for tenants' parties and the management does not wish to be sued by widows whose husbands have been accidentally splattered onto the far-down pavement below. The wire is threaded discreetly with green-leafed vines, placed with just enough gaps to provide one view of the city on each side. On top of the leaves, at regular intervals, small pink plastic flowers have been attached, as being more reliable than the live variety. Round white-painted tables with scrolled white-painted metal legs are sprinkled here and there, and potted rhododendrons still bear the brown corpses of this spring's flowering. At one end is the bar, draped with a purple and gold RICHALIFE banner, and behind the arrayed bottles and siphons stands a worried-looking boy in a white drill jacket.

Most of the salesmen and their wives and the office staff are already here, in knots and clusters, drinking rye and proclaiming in voices which will carry as far as Thor their intentions of alternating each one with plain ginger ale.

Stacey grins and nudges Mac in order to overcome the ice which seems to have become lodged in her stomach.

So much for his tomato juice campaign, eh?

Sh. And for God's sake don't point it out. And don't

Stacey's upsurge of rage wipes out all memory of Mac's pain over Buckle, all memory of his worry about Thor.

Okay. Fine. I get the message. I'll be a campaigning teetotaler if you like. How be if I get an ax and break up the bar?

Christ Christ why do you always   if you're going to start *that*, then we may as well turn around right now and go home

Sh, for heaven's sake. I won't. I promise. Don't talk so loud.

Me talk loud? What about *you?*

Sh sh sh   here comes the angelman

Thor approaches like a mobile tower. He is dressed in a suit of pale pigeon-grey, and his turquoise eyes gleam flatly, exuding cordiality but betraying nothing of himself. His silver hair is ruffled very slightly and attractively by the light night wind.

Stacey   Mac   well, *hi* there. Wonderful to see you. How have you been, Stacey?

Oh just fine thanks

No more stigmata ha-ha?

Oh   yeh   well   ha-ha   no

—— Mean bugger.

Now—what'll you have to drink, Stacey?

Mm—Coca-Cola, please.

What? Hey, you don't *have* to.

Mumble

Could it be that the Program is reducing your need for stimulants? How do you find you are, smoke-wise?

Madness seizes Stacey. Her smile glints up into his face.

Oh, I'm tons better. I hardly smoke anything at all now. And caffeine-wise I'm like a new woman. And golly, the kids have got so much energy now that I may have to put them back onto dreary old cod-liver oil, in sheer self-protection ha-ha.

She feels Mac's fingers digging into her elbow. Thor turns the microscope of his eyes upon her.

Well well. You don't say. Well, that's great, isn't it? Now, if you good people will excuse me, I see the Storeys have just come in.

He departs. Mac glowers.

You certainly overdid *that* bit.

Stacey shrugs. She is light-headed, euphoric, adrenalin-laden.

Not to worry. Nobody wins them all.

— I couldn't care less. Less than absolute nothing do I care what Thor thinks of me. Am I deliberately trying to sabotage Mac's job? There's a thought. I don't think so, but I might be. How can you tell? Oh Katie, imagine thinking that I always knew what to say. Well, the hell with it. I will not be intimidated by that white-haired boy, that hybrid offspring of a moronic lion and a lady wrestler. Thor—what a name, anyway. Even if you were christened that, imagine keeping it. If I knew any good hexes, I'd sure put one on him. I will carry off this evening with tremendous dignity and poise if it's the last thing I ever do. I'd give my eyeteeth for just one large Scotch. But I won't. Damned if I will.

Mac has drifted off to talk to Mickey Jameson. Stacey perceives that a small detachment of lone wives is making its frilly way towards her. She recognizes them but is totally unable to remember any of their names.

Hi there, Stacey.

Oh, hi. How *are* you? Nice to see you again.

Yeh. Say, this is some *place*, eh? I was just saying to Joanie, here, this really is a lovely spot for a party, isn't it?

Yeh lovely

— Joanie Storey. Praise the Lord. Now get to work on detecting the others, oh female Saint.

The babble and babel of voices go on, rising to crescendo, to cacophony. Stacey shouts questions and answers. How many kids you got? What grades are they in? It's been a pretty good summer so far, hasn't it? Yeh, no rain to speak of.

> The shore of the Sound. The huge water-whitened log, and herself perched on it. The black water lighted streakily by stars. Luke. The A-frame. *What's the bad news? What's*

with you? I took off. *Well, don't worry. Sometimes people do.* Then, later, after what he
said about the kid in the Cariboo, the one
whose mother took off. *Stacey, you don't need
to be sorry. It hurts?* Yes. *Well, go ahead and
bawl. No shame in that. You're not alone.*

— I am, though. I am now. Why did it have to happen
like that? Why couldn't it have been different—Luke older—me
unattached? If only I could get out of here. *If only I could get out.*
What if everybody is thinking that, in some deep half-buried
cave of themselves? What an irony that would be. If that were
so, you'd think we ought to be able to move mountains. But it
doesn't happen that way.

Stacey's resolve breaks at eleven thirty and she goes to
the bar for a double Scotch. She drinks half of it in a mouthful.
Then she sees the diversion which is happening on the other
side of the plateau, an entertainment for men. Somebody has
produced a large number of beach balls, in as many colors as
Richalife pills, scarlet jade azure apricot. The men are busily
pelting one another. The laughter is hoarse, explosive.

Here y'are, Mick. Catch!

The ball flies strongly and catches Mickey Jameson on
the shoulder and off guard, nearly knocking him over. The
thrower roars gleefully.

Pow! Gotcha!

Stacey stares as the game gets rougher. A number of
other women are also watching. Some of them are clapping and
cheering. Some are standing in silence. Then Thor bounds like
an outsize faun into the middle of the group. He, too, is laughing.
He picks up a beach ball as though it were the world and hovers
for a moment with it, searching.

Mac has not been participating. He is standing with a
glass in his hands at the extreme edge of the group, looking on.
Thor makes as though to throw the ball directly ahead, then
abruptly swings around and sends it in the opposite direction.
Mac sees it coming too late. It catches him squarely in the face.

His neck jerks back, and Stacey's guts turn over. A few men gasp and a few women shriek titteringly. Then the clapping and laughter go on as before. Mac's head rights itself and Stacey can now see the dribble of blood from his nostrils. His fists clench and unclench and clench again. Stacey can see his jagged breathing. Then Thor's voice.

Hey—*sorry*. You oughta been looking *out*, fella.

Mac's voice is low but steady.

Yeh. I'll know better next time.

You're not *hurt*, are you?

No. It's nothing.

The game breaks up and chatter fills the gaps. Somebody puts a record on, and dancing begins. Stacey sees Mac going through the door which leads to the lower regions. She follows him. He is wiping his face with his handkerchief. They go into the elevator without speaking. Then outside and into the car.

Do you want me to drive, Mac?

Yeh. I guess you better. Still a certain amount of stars inside my head.

Goddam him. Goddam him. Goddam him.

Mac's voice is tight and controlled, grating.

Yeh. It would be nice to know why he's got it in for me. One of life's mysteries.

At home, Stacey makes coffee and takes it upstairs. Mac is already in bed, sitting up and smoking.

How is it now, Mac?

Oh, okay. It wasn't anything much. It's what's behind it I know.

He turns to her, propping himself on an elbow.

You know something, Stacey? I damn near hit him as hard as I could. For a second, there, it was almost like an automatic reflex. I didn't care about anything. I couldn't even look ahead as far as any consequences. I though afterwards—I wonder if a lot of murders are done that way? Not that I would've been able to do him that much damage—but you know what I mean?

Yes. I know. What stopped you?

Mac shrugs and lights another cigarette from the end of the first.

I don't know, really. You, I guess.

Me? How come?

Well—the kids and you, and me with no job at my age

Mac, you're forty-three. You talk as though you were a hundred. Has it bugged you so much? The possibility of being without a job? You're a damn good salesman. They're in demand.

Yeh, I know all that. It's a hangover from the past, I guess. Also, it isn't so easy to re-establish yourself. I've done better, at least financially, in this job than I ever have. Not that that's saying much.

Stacey is shocked by the bitterness in his voice.

What do you mean? You've done all right, Mac.

I would've liked to do better. You know—something that meant something. I won't, now. I guess that's why I had to convince myself that Richalife was pretty terrific.

Stacey's hands are shaking. She sets the coffee cup down on the bedside table.

—— Now is a fine time to tell me. Why didn't he tell me before? Okay, I know why.

Mac—why didn't you say all this before? What do you really think?

About the firm? I think it's a load of crap. I don't suppose the bloody pills actually do anybody any harm, though. But probably I'd sell them even if they did.

Stop it. You've got to. You mustn't be that tough on yourself. Look what all you've done.

Yeh, just look

But why didn't you ever say? Why didn't you level with me?

233

What good would that have done?

It would've   it would've

Mac's voice is abrasive, bound with ropes of an effort not to let go, an effort which almost doesn't work.

No, it wouldn't. It's my problem. Can't you see? It's got to be.

— I see. Maybe I do begin to see. If he doesn't deal with everything alone, no help, then he thinks he's a total washout. Thanks, Matthew—you passed that one on all right, but at least you had your Heavenly Father to strengthen your right arm or resolve, to put the steel reinforcing in your spine. Mac's got only himself. And if he doesn't speak of it to some extent, one of these days he'll crack up.

Okay, I guess it has to be that way, Mac. If you insist. It would've helped me, though. It would've made me feel you needed me, even just to talk to.

You mean you ever doubted *that*, Stacey?

Yeh. I doubted it all right.

Oh Christ. How could you?

I don't know. But I did.

Mac turns away from her, as though at the moment of turning closer or being forced there by innumerable and to her unknown memories, he still must keep private his face, his eyes.

How could I tell you it scared the hell out of me when Thor needled me? He's been doing it in various ways a lot of the time. That would've made me look pretty useless, wouldn't it, to be bugged that much by a thing like that?

Not to me. Only to yourself. And that's crazy, Mac. You're not made of granite. Nobody is.

Why do you think I've worked like the devil? Just so he couldn't point to anything which would give him a real excuse to get rid of me. What else did you expect me to do? Christ, Stacey, the mortgage company isn't going to wait for the payments, is it? And Katie'll be ready for university in another three years.

—— He took us all on at a time when most of us didn't then exist. I guess he wouldn't ever believe he's brave.

I know. I know. I know. I didn't expect you to do anything else. I always blame myself that we've got so many kids. Not that four is all that many but you know what I mean like, Duncan

You blame yourself? But that's insane, Stacey. Anyway, that's all in the past.

The past doesn't seem ever to be over.

Mac stubs out his cigarette and she does the same. He leans across and switches out the light.

We've gotta get some sleep, Stacey. It's past one. I got a million things to do tomorrow.

Yes. Mac—are you going to stay? With the firm? Now?

He hesitates before replying. Her eyes, unused to the darkness, cannot discover anything from his face. When he speaks, it is very slowly.

I don't know. I just don't know. I don't see how I can stay and yet I don't see how I can leave, either.

—— I know what you mean. I've felt the same myself. What can I say that'll be any use?

Nothing comes to her, so at last she turns over on her side and after a while she falls asleep.

The place is a prison but not totally so. It must be an island, surely, some place where people are free to walk around but nobody can get away. The huts are made of poplar poles chinked with mud and they have flat roofs where the people sleep. There is a ladder leading up to each sleeping plateau, and when she and Mac are safely on top, they pull up the rope ladder after them. The children are not here. They are in another place, grown and free, nothing to worry about for her at this moment. Lying together on the bed of leaves, she and Mac listen to the guards' boots. The legions are marching tonight through the streets and their boot leather strikes hard against the pavements and there is nowhere to go but here

235

NINE

꒰ꞈꞈꞈꞈꞈꞈ꒱

The gulls fly flashingly above the sun-lightened water, then latch on to air currents and glide so slow-motion that they seem to be hovering unmoving in the morning bright air at the city's rim where the longshoremen shout and the vessels move in ponderously to be unladen like great sea cows swimming in to be milked.

Stacey looks at the harbor, half an eye on her watch. She has not come down here to observe the gulls and ships, but she cannot yet bring herself to walk along Grenoble Street and enter the one door she must enter.

— I've got to. Can't stay away from home much longer. It isn't fair to Katie, to expect her to look after Jen all day. Come on, Stacey. Okay, in a minute when I feel stronger. Just a minute. You haven't got the guts of a grasshopper, that's your trouble. Come on. Not later. Now.

She turns and walks quickly. She reaches Grenoble Street and her footsteps dwindle, dawdle past cafés and the cheap hotels where old men doze in the barely waking lobbies which will blare and brawl when night falls. Stacey finds Honest Ernie's cut-price children's clothes, and enters the doorway at the side. Up the brown linoleum stairs to the second landing. She stops, then, being unable yet to knock.

> The gigantic woman, outspread like rising dough gone amok, swelling and undulating over the stiff upholstery of the chair, gaping body covered with tiny-flower-printed dress huge and shroud-shaped, and beside her on a low table the pink-pearl glass mug and the port-filled teapot. Buckle laughing.

— I can't go in. I can't. My head's spinning. I feel really awful. What if I throw up here? It wouldn't alter the smell of this hallway much, that's for sure. Go on—knock. I should've come before. I should at least have inquired. Maybe nobody found her, and she's dead, and when I open the door there she'll be, decomposing away like sixty in the chair, her head lolling and her eyes just as blind in death as they were in life. It was crazy to come here. I should've phoned the police, the day after Buckle crashed. But I didn't. And now I can't. They'd say *This is a hell of a fine time to be telling us, lady.*

Stacey knocks. There is a flurry of movement inside the room, and Stacey's stomach begins to cramp in apprehension. Then the door is opened, only a crack, and a face peers out. A girl with long uncombed hair, sharp catlike features breathing suspicion.

Whatcha want?

I—didn't Mrs. Fennick live here?

Who? Oh, you mean the old blind dame? Yeh. But her son got himself wiped out in a crash. He was a trucker. I used to live on the top floor but I moved, see? This place is better. Anything else you want to know? Such as the story of my life, for instance?

What   what happened to her?

Oh, they took her away.

They?

Yeh, Salvation Army or some do-good bunch like that. It was real funny, the way it happened. The way I heard it, they told her about the son and said they was coming back the next day to fetch her off somewheres, one of them homes, like, I guess. Well, she tries to cut her throat, see? Only she can't find the butcher knife. When they come in the morning there she was, still crawling around the floor, feeling everything, but she still hadn't found it. Ever see her? Built like the back of a barn, she was. She must've looked real cute, crawling around on her hands and knees, with her great big tits bumping along on the floor, there.

I see. Well   thanks very much

The girl laughs, and Stacey can hear Buckle's laughter again, the stone-grained quality of laughter long used as both weapon and wall. The girl imitates what she has presumably heard as phony politeness in Stacey's voice.

Oh, don't mention it, I'm sure. Always glad to oblige.

The door slams. Stacey walks down the stairs and out into the street. She walks without noticing the sidewalk, the people, the buildings.

—— She may not have been much, but she didn't abort him all that time ago, at least not before his birth. She had him and brought him up. She did that. What could have been in her mind that day I came here with Buckle? Or any of the days, for that matter. But he never turned her out, whatever else he may have said or done. When I think of the number of times I felt like clobbering him for coming around so often to our place, for coming around at all. Buckle—you can't be dead. I can't cry here. What would everybody think, passing by? But I am, damn damn damn. That's right, Stacey—requiem for a truck driver. You really time things well.

238

Stacey hears, strangely, her name being spoken by a woman's voice, a voice raucous as the gulls'.

Stacey   hey Stacey

She blinks. Coming towards her is a woman whose black hair has been upfrizzed until it resembles the nest of some large wild bird. Her dark eyes and her features are prairie Indian but not entirely. Her skin, or what can be seen of it under the thick crust of make-up, is a pale brown. Her mouth has been lipsticked into a wide bizarre cupid's bow. She is wearing a smeared hem-drooping mauve silkish dress which reveals her body's blunt thickness, the once-high breasts that are dugs now.

It *is* Stacey, ain't it? Stacey Cameron? I dunno your married name.

Yes   that's right   I   I

Valentine Tonnerre. Val. Doncha remember me?

Well, for heaven's sake. Well, sure I do. Of course.

> The Tonnerre family shack, surrounded by discarded tin cans and old car parts and extending in a series of lean-tos, at the foot of the hill in Manawaka, originally built a long time ago by old Jules Tonnerre, who was a boy then, when he stopped off and stayed in the Wachakwa Valley on his way back from the last uprising of his people, on his way back from Batoche and Fish Creek, from the last and failed attempt to save themselves and their land, the last of their hopeless hope which was finished the year that Riel was hanged in Regina. After that, the *Bois Brûlés,* the French-Indians, the *Métis,* those who sang Falcon's Song, once the prairie horse lords, would be known as half-breeds and would live the way the Tonnerres lived, in ramshackledom, belonging nowhere. And Jules begat Lazarus, and Lazarus begat a

239

multitude. Stacey Cameron at school saw the straggling tribe of kids only as *those Tonnerres*. Their name meant thunder but she did not know until a long time later.

Stacey does not know what to say. She would like to go back in time, to explain that she never meant the town's invisible stabbing, but this is not possible, and it was hers, too, so she cannot edge away from it.

— Valentine. So-named because born on February 14. Her sister once told me when I said it wasn't a girl's name. Val must be three or four years younger than I am. My god, she looks ten years older. Her sister? Her sister? What was it?

You were younger than I, Val. It was your sister who was my age. Piquette. What I heard something what was it

Valentine's face, expert at concealment, takes on blankness.

Yeh. You seen it in the *Manawaka Banner*, maybe. They wrote it up there. Maybe you remember she had TB in the bone, one leg. She used to limp quite a lot. Doctor Macleod, there, got it fixed up, after quite awhile, when she was a kid. So then she kind of took off, like, soon as she could. She married this guy from Winnipeg, English fella. Bastard walked out on her and the two kids. She went back to the old place. You know, cooked and that for Dad and the boys. Happened in winter. They used to make red biddy down there. If I know Piquette, she was stoned out of her mind, most likely. The others were out. We had one of them big old wood stoves. Place caught fire. She never got out. The kids neither.

Val I didn't know

— Or did I just forget, put it from mind?

Yeh well. You feel like a cuppa coffee?

Sure. Gosh, it's nice to see you. I don't often see anybody from Manawaka.

— I'm overdoing it and she will know. I don't want to have coffee with her. Even her presence is a reproach to me, for all I've got now and have been given and still manage to bitch on and on about it. And a reproach for the sins of my fathers, maybe. The debts are inherited and how could the damage ever be undone or forgiven? I don't want to, but I seem to believe in a day of judgment, just like all my Presbyterian forebears did, only I don't think it'll happen in the clouds or elsewhere and I don't think I'll be judged for the same things they thought they'd be. Piquette and her kids, and the snow and fire. Ian and Duncan in a burning house.

Well, c'mon then, Stacey. Here's the Emerald Café, right here. They'll put it on the cuff sometimes. But I don't guess you'd have to be too interested in that.

Well   sure, let's go in

—   And yet I resent her making a crack like that.

They sit down in a booth and order two coffees. Stacey lights a cigarette and offers one to Valentine, who takes it.

How long you been here, Val?

Oh, going on three years now. Won't be here much longer.

Why? You going somewhere?

Valentine smiles, the ruby creamed mouth now askew.

Yeh. Long trip. The last one.

How do you mean?

Don't ask, Stacey. You don't want to know.

—   Heroin? Booze? Sickness? A knife under the ribs? Luke was right. You can't ask. You don't have the right. You haven't lived in that particular cave.

Okay. I'm sorry, Val.

For what? I don't give a fuck. Today tomorrow next week, it's all the same to me. How you been, Stacey? Lived here long?

Yeh. Quite a few years now. I'm   okay   I guess

You sound pissed off.

Yeh, well. My husband works for a guy who's got it in

241

for him for no reason and there's the four kids and things get kind of

What's he do, your old man?

Salesman. Ever heard of Richalife?

To Stacey's astonishment, Valentine Tonnerre leans back in the booth and laughs, smoking at the same time and then going into a spasm of coughing. She fumbles for the coffeecup, drinks, and then looks at Stacey with uninterpretable eyes.

Yeh. I heard of it. Especially the guy they got there now. I seen his picture in the paper and then I seen him once on the street. God, I laughed so hard I nearly puked. You must've laughed too.

Stacey stares.

Laughed? What at?

You mean you never recognized him? Well, he was younger than you, a few years, so you probably never knew him, to speak of. I knew him, though. Jesus, I often thought of touching him for a few bucks, but then again, I'm not that smart and it might not work. Someday when I'm high maybe I'll do it.

Val—what are you talking about?

Him. Thor Thorlakson or whatever the hell he calls himself. Yeh, sure, he's had his pan all jazzed up by doctors whaddya call it some kinda surgery and I am damn sure he wears built-up shoes. When he took me into the bushes way back when, he was in high school but he sure wasn't that tall, and his name was Vernon Winkler.

Stacey's stunned disbelief alters only gradually, as the recollection filters blurredly back.

A kid in the graveled schoolgrounds of Manawaka Public School. A kid maybe eight or nine years old, surrounded by a gang of older, fiercer kids, scorn-chanting. *Ver-non Ver-non Ver-non.* A series of hard knees in the crotch until the teacher came along and distractedly said *Boys boys boys*. The kid crying, mucus pouring from his nose. Stacey and Vanessa and Mavis watching from a distance, disgusted and excited

Val I didn't I didn't know I didn't know

Whatsamatter? You look scared. You scared or something?

Stacey is hardly aware of speaking aloud, or to anyone.

That's why he was down on Mac. Nothing to do with Mac. Only with me. But how could I have known that? And he didn't have to worry. I didn't recognize him. How could I? I never knew him at all, not really. I only ever noticed him that once, as far as I can remember, but I wouldn't have associated *that* kid with Thor, for heaven's sake. Maybe he remembered me, once he knew where I came from, or maybe he was only scared because he didn't know whether I knew all about him or not. My God, he probably thought there was something ominous about it, every time I mentioned the prairies or the name Thor—but there wasn't. There wasn't. And now he'll find an excuse to fire Mac or else he'll keep on needling until Mac has to quit. Mac can't stand to be without a job not now

Stacey pulls herself together and looks across the café table. Valentine Tonnerre is leaning on the red arborite surface, her chin in her hands. Her eyes are watchful, unsympathetic, even pleased.

Shit, Stacey, you got worries? Go ahead—make me laugh.

You could be right. Then again, maybe not. I got to get home now, Val. My kids will be wondering where I am.

Yeh. I guess your kids would.

Val did you ever you know have you got any

The known and total stranger sitting opposite shakes her head, laughs her coarse-textured laugh and takes a cigarette out of Stacey's pack on the table.

I got a couple somewhere I kind of lost track

— The necessary lie. Where? How many? With whom?

How much does it hurt? The questions that can't be asked or answered. All I can do is go. Now she wants me to go. Too little can be said, because there is too much to say. And I'm relieved to be going, because I can't cope here.

Val come over some evening. Phone me. We're in the phone book. MacAindra. Bluejay Crescent. We'll kill a bottle.

— Stacey, you are phony as a three-dollar bill, and she knows it.

Valentine Tonnerre looks at her, unsmiling. Then she reaches under her left breast and scratches, a long slow deliberate gesture.

Yeh well

So long, then.

But Valentine does not appear to have heard, so Stacey rises, dutifully pays and goes.

— God of thunder. Vernon Winkler. I'll bet a nickel to a doughnut hole that he puts vodka in that tomato juice of his. How can I tell Mac, and what will I say? *You've been scared by a strawman.* How could anybody say that? If we're scared, at least there is some dignity in being scared of genuine demons. Aren't there any demons left in hell? How in hell can we live without them?

Bluejay Crescent. Stacey parks the car in front of the house and goes quickly up the steps, inside, through the house and out the back door. Duncan is swinging Jen on the low swing and she is shrieking with laughter and excitement. Ian and assorted friends are constructing a new and larger bug, and the grass around them is littered with wheels, boards, nails, hammers and other essentials. Katie is rubbing her newly washed hair with a towel.

Hi. Everything okay, Katie?

Sure. Why shouldn't it be?

I didn't mean it that way. Sorry I was so long, honey. Do you want to go now?

I can't until my hair's dry. If you'd come back half an hour ago, I could have gone to the beach with Marnie and washed my hair tonight.

Sorry. I was delayed

Seems like you're always delayed when it's me who's looking after Jen. When it was Mrs. Fogler, you used to get home when you said you would.

My heavens, Katie, I've said I'm sorry—what more can I

Okay okay okay

The phone rings. Katie leaps to her feet and sprints towards the house.

I'll get it, Mother. I'm expecting a call.

All right.

—— You are, eh? Who from? Why doesn't she say? She's getting very secretive all of a sudden lately. Oh for heaven's sake, Stacey, what do you expect?

In a moment Katie emerges and looks oddly at Stacey.

It wasn't for me. It was for you. It was Mr. Fogler, but he's rung off now. He sounded kind of strange. He wants you to go over right away. I think Mrs. Fogler must be sick or something.

Stacey goes swiftly. When she reaches the Foglers' doorstep, Jake opens the door before she can ring the bell. It is the first time Stacey has ever seen him without his glasses. He looks younger and less owlish. But then she sees why he has taken his glasses off. He grinds away at his eyes with his palms as though his tears are repugnant and shameful to himself.

Jake—what is it?

It's Tess

But he cannot say anything more. He takes Stacey's hand and draws her into the living room. He motions her to the chesterfield, and then he gropes over to the liquor cabinet, pours two brandies and hands one to Stacey. He drinks his own quickly, pours another and then lowers himself into an armchair. His voice is steadier now, but there is a kind of self-dramatizing hysteria in it which repels Stacey despite herself.

I found her this morning, Stacey. Here. Right here, where I'm sitting now. She'd swallowed Christ knows how many sleeping pills and nearly a whole bottle of rye.

Stacey's hands around the brandy glass begin to shake.

Jake   that's   is she

No. She's not dead.

Thank God

I took her to hospital   Stacey it was terrible   I got her into the car all by myself   I should've phoned for you or Mac   or phoned the ambulance   but I wasn't thinking straight at all   I just thought I had to get her there right away and she was limp and I couldn't tell whether she was breathing or not   her breathing was so shallow and faint

Jake   I'm sorry

They pumped her out and it was touch-and-go for most of the day and then they said they thought she'd be okay   Stacey she has to go to to   you know   the mental hospital

Listen, Jake, don't feel badly about that. They'll be able to help her.

Now he is not dramatizing. His voice is only pain and bewilderment.

Yes but why?   Why would she?   What's the matter with her?   What did I do wrong?   Was it me?   What was it?

I don't know

—— I don't know and I do know. Dog eat dog and fish eat fish. How many things added up? But I didn't get the message either. Why didn't I? I always envied her for being so glamorous. I couldn't see anything else.

Jake   I'm so damn sorry   I did know she was upset sometimes and I might have tried   but I didn't

You shouldn't think that way, Stacey. It was me. I guess. But what did I do or not do?

Maybe it wasn't you, Jake. Everything starts a long time ago.

Do you think so? Do you really think so?

Sure. Of course. It's well known.

—— He was the one who used to tell me slickly that I had a death wish because I would have liked from time to time to be on a snow mountain by myself, no voices. Now he clutches at any naive theory that might totally exonerate him. Never mind. Who could blame him for wanting that? *It wasn't me*, the kids say. It is always the other guy who starts the trouble. And I say furiously, *How am I supposed to find out? How can I sift it all?*

Jake pours another brandy for them both.

Maybe I should've agreed years ago for her to have kids, Stacey. But whenever we talked of it, she seemed so damned scared. I thought that was what she *wanted* me to say—that she was enough and that I didn't feel the need of any

Maybe that's what she did want you to say. Or maybe she did and didn't.

Jake puts his head in his hands and once again there is the faintly shrill teetering quality in his voice.

I don't know what the hell she *ever* wanted, to tell you the truth. She was so goddam beautiful it seemed incredible that she would marry me at all

I think she thought she was stupid

Christ, Stacey, surely you realize that if I kidded her sometimes it was only because she was so goddam beautiful and I look like some kind of chimpanzee and I thought she could take the odd crack   how did I know

Jake—stop it. This could go on and on. Come to our place for dinner tonight. And for as long as you want or until

Thanks, Stacey. But I couldn't do that. It may be months. I'll come tonight if I can

—— He won't, though. He couldn't sit there and talk. He couldn't bear the glances of my kids. He'll have a light delicious dinner of brandy.

He sees her to the door and she walks home slowly, wondering how to tell Katie. The boys don't need to know, but Katie has to be told.

Katie?

What happened to her, Mum? Is she dead?

No   she's not

Did she try to kill herself?

Yes. How did you know?

Kate shrugs, throwing back her half-damp hair. Under the flippancy of her voice there seems to be an undertone of something else, perhaps fear.

Oh well, that's the usual gimmick, isn't it?

Not that usual, I'd say.

You never read the papers? Mum—will she be all right?

I hope so. She needs

Yeh, I know. Treatment. Mother

Yes?

You couldn't have done anything. It must've been past that point. So let's not get all worked up, eh?

Oh Katie

Hey don't   worry   please   please   just   don't   cry Mum   *please*   you're okay   there there you're okay now

Yes. Thanks, Katie.

—— One day she will have to take over as the mother, and she's beginning to sense it. No wonder it frightens her. It damn near terrifies me, the whole business, even after all these years. And then I give in like now, and lean on her. I mustn't.

Mum?

What?

Don't ever pull that stunt   like she did   will you?

No. I won't.

—— I promise you, Katie. I give you my word. But what if the day ever comes a long time from now when Katie is worn out and would half or even three quarters wish to release me

248

from that kind of promise? Shut up, you. We'll have to deal with that one when the time comes.

Stacey goes next door to tell Bertha Garvey. From the front porch she can hear Julian's voice ranting in his accustomed manner at Bertha over some offense real or imagined. Then when he comes to the door he is calm, smiling, almost courtly.

Stacey. How nice to see you. Do come in. Bertha's in the kitchen.

— Where else, you old fraud? She spends her entire life there.

Bertha is making applesauce. She listens silently and then she turns and faces Stacey. She does not gasp or make horrified noises. Her voice is as ordinary as always.

She never ate enough, Tess didn't. She starved herself. No wonder she got so rundown and keyed up. When she gets home, I'm going to make good and sure she eats.

Stacey cannot help smiling.

Bertha, you're great. You know that?

Bertha motions with the wooden spoon towards Julian. Try telling him.

— What does Bertha concoct for her personal theater? The lumberjack she never married, the one who would have loved her with perfect admiration just as she is?

As she is going out, Stacey can hear their voices, Julian's crotchety and yet frightened.

Don't you go letting that Tess give you any fancy notions, Bertha.

And Bertha's voice, plain and solid as a pine board.

Don't you ever worry. I'm too stubborn to die yet for a while.

The march winds its way across the bridge, and Stacey, glancing backward, can see the banners, each carried by two people, the words curving and only partially visible as the marchers pace.

THE FIRE-DWELLERS

Beside Stacey, a girl in a green corduroy slacks suit takes long slow measured steps. She has informed Stacey that this style of walking is less tiring. Stacey, however, is not able to take the advice because her own legs are not long enough. Also, she has not had the foresight to wear slacks. She is wearing a blue-and-white-striped cotton dress and sandals, and apart from one or two elderly tweed-clad ladies near the rear of the column, she is the only woman wearing a skirt. She looks around, flinching, trying not to notice, trying not to let it make any difference.

—— Something like this is supposed to be serious, and here you are, Stacey, worrying about how you look. I know, I know. But I'd feel easier and less conspicuous if I'd worn my slacks. What if Mac should drive past and see me? He'd have a fit. Why can't I tell him? There's nothing furtive about it, for heaven's sake. In fact, it was with the opposite in mind that I came. *I don't kid myself that it's going to change the world, but I plod along —it makes as much sense as anything else.* That's what Luke said. Why did I think of that? I wish I hadn't. Because now I don't know if I am really plodding along out of conviction or only because it was in the back of my mind that he might be here and I might see him again. I must not want to see him again. I mustn't. But I do. I can help what I do but not what I feel.

Someone starts singing "We Shall Overcome." Most of the marchers are young. Their voices are strong and certain. High on the bridge, with the gulls' mocking birdvoices around them, the marchers sing. Stacey tries to sing, but she cannot. The green corduroy girl gives her a wry look, so she tries again, but no music emerges from her open mouth.

—— I see myself tromping along here, this slightly too short woman, slightly too heavy in the hips, no longer young. And all I can feel is embarrassment. I might at least have the decency not to feel embarrassed. Maybe I'd feel differently if I had faith. But I can't seem to manage it.

They have crossed the bridge, and at a street corner a small group is waiting to join the march. One of them is Luke. The same clothes, the same Indian sweater. He still wears his beard, except that now it is thicker and looks as though it belongs. Standing beside him is a girl about twenty, with long fine brown hair, wearing white jeans and sweater, and carrying a sign. PEACE. Luke has his arm around her.

Stacey turns to the green-corduroy girl.

Gosh I'm sorry but I just have to go to the bathroom. I'm going to have to drop out at this corner and find a john somewhere.

Gee, bad luck. Never mind. If you hurry, you can catch us up.

I'll try

Stacey, conscious of disapproving looks which she feels convinced must be aimed at her retreat, darts out of the line of marchers. Quickly, then, into the anonymity and shelter of the nearest doorway, which happens to be a hamburger place. A boy is mopping the counter with a wet and greyish rag.

Yes ma'am?

Oh—coffee, please.

She drinks it slowly, to make it last as long as possible, and watches through the window the remainder of the marchers going past. They are singing "Where Have All the Flowers Gone." Their voices reach back to the bridge where the gulls eternally whirl. Perhaps they reach to the city as well, or perhaps not.

When the last marcher is out of sight, Stacey goes out and gets a bus back home.

—— I might at least have seen it through. For what, though?

It's like church—you think maybe if you go, the faith will be given, but it isn't. It has to be there already in you, I guess. Or maybe you have to persevere. I wish I'd stayed. Despite Luke. Despite embarrassment. Despite no faith. But bravery has never been my speciality. All I know how to do is get by somehow. I'd like to talk to somebody. Somebody who wouldn't refuse really to look at me, whatever I was like. I'd like to talk to my sister. I'd like to write to her. I'd like to tell her how I feel about everything. No. She'd think I was crazy, probably. She's too sensible ever to do this sort of thing, like today, or like with Luke and all that. She'd think I must be mad, not to be perfectly happy, with four healthy kids and a good man. I couldn't write to her. She'd never see. She'd think even worse of me than she already does. Luke? I couldn't let you see me. All right—you showed me where I belonged, when you said *What can't you leave?* I guess I should be grateful. I *am* grateful. Maybe not for that, so much. I guess I knew it anyway. For the way you talked to me and held me for a while—that's why I'm grateful. I said unspokenly *Help* and you didn't turn away. You faced me and touched me. You were gentle. You needn't have been, but you were, and that I won't forget or cease being glad for. Even if you'd been older, or I'd been younger and free, it wouldn't have turned out any simpler with you than it is with Mac. I didn't see that at one time, but I see it now.

The bus pulls to a halt. Stacey gets out and walks down Bluejay Crescent. Katie is in the back yard with Jen. Stacey stands on the back porch.

Hi. Where are the boys?

Over at Weller's. Jim's got a new bike. Are you going to pay me for minding Jen?

I said I would, so I will.

How did it go?

Oh—all right, I guess. I quit before the end.

Never mind. It's quite a walk. Why don't you want Dad to know you went?

I don't know. I guess it doesn't matter one way or another if he knows. Maybe it should've been you who went.

Katie looks up, smiling but not in a way which Stacey finds possible to decipher with any certainty.

You mean—athletic me?

Stacey wants to touch her, to hold fast to her and at the same time to support her. But she expresses none of these, having to be careful, unable to gauge accurately, having to guess only.

Yeh. Athletic you.

Stacey goes back into the kitchen, finds the notebook she uses for shopping lists, tears out a page, writes on it and sticks it up above the sink with Scotch tape.

No Pre-Mourning

She stands for a while and looks at it.

> Newspaper photograph—slash-eyed woman crouched on some temporarily unviolated steps in the far city, skull and bones outstanding under shriveled skin, holding the dead child, she not able to realize it is actually and unhelpably finished and yet knowing this is so. The woman's mouth open wide—a sound of unbearability but rendered in silence by the camera clicking. Only the zero mouth to be seen, noiselessly proclaiming the gone-early child.

Now Stacey cannot recall what it was that might have been meant by *Pre*. Also, she cannot figure out a way of explaining the sign to Ian and Duncan. So she takes it down and puts it into the garbage.

Sunday. They have taken the kids to the beach in the morning. In the afternoon Matthew has arrived and has been pacing the kitchen floor while Stacey prepares dinner. Turning from sink to stove, Stacey nearly bumps into him. They both step aside and once again nearly collide. But Matthew is not aware of Stacey's teeth-grinding fury, so the small gauche ballet continues. Mac is out cleaning the car, assisted by Ian. Jen is playing under the kitchen table. Duncan stands in the doorway. Stacey, angry at Matthew, flies at Duncan.

For heaven's sake, honey, can't you find something to do? Why don't you go and help Dad and Ian with the car?

Duncan mumbles indistinguishable words.

Speak properly, Duncan. What did you say?

His voice is now abnormally loud and high.

I said they don't want me

Stacey stops and looks at him.

Did you ask?

Yeh. He said to buzz off—he was busy.

Duncan   he didn't mean

It's okay. I don't care.

— Not much you don't.

Duncan goes upstairs. A moment later, Matthew also walks up the stairs to the bathroom, and Stacey with relief pours herself a gin and tonic. She has gulped only half of it when she hears a thudding sound, followed by Duncan's frightened voice.

Mum! C'mere—quick!

What is it, Duncan? What's happened?

It's Granddad—he's fallen.

Stacey runs through into the front hall. Matthew is lying at the foot of the stairs, having evidently missed his footing on the bottom steps. He does not seem able to rise, but Stacey can detect no broken bones. More than anything, he is humiliated and apologetic.

Stacey   I'm so sorry   it was so stupid of me

No   no   you mustn't say that. Here, Duncan, give me a hand, will you?

Between them, they manage to get Matthew into an armchair in the living room.

254

Okay, Duncan. Granddad's okay now.

You sure? Should I call Dad, maybe?

No. It's all right. Would you just go and make sure Jen's all right, though?

Duncan looks once again at Matthew, who is moving one hand across his forehead. Then he looks away, as though he has witnessed something not intended for his eyes. He walks into the kitchen and stays there. Matthew is breathing heavily but making a strained effort to breath normally.

What happened?

As soon as she has spoken, Stacey realizes that her voice has been more incisive than she meant it to be, more piercing and demanding. Matthew leans his head back against the chair, as though at last having to accept the unacceptable.

Stacey   I'm sorry

You're sorry? What for?

Well, I guess I've got glaucoma. The eyes aren't much good any more. That's why I fell. The doctor told me sometime ago but I didn't want to let you know. I have drops for them but

Stacey looks at him, appalled.

You should have said. You should have told us.

I suppose so. But I didn't want   well   I didn't want you to feel you had to

Dad?

—— Dad. I've never called him that before. I might as well begin. I'm going to be seeing a lot of him from now on. Strange —it's only a name now, that, only a way of identifying Matthew. Niall Cameron has been dead a long time. If someone else needs the name, no point in not using it. It doesn't mean anything to me any more. I never knew until now.

Yes? What is it, Stacey?

Wait. I'll be back in a sec.

Stacey flashes into the kitchen and snatches her drink from its cave concealment in the blue Mixmaster bowl.

—— Well, Dad, old buddy, you may as well get used to it,

because I am certainly not taking to tomato juice with invisible vodka, for you or anyone else. For what I am about to say, I need this.

She returns to the living room and sits on the chesterfield. Matthew eyes the glass but says nothing.

Listen, Dad. You can't live there any more. Not now. Not with this. You'll live here. With us.

— Oh Christ, will I ever regret it. I'll regret it every day of my life. It'll be pure bloody murder. We've got enough to deal with, without him. He'll follow me around all day long. Move over, Tess—I'll soon be out to join you. No, I damn well won't. I will not let this get me down. I just damn well will not. Oh heavens—I'll have to take him up and down the stairs to the bathroom. I can't. I can't. Yes, you can. If you think it'll be awful for you, doll, how do you think he'll feel about it? Matthew, who doesn't even like to admit he has any natural functions. Matthew, always so neat and so proud.

Stacey   thank you my dear but I can't impose

No. You mustn't feel like that. That's—unrealistic. We want to have you. Naturally. Of course. There's no question.

— Naturally. Of course. Oh brother. Why did I ever once feel that to tell the truth the whole truth and nothing but the truth would be a relief? It would be dynamite, that's all it would be. It would set the house on fire.

Stacey, I don't know what to say. I would like to come and live here. I can't deny that. But—it's Mac.

How do you mean?

Matthew turns his face away from hers. It is Mac's gesture and Matthew's voice could almost be Mac's voice at the moments of difficult telling.

I didn't do very well by him when he was a boy.

Dad   I don't think he thinks that

He must. It isn't easy for a minister's children. Everyone expects them to be some kind of example. I see now that I expected too much of him. Strange—I could even see the unfairness of it then, from his point of view. But I never told him that. I wanted him to grow up with some strong background of faith. But he didn't. The reason must be that I had so many doubts myself. I must have passed them on even though I never spoke of them.

I never knew you had any doubts at all. I don't think Mac ever knew, either. Maybe it would have been better if he had known.

— And Matthew's despair.

Oh no—that couldn't have been better for him or his sister or anyone. One should be certain. A minister should be. If he isn't, he must at least try not to put anyone else's faith in jeopardy. That always seemed to me to be the least I could do. But with Mac I failed. Perhaps there is something contagious about doubt. He must have known all along about that essential flaw in me.

Dad   you've got it all wrong

I'm afraid not, my dear.

Mac would have been relieved if he'd known you weren't always certain. But he didn't know.

Matthew hears her words but not their meaning. He has to continue in his own groove.

Stacey—I always wanted to talk about it to someone, but I couldn't. I wish now that I had talked of it. Not to Mac, but perhaps to my wife. But she was—well, I don't think she ever had any doubts about anything, so how could I? It would have weakened me so much in her eyes.

Maybe she wasn't all that sure.

Oh yes, she certainly was. I used to admire her for it. She never needed the things that some people need. Her faith was very strong and

— And she didn't like to be fucked. But not because her faith was very strong. Something else. Poor goddam her. Poor Matthew. Too late now.

257

Sh. It's all right, Dad. Everything's going to be all right. Listen, you rest here for a minute, until dinner's ready, and I'll go see Mac. Don't worry.

She goes outside and calls Mac. When they are in the study, she hands him a gin and tonic.

Mac

Yeh? What's the matter?

It's your dad. He fell down the stairs.

Oh Christ, what next?

He's got glaucoma. Mac, we'll have to have him here.

Stacey, we can't. Where's the room?

We'll have to turn the study into a bedroom and build a study for you in the basement.

Great. Wonderful. You got it all figured out, haven't you?

For God's sake, then, what's your suggestion?

Stacey   I don't want him here   I can't

You were the one who always said he had a right to walk in without knocking and that we should send the kids to Sunday school so as not to upset him and all that.

I know I know I know. Lay off, can't you?

I'm sorry. Mac—what is it?

He looks at her as though they have never before met, as though she is the stranger on shipboard to whom he may possibly be able to relate his edited past.

I never bought what he was preaching about, but still, he was doing something, you have to admit it. He didn't spend his life doing nothing.

—— Like you? Is that what you mean? Mac, you can't mean that. It isn't true. What to say that'll do any good?

Mac—he thinks he didn't do well by you.

I'll bet.

He does. He said so.

In the heat of the moment, maybe. Don't kid yourself. He doesn't think that. He thinks the other way around.

What do you think, yourself, about the boys, Mac?

258

What? What's that got to do with it?

I just wondered. Because they quite often have the notion that they'll never be as smart as you are. Especially Duncan.

They'll learn differently.

Yeh? Thanks for reassuring me.

Mac dredges up a kind of laughter and puts an arm around her shoulders. Suddenly Stacey is filled with the knowledge of what it will mean to have Matthew in the house.

Mac—what'll we do? It'll be impossible. I just can't

Well, as you say, there's nothing else we can do. Hush, honey. It'll be all right. We'll manage. But I'll have to use the TV room as a study until we can get another room built down there. The kids will squawk like hell, I suppose.

Let them squawk. Mac—

They hold on to one another for an unpredicted moment. Then Stacey goes out to the hall and bellows at Ian and Duncan.

C'mon you guys! Is Katie home?

Katie's voice floats down.

I'm here. And I'm not deaf—yet.

Stacey picks up Jen and plonks her onto the cushion-heightened chair in the dining room.

—— A few more years of this life, God, and if I'm not dead or demented, I'll have a hide like a rhinoceros. Odd—Mac has to pretend he's absolutely strong, and now I see he doesn't believe a word of it and never has. Yet he's a whole lot stronger than he thinks he is. Maybe they all are. Maybe even Duncan is. Maybe even I am.

TEN

ᎶᏙᎩᏙᎩᏙᎩᏙᎩᏙᎩᏙᎩ

Stacey still cannot decide whether to tell Mac about Thor or not. Mac has said nothing about the job since the evening of Thor's party. Stacey vacillates inwardly for several days, being careful to keep outwardly busy. She takes the three younger children to the beach, does baking, writes letters, has Bertha in for coffee. She watches Mac covertly but cannot discover anything from his manner. He works just the same, grindingly. But one afternoon he comes home early. Jen and Stacey are in the back yard, Stacey dutifully spread out on the lawn, wearing her bathing suit, trying to gain more tan.

— I must be out of my mind. I don't give the smallest damn whether I've got a tan or not. But every summer I do this, because it's taken for granted that everybody wants a tan.

She looks up and sees Mac standing in the back doorway. His brush-cut has completely grown out now and his russet hair looks like himself once more.

Mac—what're you doing home?

—— Has he quit or been fired? Lord, please let it be that he's quit, not the other.

Hi. I came to tell you something. C'mon inside, eh?

Stacey snatches up Jen and carries her, wriggling and protesting, into the house. Jen begins screeching, a piercing enraged voice which proclaims her intention of going on and on until Stacey takes her back to the garden. Stacey shakes her.

—— Shut up shut up shut up you goddam little nuisance.

She has not said a word aloud, but she can feel her own anger mounting in direct proportion to her tension, assaulted eardrums and sense of apprehension about Mac. She pats Jen's shoulders.

Hush, flower. It's okay. Please, honey, please. *Jen*. Listen, if you don't shut up, I'll smack you, see?

—— Oh God. Now she'll roar forever. Why why is Mac home?

In the kitchen, Jen suddenly stops screaming, as unreasonably as she began. Mac is in the process of pouring two gin and tonics. Stacey looks at him in surprise.

Hey—what's this in aid of?

He hands a glass to her and raises his own.

Guess what's happened, Stacey.

What?

Thor's been offered a head office job in Montreal and he's decided to take it. They want me to be manager here.

Mac! You don't mean it.

—— *Thor* is leaving? Thor is *leaving*? But he was the god here, and he won't be that in head office. Was he really invited to go, or did he ask for a transfer himself, for his own reasons? Val, did you get stoned one night and go to see him? You didn't have any cause to do me a favor, that's for sure. I couldn't even bring myself to ask you around—I didn't want you swearing in front of my kids. Did you say something to Thor? Was it settling an old score, for you? I'll never know. And I'll never find out from you, either, because I'll never find you. No fixed address. Val—I'm sorry. I'm sorry. Too late. *Was* it you?

Mac is smiling.

Yeh, it's true all right. I was pretty taken aback myself. Anyway, I'm going to accept. It's a funny thing—I had just about decided to quit. In fact, I was going to hand in my notice this week.

You didn't say anything.

Yeh, well I was going to tell you

— Thanks.

I can't take it in all at once, Mac. When—when did you hear about Thor?

Just today. And the offer came to me at the same time.

Mac   that's great   it's really wonderful

I thought you'd be pleased. Apparently they decided to offer me the job on account of the fact that I've actually sold more than any of the other guys here. I'm going to change a few things. A lot of the jazz in the campaign was Thor's, not head office's. The charts and quiz and that. We can cut out that crap. It'll be a pretty good job. It's a going firm.

Sure. I know it is. Gee, that's just fine, Mac. It's marvelous.

—— Life's games. He knocks himself out because he thinks Thor's got it in for him, and he winds up manager in an outfit he really thinks is a load of phony baloney. Dear Lord and Father of mankind, forgive our foolish ways, as some goon once said. Reclothe us in our rightful mind. And so on. But what if this *is* our rightful mind, or at least the only one we're likely to have? Anyway, it *is* a good job. It's somewhere. It's better than nowhere.

> Luke. *I think I'll just hitch and see what happens. I'd like to go north. That's a great country, Stacey. Up the Skeena River—Kispiox, Kitwanga, crazy names like that. Northern jungle, rain forest—*

—— Okay, Stacey, simmer down. The fun is over. It's been over for some time, only you didn't see it before. No—you saw it all right but you couldn't take it. You're nearly forty. You got four kids and a mortgage, and in just over three years Katie will be ready for university if she works hard enough, which is dubious. I guess the fun's been over for Mac for quite a while. It would be nice if we were different people but we are not different people. We are ourselves and we are sure as hell not going to undergo some total transformation at this point. That's right, doll. Mrs. C. MacAindra, by an overwhelming majority voted The Most Sensible Woman of the Year. We can save our money. When we've got all four kids through university or launched somewhere, and Mac retires and is so thin you have to look twice to see him and I'm so portly I can hardly waddle, we can go to Acapulco and do the Mexican hat dance. I can't stand it. I cannot. I can't take it. Yeh, I can, though. By God, I can, if I set my mind to it. And I'm not going to tell him about Thor. It's not actually like lying. It's just refraining from saying. The silences aren't all bad. How do I know how many times Mac has protected me by not saying? He probably noticed the burn on my hand that time.

Mac, I don't know what to say. I think it's just terrific.

Yeh. It's good. We're getting somewhere.

Only one thing

What?

Let's not move, eh? I mean, we'll be able sometime to afford another house—you know, bigger or like that—but I don't want to.

For Christ's sake, Stacey, why not?

I just don't

You can't mean it. Listen, honey, it'll be me who has to have the staff parties and all that. Can you see us having them here? There isn't room to swing a cat, and the kids' stuff is littered all over the place. We need at least a decent-sized living room, and for the boys to have their own bedrooms, and now that Dad is here it would be pretty convenient to have a house that had a downstairs john as well as an upstairs one.

You've got it all figured out, eh? That was quick work.
Now, listen Stacey

I don't want to move. I like this old dump. I'm used to it.
It's not you who has to be around the house all day long.

I know. I know. I'm only saying I just don't see how we
can manage here indefinitely. That's all I'm saying. I'm not suggesting we should move tomorrow. I'm only saying that at some
point it's going to become

Okay. So we'll move, if you want to that much. But don't
be stunned if I bitch about it, eh?

Oh for God's sake what's the matter now?

Nothing   nothing's the matter

The sand of the beach is fine and pale brown, lightly strewn with
fringed yellow-green fronds of seafern and bulbous kelp cast up
and drying in the late August sun. Stacey and Jen walk barefoot,
picking up grey-white coarse clam shells, small purple shells
paired and open like moth wings, greenly iridescent shells
shaped like miniature coolie hats.

Hey, that's a nice one, angel bud. Shall I put it in my
bag?

Jen nods and Stacey gravely takes the cracked shell and
stows it away. The tide is low. Some distance out, Ian and
Duncan have gone to the retreating sea. Stacey glances up
and sees the two auburn heads. Then she looks back to Jen.

C'mon, flower. What've you got? That's a crab claw—you
don't really want that, do you? Oh, all right.

Ian's voice, thin and far.

Mum!

Stacey looks up and sees Ian's hair caught by the sun.
Not Duncan's. She places her hands briefly on Jen's shoulders.

Stay here, Jen. Don't move. Don't follow me. Understand? I'll be right back.

Then she runs. Through the dry sand and after that the wet heavy sand and the shallow water, until the water is halfway up her thighs. Ian's face is unrecognizable and he is straining, tugging at one of Duncan's arms. By the time she reaches Ian, he has pulled Duncan out of the water, but only part of the way.

Mum—I think his foot is caught under the rock

What happened? Ian—*what happened?*

She is not aware of having spoken. She kneels and manages to dislodge Duncan's foot, hauling him up and out of the now-brown muddied water. Ian's voice comes to her, treble with fright.

He tripped—I don't know how—I guess the seaweed. I looked and he'd gone down and I thought he'd get up right away. It's not even deep, Mum. But the tide's low. So we came out as far as the rocks. Look—he hit his head when he fell. Maybe it sort of stunned him, but it didn't knock him out or anything, because I saw him thrashing around and I thought he was okay. But he must've got his foot hooked under the rock. By the time I got to him, he wasn't thrashing around any more. He was just lying there.

Duncan   Duncan

His head is bleeding and the sea pours from his nostrils. His mouth is open, and his eyes. But he is not seeing anything and he does not seem to be breathing. His seven-year-old body is heavy in Stacey's arms, a dead weight. She flounders through the water and weed-netted mud, back to the damp exposed sand. She puts Duncan down. She cannot think what to do. She cannot seem to think at all.

Ian—get my bag and take the change purse and go phone Dad. You know where the call box is?

Yes. Sure.

Ian runs, sprints, and she does not even know that he is no longer beside her. She places Duncan on his front and presses down on the place where she thinks his lungs are. Seawater trickles yellowly from his mouth. But he remains inert.

— I don't know what to do. I never learned artificial respiration. How could he fall like that? So quickly? I wasn't watching. I should've been watching. Why wasn't I? I thought they were all right. The tide was out. It was shallow, the water. The rocks covered with barnacles. But he knew they were there. He's been there dozens of times. How could it happen like that, so quickly? It couldn't. But it did. Duncan! You've got to be all right.

Duncan! You've got to be all right.

The words have been screamed, and although she does not hear her own voice, she is suddenly aware of the words' total lie. They are rune words, trinket charms to ward off the evil eye, and that is all. There is nothing she can do.

Now several people on the beach are running towards her, two women and a man, but when they get there, they stand talking at her because they do not know what to do, either.

What happened?

What's the matter?

How did it happen?

I saw those two kids out there and they were perfectly okay and then

Stacey does not hear their voices.

— God, let him be all right, and I'll never want to get away again, I promise. If it was anything I did, take it out on me, not on him—that's too much punishment for me.

She wants to hold Duncan in her arms, but some vestigial knowledge tells her this might be harmful. She is still pressing down on Duncan's ribs, on his warm limp back, her hands filled with the fear of their own ignorance. Then she feels herself pushed aside by a pair of unknown hands and a man is kneeling over Duncan, kneading his body until the brackish water gushes again from his mouth. The man is no more than twenty, tanned, wearing a red swimsuit. One of the lifeguards.

Your other boy fetched me. Just keep a little aside, eh?

266

He turns Duncan over onto his back, and puts his mouth to Duncan's, breathing from one pair of lungs into the other. Stacey, crouched on the sand, is momentarily blinded, her sight extinguished by saltwater not from the sea. Her mind is empty of everything except Duncan's name which repeats itself over and over. When her sight clears, Duncan is half propped up by the man's arm and is vomiting and also struggling to breathe, his breath creaking and uncertain. Then he begins to cry, the attenuated wail of a very young child, an infant voice, not his own voice at all. Stacey puts her arms around him. Once again she cannot see him because of her sight-destroying tears, but she can feel him moving even through her own trembling.

Will he be okay? Mum—will he be okay?

Ian. Stacey does not know the answer. She looks at the young man, who nods and replies for her.

Yeh. He'll be okay, I think. Good job you fetched me, though. It wouldn't have been too good for him to have gone that much longer. He swallowed quite a bit of sea.

Ian does not say anything. He turns away because he does not want either Stacey or the university student to see his face. But Stacey sees that his shoulders are shaking with his dry sobbing, which he has to deal with himself. Then she turns again to Duncan.

His head

Yeh. Well, if you'll bring him along, we can patch that up until you can get him to a doctor. He had quite a wallop, but I don't think it's all that deep. Scalp wounds always bleed a lot.

Stacey! Duncan—I got here as soon as I could—is he

Mac is on his knees beside Duncan in the sand, uncaring about the vomited slime in which he is kneeling.

He's okay now. I think. I think he is. Mac—he nearly

I know. Ian said. Is he really okay?

Duncan has almost stopped crying now. His eyes are half closed. The young man, semi-embarrassed, tries to explain, seeing that Stacey cannot.

He'll be okay, I'm pretty sure. Shock—he'll probably go to sleep. If you want to bring him along to the first-aid post, I can mop up that

But Mac somehow replies unequivocally.

No. Thanks. I think we better take him straight to the Emergency. Thanks all the same. What did you do?

Mouth-to-mouth

My God. Not much point saying thanks, is there? But thanks

That's okay

Mac lifts Duncan out of Stacey's arms. For a moment, she protests.

It's okay, Mac. I can take him.

No. Let me. I'll carry him.

She looks at Mac dazedly. His face is under control, but only just. He picks up Duncan carefully, and for an instant, his own head bowed over Duncan's, holds him tightly, almost cradlingly.

—— He's never held Duncan before, not ever. Why did I think he didn't care about Duncan? Maybe he didn't, once. But he does now. Why didn't I see how much, before? He never showed it, that's why.

We'll take my car, Stacey, eh?

Yes. But—Mac, I don't think I can drive.

That's okay. I never meant you should. You take him in the back seat.

All right. Mac—I never thought to call the lifeguard. I wasn't thinking straight. It was Ian, on his way to phone you.

Mac puts Duncan in the back seat of the Buick. Stacey and Jen climb in beside him, Jen very quiet. Mac and Ian go into the front seat. Duncan is nearly asleep. Stacey holds him. Mac starts the car and speaks to Ian in a low gruff voice.

Ian?

Yeh?

You did fine.

Stacey looks at the two unbending necks in the front seat.

—— That's the most Mac will ever be able to say. They're not like me, either of them. They don't want to say it in full technicolor and intense detail. And that's okay, I guess. Ian gets the message. It's his language, too. I wish it were mine. All I can do is accept that it is a language, and that it works, at least sometimes. And maybe it's mine more than I like to admit. Whatever I think that I think of it, it's the one I most use.

Unbiddenly, then, she remembers what she was thinking out there on the sand when she did not know what to do and when Duncan's still-warm but nearly unhuman body seemed to be going beyond reach.

> *God, if it was anything I did, take it out on*
> *me, not on him—that's too much punishment*
> *for me*

—— Judgment. All the things I don't like to think I believe in. But at the severe moments, up they rise, the tomb birds, scaring the guts out of me with their vulture wings. Maybe it's as well to know they're there. Maybe knowing might help to keep them at least a little in their place. Or maybe not. I used to think about Buckle that he was as superstitious as a caveman. I didn't know then that I was, too.

Duncan sits up in bed and sips ginger ale through a straw.

Dad   I almost

Duncan knows that Mac carried him from the beach. Mac did not tell Duncan. Stacey did, when Mac was not around. Now Mac is sitting on Duncan's bed.

Yeh. Well, lucky for you that you didn't, eh? Next time you better watch out for your footing.

Next time?

This is not something that Duncan has previously considered. Stacey, standing in the doorway, examines his face and wonders if he has taken for granted that the sea and himself will in future no longer be on any kind of terms.

— Mac's right. I know. But at the same time, it's not Mac who has to go through with it. I don't ever want to take that kid to the beach again.

After a week, Duncan is back to himself. It is the last week of the summer holidays, so Ian is agitating to be taken to the beach. Katie has gone with her friends. Mac, entrenched in myriad administrative responsibilities, has gone to work that morning absentmindedly. Matthew roams the house.

Dad—how be we take the kids to the beach?

Well, that would be quite nice, Stacey.

Okay, you guys—c'mon, then, get your swimsuits and let's get going. C'mon, flower—you, too.

Stacey, Jen and Matthew station themselves fairly high up on the beach, equipped with plastic shovels and sandpails. Ian looks at Duncan and then flashes off on his own towards the sea.

— Ian. If Duncan goes to the sea, Ian will keep an eye on him. But he doesn't want to be responsible. I don't blame him. Maybe he only thinks it would be an insult to Duncan, to watch over him.

Ian rushes into the high-tided water alone, plunging outward and then turning and swimming in, as he has been taught to do. Never swim outward, or you'll get too far beyond your depth. One day he will disobey, and that will be right, then.

Duncan plays in the sand by himself, constructing a moated fort, shoring it up with walls of hard-packed sand. Then, after a while, as though it is something he knows has been laid upon him and which he cannot deny, he walks by himself along the wet reaches of the sand down to the sea.

Stacey watches him, but she makes herself not move.

Duncan reaches the edge of the water and then he walks, plod-dingly, into the sea.

—— I wonder how deep it is, at the deepest? How far out does it go? How many creatures does it contain, not just the little shells and the purple starfish and the kelp, but all the things that live a long way out? Deathly embracing octopus in the south waters, the white whales spouting in the only-half-melted waters of the north, the sharks knowing nothing except how to kill.

Duncan looks incredibly small on the rim of the ocean. But he keeps on walking outward until he reaches what he judges to be a decent and to himself acceptable distance. Then he turns and swims back to shore.

September, and the kids go back to school. Stacey, half ashamed of her own relief, waves at them from the veranda. The morning is warm, so she fetches a lawn chair from the garage and sets it up in the back yard.

Dad—it's such a lovely day, I thought you might like to sit in the garden for a while.

That was thoughtful of you, Stacey.

Stacey helps him down the steps.

—— I never know whether he's being delicately ironic or genuinely grateful. If it's the latter, I ought to warn him. Thought-ful, hell. I just don't want him under my feet all morning, that's all. He pussyfoots behind me until I begin to feel he's my shadow, but a shadow that has to be spoken to, taken notice of, and then all I want to do is speak the unspeakable. Okay—so in some ways I'm mean as all getout. I'm going to quit worrying about it. I used to think there would be a blinding flash of light someday, and then I would be wise and calm and would know how to cope with everything and my kids would rise up and call me blessed. Now I see that whatever I'm like, I'm pretty well stuck with it for life. Hell of a revelation that turned out to be.

Stacey goes back into the house. Jen is in the kitchen and has dragged a chair over to the sink, climbed up on it and filled her plastic teapot from the tap. She holds it up for Stacey to see.

Hi, Mum. Want tea?

Stacey stares. Then quickly, she recovers and manages nonchalance.

What did you say, flower?

Want tea, Mum?

Why—yes, thanks, Jen. I'd love some.

When she has drunk two plastic cupfuls of water, Stacey flies to the telephone in the hall. She speaks guardedly, glancing towards the kitchen, as though imparting top secret material to a co-spy.

Mac? That you?

Yeh. What's the matter, Stacey?

Nothing. It's Jen—she just talked.

Oh?

What d'you mean—*oh?* She *talked*, Mac. A whole sentence. A short one, mind you, but all the same

That's great, honey. I always knew she would.

Well, I just thought I'd let you know. Sorry for phoning you at work. So long.

So long, Stacey.

—— What the hell. It may be nothing to him, but when you've listened to this child's garbled gargling for the past year, and all the other kids talked before they were two, then it's like brass bands and banners to me.

Flower, you're a genius.

Want tea, Mum?

Sure.

—— Ye gods. What if she never learns to say anything else?

That afternoon, Katie comes home and goes into the back yard where Jen is playing and Stacey is reading.

Guess what, Katie?

What?

Jen talked—a whole sentence.

Katie picks up Jen and swings her high.

Hey—clever kid. What's your name, eh?

Jen.

That's right. My, my, such ability. You're the best two-year-old talker in this entire house. Hey—Mum?

Mm?

I'm going out tonight.

Who with?

Oh—just this boy.

Stacey fights the impulse to ask instantly for a total record—name, age, ambition, appearance, scholastic performance, religion (if any), principles, scruples, manners?

Oh? What's his name, Katie?

Don.

Don who? What's his last name?

How should I know?

—— Good God. If it had been me, the name would be embossed on my mind in letters of silver, ten feet high. Maybe she's not quite so desperate to latch on and get the hell out as I was when I was her age? Or is that only my wishful thinking? She's always gone out before with a group of kids. This is the first time alone. It's been bugging her, too. Why, I can't think. At her age. Fourteen. To hear her, you'd think she was thirty and never been kissed. Oh, Katie, love. I hope everything goes well for you.

Okay, Katie. Where you going?

Just to a movie. He's a funny kind of guy, in a way. His home background sounds all loused up. He was telling me about this pot party some of them had last summer, and his dad found out and actually took him to the police. Can you imagine?

You mean he smokes marijuana?

Well, he did that time. That wasn't what I was trying to say. Didn't you hear?

273

— Katie, I'm sorry. I guess I didn't hear. I only heard what was pertinent to you or what I imagined to be pertinent to you. In the same way that I used to wonder if my mother ever really listened to what I'd been saying. Sorry, Mother. Now I see why. I'm a stranger in the now world.

Sorry, Katie. Yeh—I agree. It seems a pretty low thing, for a person to take his own kid to the police. I guess the father felt desperate and worried and—you know—helpless. I don't know. You don't—you haven't—have you, Katie?

Stacey Cameron, standing very still in her blue dirndl skirt and yellow blouse, waiting to be released from the querulously probing voice. *Stacey, some of these boys drink—I know they do—all I hope and trust and pray is that you're not so foolish that you'd accept if one of them offered you a drink.* Of course not, Mother.

You mean have I smoked pot? No. But it's not up to me to judge what other people do, is it? That's his business. It's got nothing to do with me.

Well   I guess I can't really argue with that

— It's odd. I believe her. But I guess my mother believed me, too, although I certainly wasn't telling her the truth. Do I know if this particular stuff will lethalize more than the tobacco and booze which are my cup of tea? No. I do not know. I, who may well expire from lung cancer or cirrhosis of the liver. It's partly fear of the unknown, this, with me. But it scares me all the same. I don't know what to tell Katie. I have the feeling that there isn't much use, at this point, in telling her anything. She's on her own, so help her. So help her. At least my mother had the consolation of believing herself to be unquestionably right about everything. Or so I've always thought. Maybe she didn't, either. Although I really do wonder if she ever saw her codeine and phenobarb in anything like the same terms. She always put such a patina of respectability upon them. Probably Katie thinks Mac and I do, too, with the gin and tonic. Ritualized props.

274

Stacey takes Jen and goes into the kitchen to start dinner. She turns the radio on and begins peeling the potatoes. The tune that is playing is "Zorba's Dance."

She is dancing alone. The café is in a village, a village of low whitewashed huts, surrounded by and threaded through with whatever kind of trees they have in Greece. Olive trees. Yeh, those. However they look. The café is small, and the band is only two or three men playing (unspecified string instruments). She starts slowly, following the beat of the music, her bare feet certain, confident. The sudden upswirling of the tune, and she is whirling, wrists gyrating, possessed by the god. Swifter, swifter, with the freedom of wild horses, the music races the wind. Then he is beside her, the man who also is enabled to hear the music, who also is directed by the god

AND NOW A WORD FROM OUR SPONSOR   ARE YOU TIRED OF WAXING FLOORS?

Stacey, immobile beside the sink, except for the movement of the potato peeler in her right hand, laughs with minimal amusement.

— I was wrong to think of the trap as the four walls. It's the world. The truth is that I haven't been Stacey Cameron for one hell of a long time now. Although in some ways I'll always be her, because that's how I started out. But from now on, the dancing goes on only in the head. Anything else, and it's an insult to Katie, whether or not she witnesses the performance. Well, in the head isn't such a terrible place to dance. The settings are magnificent there, anyhow. I did dance at one time, when I could. It would be a lot worse if I never had. Funny—I recall one of my mother's bridge cronies in Manawaka, and every time she came over, she'd ask my mother to put on a record, and Mother would play the old-time one with a polka on one side and a schottische on the other, and the old dame would sit there as

K

though under heavy sedation. Maybe she was dancing in her head.

The next morning the letter from Stacey's sister arrives. She tells Mac about it after dinner that evening, when he has gone down into his temporary study in the TV room.

Mac—guess what?

What?

Rachel and my mother are moving out here. Here. This self-same city.

Oh holy Jesus   that's all we needed

Yes. I know. But the fact remains that Rachel has had her all alone all these years. We can have them over for Sunday dinners, I guess, and pray it won't be much more than that. That's a fine thing to say about your own sister and mother, isn't it? But I can't help it, Mac. I just can't   I don't want

I know. I know, honey. Well

Never mind. Maybe my mother will strike up a rewarding relationship with your dad.

Mac laughs.

I can just about see that happening, can't you?

Yeh. In a magazine story. Well, it'll mean a lot to her to see the kids. I can't begrudge her. She's had her troubles. As I know now. You know something, Mac? I'll be forty next week.

So you will. I'd forgotten. Do you mind?

To tell you the truth, I mind like hell. But there it is.

Yeh. There it is.

The butterfly priestesses flutter in winglike robes of pale mauve. The hairdryers sing whirringly like insects from another planet. Stacey flicks the heat control from high to medium.

—— It's an ill wind and all that. At least since Tess's break-down I can get my hair done again. There's a charitable thought.

She picks up a shiny-paged magazine and thumbs through until she finds the current pop psychology article. It is entitled "Mummy Is the Root of All Evil?"

What do you want for your birthday, Mum?
I don't know. I can never think of anything. What about a nice wheelchair?
Katie laughs obligingly.
No—we're saving up for that one next year.
Thanks, Katie. That's big-hearted of you.
But then Katie swings away, turns into herself.
Ah, drop it, can't you?

EVER-OPEN EYE STREETS IN CITIES NOT SO FAR AWAY ARE BURNING BURNING IN RAGE AND SORROW SET ABLAZE BY THE CHILDREN OF SAMSON AGONISTES   VOICE: RIOTS ARE SAID TO BE WELL UNDER CONTROL IN

—— I see it and then I don't see it. It becomes pictures. And you wonder about the day when you open your door and find they've been filming those pictures in your street.

On the bedroom chair rests a jumble of Stacey's clothes, off-cast stockings like nylon puddles, roll-on girdle in the shape of a tire where she has rolled it off. On another chair, Mac's clothes are folded neatly, a habit he acquired in the army, as he has re-marked countless times. Two books are on the bedside table—*The Golden Bough* and *Investments and You,* Hers and His, both unread. On the dressing table, amid the nonmagic jars and lipsticks are scattered photographs of Katie, Ian, Duncan and Jen at various ages. Above the bed is hung a wedding picture, Stacey twenty-three, almost beautiful although not knowing it then, Mac twenty-seven, hopeful confident lean.
Stacey is already in bed. Mac crawls in beside her.

Christ, am I ever beat.

You better get to sleep right away, then, Mac.

I've got to.

It's okay. I know.

—— I can't very well say—look, don't worry, you're fine and what I'd really like from time to time is someone I've never been with before. No doubt he'd like that, too.

Well

Mac, it's okay. It's okay if you want to, and it's okay if you don't want to. Only—just talk to me sometimes when you can, eh?

What in heaven's name do you mean by that, Stacey?

Well you know like about what's bugging you

They are silent for a moment. Then Mac turns to face her.

Stacey?

Yes?

What did you ever do with your dad's old revolver?

She sits up in bed and looks at him.

What?

The one you brought back that time from Manawaka.

How did you know?

I was looking for a tin of nails I'd stuck up on one of the rafters in the basement, and I found it. Couple of months later it was gone.

I chucked it into Timber Lake that summer. Why didn't you ever mention

I don't know. I didn't know what to say. I wanted to throw it away myself, but then I thought that might make you even more determined if that was what was in your mind

What? What did you think I planned to do with it?

Maybe it sounds crazy, Stacey. I was kind of afraid you might you know like Tess

Mac that wasn't it at all

278

Slowly, Stacey tells him how she felt then and how she came to realize there was no use keeping the gun. She finds it neither easier nor more difficult to explain now than she did when she said the same thing to Luke. Mac scrutinizes her face.

You thought all that?

Yeh. Didn't you ever?

His voice is in low gear, with brakes on.

Yes. I guess. Sometimes.

She moves towards him and he holds her. Then they make love after all, but gently, as though consoling one another for everything that neither of them can help nor alter.

Finally, Stacey disentangles.

Mac, we better get some sleep.

I know. Good night, Stacey.

Good night, Mac.

> *Ladybird, ladybird,*
> *Fly away home;*
> *Your house is on fire,*
> *Your children are . . .*

—— Will the fires go on, inside and out? Until the moment when they go out for me, the end of the world. And then I'll never know what may happen in the next episode.

As she tries to settle herself for sleep, Stacey feels a nudging pain like a fingernail scrawling fitfully under her ribs at the left side.

—— There it is again. Should I phone Doctor Spender tomorrow? It's nothing. It'll go away. But what if it doesn't? What if it's the heart? Is the heart on that side? Well, so what? No one is indispensable. Maybe not, but it's myself I'm thinking about, as well as them. If I could absorb the notion of nothing, of total dark, then it would have no power over me. But that grace isn't given. My last breath will be a rattle of panic, while some strange face or maybe the known one hovers over me and says

Everything's all right. Unless, of course, it meets me with violent quickness, a growing fashion.

She lies stiffly, listening.

— Maybe the trivialities aren't so bad after all. They're something to focus on. As I'm forty tomorrow, that would be a good day to start a diet. Not the banana diet—it's too repulsive. High protein. How would it be if I did myself a steak at lunch and then only had soup at night? Yeh, you do that, doll. You'll lose the same ten pounds you've been losing for ten years. All right. I know. It's not necessary to spell it out. I won't be twenty-one again. I'll never have a really decent-looking pair of hips again as long as I live. I don't claim that's any tragedy. I don't even claim it's anything except ludicrous. But it's enough to make me feel relatively lousy on occasion. Like today when I took the prescription into the drugstore to get more of the wonder pills. I hate getting them. I always think the pharmacist is looking at me and thinking *Who in hell would want to make love with that old cow?* On the other hand, they're a kind of proof that somebody still does. I would have liked to be a great courtesan, like that one in France who went on until she was about ninety-five. Still beautiful, it is said, although personally I find that hard to credit. Well, such was quite plainly not meant to be your lot, Stacey. Never mind. Give me another forty years, Lord, and I may mutate into a matriarch.

Stacey heaves over onto her side. The house is quiet. The kids are asleep. Downstairs in the ex-study, Matthew has been asleep for hours, or if not asleep, meditating. Beside her, she can already hear the steady breathing that means Mac is asleep. Temporarily, they are all more or less okay.

She feels the city receding as she slides into sleep. Will it return tomorrow?